RACE WITH DEATH

RACE WITH DEATH

GILBERT MORRIS

Fleming H. Revell
A Division of Baker Book House Co
Grand Rapids, Michigan 49516

Published by Fleming H. Revell
a division of Baker Book House Company
P.O. Box 6287, Grand Rapids, MI 49516-6287

Printed in the United States of America

Library of Congress Cataloging-in-Publication Data

Morris, Gilbert.
    Race with death / Gilbert Morris.
        p.   cm.
    ISBN 0-8007-5498-0
    1. Ross, Danielle (Fictitious character)—Fiction. 2. Private investigators—United States—Fiction. 3. Women detectives—United States—Fiction.
PS3563.O8742R3   1994
813'.54—dc20   94-14532

Scripture quotations in this volume are taken from the King James Version of the Bible.

To Paul Root, who hasn't read a book since he read *Black Beauty* in the ninth grade—and who will not read this one. However, it's good to have one friend whose mind is not messed up with literature, and who can still think straight. The good old days when Sam and Jesse rode the range are never far out of my mind, Paul. And you have proven that friendship is not based on time and geography!

Contents

Contents

1

Birthday Surprise

Dani Ross stood in her bedroom staring at the dresses and pantsuits she'd laid out across her bed and draped over the chairs. A perplexed expression scored her face, and she finally selected one, muttering aloud, "Trying to dress for a date with Ben Savage is impossible!" Moving quickly she replaced the garments, slipped into an ivory crepe pantsuit, then stared at herself in the full-length mirror on the wall.

She'd bought the outfit on sale at Dillard's almost a year before but had never worn it, and even now she wasn't sure about her choice. The reflection revealed a tall young woman with a figure too full to qualify for a fashion model. Nor was the face right for that profession. The jaw was too solid, the mouth too wide, and a small mole adorned the right cheek. She studied the outfit carefully—the high-waisted pants with inverted front pleats and the long jacket with mock flap pockets and pearlized buttons. Finally she shrugged, grabbed a small clutch of golden fabric, and left the room.

Reddish bars of afternoon sunlight fell through the high windows as she descended the stairs and turned to go to the kitchen. The house was very old, with heart-pine floors and high ceilings, and the gleam of fine antique furniture gave a mellow cast to the rooms she passed through to get to the kitchen. The old grandfather clock boomed out the first of six round notes as she passed, and as she glanced at it, she thought of the time she and her father had removed the old finish and had given the rosewood case a dull sheen that seemed inches deep.

Pausing by the clock, she slowly reached out and rubbed the burnished wood, the memory of her father sweeping over her—as he had been on that day. She could see his thin, aristocratic face and the smile on his lips as he'd said, "Dani, this old clock's already done two hundred years—and it'll do two hundred more. Better than either of us, eh?"

The case vibrated under her touch, and the recollection brought a sudden stab of grief so powerful that she was forced to swallow quickly, wheel around, and hurry down the hall, keeping her lips in a tight line. It had been that way since her father's funeral—not just for her, but for the whole family. No matter how noisy the house became, there was an empty silence in it now that Dan Ross was not there.

Dani pushed through the door to the kitchen, and seeing her mother sitting at the table peeling shrimp, resolutely ignored the grief that had risen inside, and said, "Well, will this outfit do?" She wheeled to give the full effect, then laughed shortly, "Who knows what to wear on a date with Ben? He may decide to go to the stock car races over at Erwinville!"

"Well, it's his birthday, Dani, so I guess you'll have to humor him."

Ellen Ann Ross was one of those tall Texas beauties with

ash-blonde hair and deep blue eyes. At the age of forty-six, she looked ten years younger—or had before the death of her husband. Physically she was changed only by the loss of a few pounds, but Dani noted the lines that had not been there before his death around her eyes and lips. Dani had not seen her mother weep after the funeral, but suspected that she did so at night lying alone in the darkness.

Dani reached over and picked up a shrimp, saying quickly, "Oh, I suppose so." She peeled the shrimp, tossing first the shell into the stack beside her mother and then the pink plump body into the bowl. "I didn't tell him about the surprise party awaiting when we return. I'll see to it that we get here early—" She lifted her head, paused, then asked, "What's *that?*"

"Sounds like an airplane landing in the driveway," Ellen said. She got up, leaned to look out the window, then turned with a smile on her lips. "It's Ben. Come on, let's see what he's driving."

The two women left the kitchen, and Dani's eyes opened wide at the automobile that Ben Savage was getting out of. "What is that?" she called out as they approached.

Savage stopped, put his hand reverently on the hood of the bright blue car, and nodded. "You don't know what this is? What do they teach children in school these days?"

Savage was a compact man of no more than average height, but there was a roundness to his body and a practiced ease to every movement. He had a squarish face with deep-set hazel eyes under a shelf of bone. His nose was short and had been broken, and his mouth was a wide gash with a thin upper lip. There was a trace of his Slavic ancestry in his coarse black hair and heavy black brows, as well as in his coloring. A scar on his forehead ran down into his left eyebrow, which he touched when he was upset or angry.

"It's beautiful, Ben!" Ellen walked around the car admiringly. "It's a Studebaker, isn't it?"

Savage moved away from the car, put his arm around Ellen, and hugged her. "Glad to see there is some taste and culture in this family," he grinned. "Too bad it didn't rub off on your daughter."

Dani saw the pleasure in her mother's eyes, but sniffed impatiently. "It was probably made before I was born. But at least it looks better than that old wreck you've been driving."

"Yep, it was made before you were born," Savage nodded. "One year before." He held on to Ellen with one arm, and made a sweeping motion with his free hand. "You are looking at a 1963 Gran Turismo Studebaker Hawk!"

The car was a sleek sports model with a sloping hood and rear deck. The grill was squarish with a red, white, and blue emblem. There was a grace about it that Dani found pleasing. "Where'd you get it, Ben?"

"From under a live oak," Savage answered. "It was in pretty bad shape, so I got it cheap from the farmer who owned it. It had belonged to his old man, he said, so the mileage is accurate."

As he spoke, Allison Ross came running out of the house, her long blonde hair flying. "Ben!" she cried out, and Savage dropped his hold on Ellen to grab the girl and squeeze her. "Where did you get that *gorgeous* car?"

"A birthday present, doll," Savage grinned. He set her down, then added, "What say I dump your dowdy sister and the two of us go out on the town? I'm tired of older women anyhow."

"All *right!*" Allison cried. She held on to Savage possessively, and stuck her tongue out at Dani, saying, "Go find yourself another man!"

"Nothing doing!" Dani shook her head firmly. "I'm all dressed up and I'm going to be fed."

Savage gave Allison a squeeze, then released her. Reaching into his pocket, he pulled out an envelope and gave it to Allison. "Happy birthday," he said.

Allison took the envelope, protesting, "It's *your* birthday, not mine." She took out two small rectangular cards, and cried out with joy, "Oh, Ben!" She beamed at the others, exclaiming, "Tickets for the Chinese gymnastic team's exhibition next Wednesday in Baton Rouge!"

"Just the two of us, doll," Savage grinned. "Well, are you ready, Boss?"

"Where are you taking her, Ben?" Ellen asked.

"Thought we might get a quarter-pounder at McDonald's."

"No, you're too dressed up for that," Dani shook her head. She eyed his charcoal slacks, maroon tie, and burgundy wingtips with surprise. He usually wore clothes that looked as though he'd picked them up at a yard sale.

Savage noted her glance, and shrugged. "First sign of depravity, wearing natty attire. Well, let's go truckin'!" He held open the door, closed it when Dani seated herself, then climbed in behind the wheel. When he turned the key the engine roared into life, and he yelled, "See you!" as he sent the car rocketing out of the driveway.

Dani looked around at the interior gleaming in off-white leather, and commented, "No duct tape like on all your other cars."

Savage turned the wheel sharply, lifting the car slightly as he glided onto the highway, then stepped on the gas. Dani was pressed back against the seat and waited until the roar of the engine modified before she was able to say, "Why is it so *loud!?*"

"Got glass packed mufflers," he nodded. A happy grin was on his lips, and he added, "It's got a 289 cubic inch V-8 engine—feel that power?"

The windows were all rolled down, and since it was a hard-top, the effect was almost like riding in a convertible. He leaned over, turned a dial, and the radio blasted out Hank Williams singing a somebody-done-me-wrong song.

"Hear that quality?" Savage shouted. "Not bad, huh?"

"Really cool, Ben," Dani shouted back. "Could we turn it down a little?"

"Well, sure." Savage turned the radio down and offered, "You can roll your glass up if the wind's blowing your hair too much."

Dani rolled up her window, and in the comparative quiet, commented, "It's a nice car, Ben. Lots of room."

"Yeah, these new sports cars, you got to put 'em on like a pair of tight shorts," he nodded. "They're all made out of soybeans and plastic. Now *this* little hummer's made out of steel, real steel! Can't dent it with your finger!"

Dani listened as he spoke glowingly of the virtues of the car—how much better it was than the ones coming off the assembly line these days—and finally observed, "You don't like new things much, do you, Ben?"

He was steering the car at eighty with his right wrist drooped over the wheel, pure enjoyment on his face. "I've seen lots of changes in the last twenty years, Boss—and I've been against every one of them!"

"You're a medievalist!"

"Yes, that too," he agreed. "If it's new, it ain't true."

"Oh, come on, Ben!"

"Name me one good thing that's come along in the last twenty years," he challenged. "The world went to pieces after George Patton died."

"Don't be silly!"

"I'm not silly, just a careful observer of the social scene. Look at any aspect of American life—say popular songs. In the good old days, we had things like 'Stardust' and 'You Made Me Love You.' Now we've got songs telling kids to dust off the cops and their parents." The wind from his inverted wing window rippled his stiff black hair, and he ran his hand through it. "And you take haircuts—used to be you could tell a man by a good haircut. Now half the male population's blow-dried or pig-tailed."

Dani leaned back, enjoying the ride and Savage's sturdy defense of the good old days. His hands were strong and square, capable of rendering a strong man unconscious—or of giving a caressing touch to a woman's cheek. Together they had been through a great deal in the past two years. After taking over Ross Investigations, Dani had needed a man in the company, and Ben had dropped into her life to fill that position. His ideas on women really *were* antediluvian, considering them best fitted for having children and washing dishes. During the first weeks of his employment, she had come close to firing him many times. But she had learned that his glib talk clothed a very sensitive spirit, so she had put up with him. They had had some close calls, and it had been the toughness of Savage that had gotten them through more than once.

Now as they sped along the Lake Pontchartrain Causeway at a highly illegal speed, she let her eyes rest on the planes of his strong jaw, thinking of the other side of their lives together. He had kissed her a few times, and his kisses had stirred her more than those of any other man. But he had never forced himself on her, which had both relieved her and puzzled her. He saw other women, she knew, but there was some sort of barrier around Ben Savage, and he stayed inside it for the most part. It was as if a high fence had been built around his house, and he had hung a large KEEP OUT! sign over the entrance.

As they left the causeway, he turned left, heading west. "Where are we going?" she asked.

"Thought we might go to T.J. Ribs," he shrugged.

"You *always* want to go there," Dani said. "Don't you ever think about trying a new place?"

"When you find a winner, stick with it."

"You miss a lot with that philosophy," Dani argued. She was amused at his attitude, but surprisingly enough had been strongly influenced by Savage's almost fierce conservatism. As they sped along Interstate 10, she bantered with him, teasing him about being monolithic, and he defended himself staunchly.

April in Louisiana was hot and steamy, a chronic condition that was never going to change. On each side of the highway, huge cypress trees rose out of the black waters of Lake Pontchartrain, their swollen bases tapering into strong trunks. The dark waters were broken by the incredible white of egrets and the floating logs. As Dani looked on, one of the "logs" suddenly opened its jaws, transforming into an eight-foot alligator.

The warm air and the drone of the powerful engine proved to be too much. Dani had slept little, and when she lay her head back on the smooth leather listening to Ben talk, she dropped off into a sound sleep. She awakened when the car slowed abruptly, and sat up, rubbing her neck, which was stiff. They were inside the city limits of Baton Rouge, and she murmured, "Nice way to treat a date—going to sleep."

Savage only nodded, saying, "You're pretty washed out, Boss."

He took the Acadian exit and pulled into the crowded parking lot of T.J. Ribs. The building was a low structure surrounded by cars and the aroma of cooking meat. Ben put the Hawk between a fire-engine red Corvette and a black Ranger pickup truck. He got out, opened the door for Dani, and escorted her toward the entrance. A small brass sign on the front door said, *We cannot take your personal checks.* They passed through a short hall, then stepped into the interior, which consisted of a large bar in the center, surrounded by a dining area. A young woman at the desk to the right smiled and inquired, "How many, sir?" When she found out, she asked, "Smoking or non-smoking?"

"Non-smoking."

"It'll be about twenty minutes, sir."

There were no seats for the ten or twelve people who waited, so Dani and Savage stood with the others. One wall was covered with the pictures of all the Heisman Trophy winners since the award had first been given. "How many of them can you name?" Savage asked Dani.

"None."

"I'll bet you can name all the presidents of the United States, though."

"Yes, I can."

"How many times has somebody called you and asked breathlessly, 'Please, name me all the presidents of the United States?'"

"And you get calls all the time asking you to name all the Heisman Trophy winners, don't you?"

"Constantly!"

They stood for twenty minutes, and then a waiter came to say, "Savage? Table for two? This way, sir." He led them through the crowded dining area, made a sharp left turn and seated them at a table set for two people. "Enjoy your meal," he smiled, then left.

As he pulled Dani's chair out, then pushed it in, Savage said, "I hate it when they say that."

"You'd rather they say, 'I hope you choke'?"

Savage picked up the menu and stared at it. "I hate meaningless words."

Dani was amused. "It'd be a pretty silent world if people didn't use a lot of meaningless talk. And why are you looking at the menu? You always have the same thing."

When the waiter came, he further irritated Savage. His name tag read "William," and he started to say, "My name is William, and I'll be your waiter tonight." But Savage said first, "My name is Ben, and I'll be your customer tonight." Then he added, "I'll have the baby-back ribs and the lady will have half a barbecued chicken. We'll both have baked beans, slaw, and cornbread. I'll have coffee, and she'll have a Coke."

The waiter was slightly rattled by his rapid words, and stared at Dani for confirmation. "It's all right, she'll eat what I tell her," Ben said. "And don't tell her about women being liberated. I'm trying to keep it from her."

"Yes, sir!"

As the waiter scurried off, Dani laughed. "You ought to be ashamed!"

"Why? He's the one who ought to be ashamed," Savage shrugged. He looked at the pictures of the basketball players on the wall, then added, "If he tells me to have a good day when we leave, I'm going to punch him out!"

Dani was accustomed to Savage's ways, and they sat there talking until William brought their food. He said nothing, but retreated as soon as possible. "You've got him scared," Dani said. "You'll have to give him a big tip to ease your conscience."

"Ask the blessing," Savage said. "A short one, if possible. I'm hungry."

Dani bowed her head and murmured a few words of thanks. As they began eating, she thought of how odd it was that Ben always made that request—that she ask the blessing. He was not a believer, but adamantly insisted on this formality. As she dissected the golden brown chicken, she wondered about this, but said nothing.

The meal was delicious, as always. The room was noisy, for the bar was not separated from the dining room, and two television sets gave reruns of basketball and football games. Finally they finished, and Dani noticed that Savage gave William a ten-dollar tip. "See?" she nudged him. "It costs to be crude and impolite."

"It's worth it, though," he grinned. He allowed her to go first, and as they made their way through the room, she felt him touch her shoulder. She turned and saw him motion with his head to a group seated at a round table by the wall. She recognized the governor of Louisiana, Layne Russell, but waited until they were outside to say, "I guess the governor is slumming."

"I've seen him here before," Savage murmured. "He knows good barbecue. I guess that's the one good thing about the man."

"Who was the girl with him?"

"One of his string, I guess. He changes them with his shirts."

After they got into the car, Savage backed out and threaded the Hawk down the narrow strip that led to the exit. He turned right, and drove onto the interstate. The sky was dark now, and Dani sat back, conscious of the throbbing of the big V-8 engine. Savage drove slowly, and Dani paid no heed to where they were going. They crossed over the Mississippi River bridge, and for half an hour, enjoyed the night air. Then Savage turned back, and as they came over the bridge, Dani saw the lights along the edge of the east bank of the river. "They look like strings of emeralds, don't they," she said with admiration. She paused, then added, "I wonder how many cases of lung cancer those petrochemical plants have caused?"

Savage glanced at the brilliant lights before answering. "Quite a few. I read the other day that Louisiana ranked first in air pollution—and I'll give you one guess which city in Louisiana ranked first."

"Baton Rouge?"

"Sure. So right now we're in the most polluted spot in the United States. Kind of makes you proud, doesn't it?"

"The governor doesn't seem to be worried."

"No. Chemical industry money got him elected. Guess it keeps him in women and fine cars even now." Savage took the exit and drove through the middle of the Baton Rouge business center—one of the most attractive in the country. The streets were lined with huge live oak trees that had been carefully preserved. Savage commented, "Glad they left those big trees. Now a person can get held up and shot in the shade."

He emerged from the business district onto the River Road, and pulled up on a cobblestone street. "Let's go out on the pier and smooch," he suggested.

Dani got out and walked with him up the steep steps that ascended the levee. They walked out on a steel structure of round tubes that arched gracefully and extended out into the Mississippi. The pier was deserted, and it was so quiet that Dani could hear the waves lapping at the steep columns as the muddy waters swept by heading for the gulf.

"Look, there's the USS Kidd," Savage said. "Took some bad hits from kamikazes in the South Pacific."

"What's it doing here?"

"Been made into a war memorial," Savage answered. "It's closed now. Someday we'll come over and take the tour. It's just like it was when it was a fighting ship. Papers still in the typewriters, stuff like that." He turned his back and leaned against the rail. "I come over sometimes and play sailor. Pretend to shoot down Zeros with the pom-poms."

"You haven't outgrown that?"

"Nope. Just a little boy at heart."

Dani leaned on the rail and stared at the sleek outline of the destroyer, then turned to face Savage. "You really are—but I didn't find out about it for a long time." Her lips curved into a smile and she put her hand on his arm. "I thought you were just another hard-nosed cop."

"Eagle scout with a heart of gold—that's me."

But Dani shook her head. "You're tough, but you still like to play games. That's why you like old cars and airplanes. And you only watch old movies. Just a romantic, that's all you are!"

Savage was very still, his eyes turned down. A brown pelican floated by, riding the breeze. From far away a hoarse foghorn moaned faintly.

"Funny you should say that," he murmured at last. He reached into his pocket, pulled out a small object and held it up.

"What is it, Ben?" Dani asked.

"For you."

Dani was surprised, but took the small box. It was, she saw, from a jeweler's. She opened it, and a small reflection caught her eye. She touched it, then looked at Savage with a startled expression.

"Why—it's a ring!" When he didn't answer, she removed the ring and held it up, where it caught the silver light of the full moon. "It's not a diamond, is it?"

Savage turned to face her, and his eyes were watchful. He seemed tense, and Dani thought that she had seen him so poised only when danger threatened.

"Yes, it's a diamond," he said slowly. He paused and added, "It's an engagement ring."

For one moment Dani had the notion that Savage had found a girl and wanted her opinion of the ring he'd picked out for her. But one quick look at his face and she knew he was asking her to marry him.

It was not Dani's first proposal, but always before she'd been able to handle the situation deftly. Now she was absolutely unable to think of one thing to say. She stood there staring into Ben's face, trying to read his expression.

And Savage was no help. He stood quietly, saying nothing, but watching her face. She knew well his ability to read her feelings, and knew that there was no possibility of deceiving him.

"Why, Ben—" she said slowly. "You've caught me off guard. I had no idea—"

Savage said, "I'm no good at this. No practice, I guess." He hesitated, then said simply, "I love you, Dani. Have for a long time."

Dani waited, but he said no more. She felt his eyes on her, then took a deep breath. "I didn't know that, Ben." The inadequacy of her reply moved her to say quickly, "We've been good friends, but marriage is more than that, isn't it?"

Savage shook his head. "Dani, I've never told a woman I loved her. And I've got a funny feeling I'll never tell another one." He pulled her into his arms and was kissing her before she could even think. Dani felt the strength of his arms, and his lips on hers were demanding. She had felt helpless and lost since the death of her father, and as she rested in Savage's embrace, she knew a security that she'd longed for. There was a need in her for a man's strength, and she recognized that Ben Savage had the same purposeful power that had rested in her father.

But then he pulled his head back and asked quietly, "Do you care for me, Dani?"

"I—I have always had strong feelings for you, Ben," Dani answered. She found that her knees were weak, and she knew that she had to say something to him that was going to hurt. "I don't know if I love—"

"Somebody else?"

Dani knew he was thinking of Luke Sixkiller, the brawny chief of the homicide department in New Orleans. "Ben, I'm so mixed up," she whispered. "It's been a hard time for me—for all of us—since Dad died." She carefully put the ring back into the box, noting that her fingers were unsteady. "I can't think about such things now. Mother's having a hard time—and so are Rob and Allison."

Savage took the box and slipped it into his pocket. Then he said, "It's more than that, isn't it, Dani?"

"Well, yes, Ben," Dani said slowly. "I could never marry any man unless he felt like I do about God. It just wouldn't work."

Savage said slowly, "I know that." He looked down at the deck, then back up and said, "And I've made up my mind. I'll become a Christian."

Dani stared at him, speechless. "Ben, you can't become a Christian just to please me!"

"I know that, too. But it's more than you and me, Dani." Savage stared out over the water, his face tense in the silver light. "It's a lot of things—or a lot of people, I guess. I watched your dad. He was the real article. I thought all Christians were really kind of soft—but he wasn't. And then there's Luke—nothing soft about him! " Savage smiled faintly. "But it's you, mostly. Ever since those days in the silo when it looked like we were all going to go belly-up, I've been watching you. Kicking your tires, too, trying to shake you up. You're like your dad and your mother, Dani." He paused, then said, "I've always wanted to think there was something in this life more than what a man could see or feel—but until I met you, I never found it."

"Oh, Ben!" Dani whispered. "It would make us all so happy to see you find Christ! Dad spoke about it so often." But then she shook her head, a warning in her tone and her eyes. "But this is between you and God, not between you and me."

Savage considered her, then nodded. "Sure. I figured that, Dani. But I had to tell you. And I know that even after I find God, that doesn't mean I get you." He smiled crookedly, then said, "Let's go home."

Dani walked with him off the pier. Ten minutes later they were in the car and headed back toward Mandeville, but she paid no heed to the dark landscape. She was shaken by what had taken place, and somehow knew that the two of them could never go back completely to what they had been.

Savage began to talk about one of the cases they were on, and she knew that he was telling her that he was not going to overburden her with unwanted attention. When they pulled up in front of the house, she said, "Ben, Mother's arranged a 'surprise' party for you. Just the family. But if you want to get out of it—?"

Savage grinned at her. "You trying to do me out of some chocolate cake?" He got out of the car and opened her door, adding, "I knew about the party. Allison gave it away."

Then he said, "Boss, don't let what I said be a weight. No matter what happens, it's okay."

They went inside, and as Ben put on a big show of being astonished, Dani was thinking: *I can't hurt him—no matter what!*

2
Trip to Angola

For several days after Ben's proposal, Dani moved through her daily rituals efficiently, despite her inner feelings of confusion. She didn't mention it to her mother, though the temptation to lean on someone was a sharp urging deep inside.

She had dreaded going to work, not knowing how to behave around Ben. But he took that matter out of her hands, for he never once referred to what had been said. Dani was relieved when he spoke with her naturally and without any sense of strain.

However, her own work suffered, for she discovered that the proposal had shaken her more than she had dreamed such a thing might. Most of the girls she had grown up with were married already, some of them having started their families. A sense of fleeting time came to her, and somehow she felt left behind and unfulfilled.

At the age of twenty-seven she had achieved a great deal, more than most young women. She had been a CPA, she had spent many productive years working for the attorney general of Tennessee, and, for the past two years, she had been the head of a successful investigation agency. She was not rich, but money had never been a problem, and she had no yearning for status symbols. And yet—the more she thought of her life, the more barren it seemed. She had never been caught up with the women's movement, considering most of the leaders to be rather mannish types, unable somehow to take pride in their femininity. She had been approached often by the local leaders in the movement to give herself to the cause, but had always refused.

On the other hand, her own concept of what a well-balanced and fulfilled woman should be had come from her own mother. She had seen from her childhood a graphic portrayal of a woman who was as lovely and feminine as a human could be—yet at the same time, had been fully equal with her husband. But part of this, Dani recognized, was due to the fact that her father had loved her mother devotedly, and that he understood women and their real place better than anyone she'd ever known.

"I always wanted to be a king, Dani," Dan Ross had once told Dani when she was sixteen and struggling with the problem of becoming a woman. She'd gone to him honestly with questions about herself, and he'd taken her for a long walk through the woods. "But the only way I could be a king," he'd said, "was to be married to a queen. So, when I married your mother, I was smart enough to make her a queen. Do you see what that meant? A man who's married to a queen is a king— so that's what I became." Dani never forgot how he'd smiled at her that day, thoughtfully and seriously, and how he'd taken her hand and finally said, "When you marry a man, Dani, be sure he understands this—that you must be a queen. A man's first responsibility is to God, but his second is to his wife. She must come before everything else, even before his children. I love you and Rob and Allison more than my own life, but Ellen will always come first. You three will all leave my house someday to find homes and companions of your own. But Ellen is mine as long as I have breath. We're one flesh," he'd said, "and nothing can change that."

Dani was sitting at her desk on Wednesday morning, thinking of that time. The office of Ross Investigations occupied the second floor of what had once been a fine home on Bourbon Street. The location had once seemed romantic, but parking was terrible—and the evil that had found a place in the Quarter hovered over the section like a dense fog.

Morning sunlight flooded into the room from the tall windows that lined one side of the room, bringing out the rich glow of the antique walnut desk she sat at, and throwing a spotlight, it seemed, on the fine portrait of her great-great-grandfather on the wall across from her. Dani looked up suddenly at the portrait, and spoke his name aloud.

"Colonel Daniel Monroe Ross—" She studied the fierce-eyed man dressed in Confederate gray with a red sash around his waist and a steel trap for a mouth. He had made the charge with Pickett at Gettysburg, and she thought of the last sentence in his terse diary entry concerning that day: *It was a bold maneuver, doomed to failure—and my heart weeps over friends I left on that dreadful hill!*

Something in even the memory of those words was so painful that Dani rose and turned to the window to stare down on the narrow street below. A battered drunk with his white shirt ripped and dangling over his pants was plodding along across the street. His face was pale as paste and he had what appeared to be dried blood stiffening his dirty blonde hair. As Dani watched, he stumbled, fell headlong, and struggled for a brief time to get to his feet. Finally he put his head down on the concrete and lay motionless.

Dani had seen such things often, but they never failed to depress her. She knew the man would be picked up by the police and would wake up in the drunk tank. She knew also that he would probably be back on the street and drunk again as soon as he could find the money for a bottle of cheap wine. She turned away in disgust, and as she did, the intercom on her desk buzzed.

"Yes?"

"Captain Sixkiller is here, Miss Ross."

"Send him in, Angie," Dani said at once, and turned toward the door. When Luke Sixkiller entered, he seemed to make the room smaller, for he was perhaps the most physical man Dani had ever known. He was an inch under six feet, but thick and solid in every way. His deep chest arched under the ivory sports jacket. The pale blue shirt, Dani knew, was tailor-made for the policeman, for no shirt on the rack would meet around his thick neck.

"Hi, Dani," he said, and came to stand beside her. He had the blackest hair possible, obsidian eyes, a wide mouth, a roman nose, and high cheek bones. He was the terror of the underworld in New Orleans, and the word was, "Don't try to buy Sixkiller. Kill him if you can, but don't mess with him."

"How about we go get something to eat?"

"It's too early for lunch. Besides, I have work to do."

Luke grinned at her and his thick hand closed on her arm. "You're under arrest. Are you going to come quietly, or do I have to put the cuffs on you?"

Dani felt like a child in his grip, and suddenly was tired of the office. "All right," she agreed. She eyed his expensive slacks and coat, then said, "You've been shopping again, Luke. I feel like a dowdy bird next to you."

Luke glanced at her, taking in the orange safari dress she wore, and nodded. "I'll tell everybody you're my maiden aunt from Mississippi," he grinned. "Come on, let's go."

They walked down Bourbon Street, which was beginning to fill up with tourists. Dani watched as they looked through the half open doors of the strip joints and bars that advertised female wrestling, their faces scrubbed and smiling in the morning light. There was in some of the younger ones an innocence that would not last in their oblique fascination with the canned sin. Careless with youth, they squandered it as though nothing ever changed, unaware that they themselves were subject to time and decay—and death. Some of them, she knew, would wake up trembling and sick the next day in a motel off the old Airline Highway, with empty wallets and memories that would sicken them.

When they reached Jackson Square, they found that Cafe du Monde was not crowded at that early hour. They sat down at one of the outside tables. They drank café au lait and munched on sweet rolls. Across the way, the twin peaks of St. Louis Cathedral scored the pale blue of the sky, and the clean, sweeping design seemed somehow, to Dani, to mock the pitiful human derelicts that passed beneath its facade.

Sixkiller lounged in his chair, watching the scene before him, taking in the skinny black drug pusher who had set up not more than fifty yards away. "Little Willie's getting pretty bold," he remarked lazily. "Have to retire him pretty soon, I guess."

Dani looked at Sixkiller's relaxed form. "I can see you're all worked up over making a big arrest."

"Take Willie out and his replacement will be right in that spot the next day." He took a bite of his roll, then asked, "You going to the FCA rally with me tomorrow night?"

29

"I don't think dragging a woman along to preach to a bunch of jocks is that great an idea."

"Then you don't know much about jocks," Luke grinned. "Taking a good-looking broad along is a great idea—one of my all-time best. Some of those guys have an attention span of maybe four minutes. But with you along, it'll shoot up to five or six."

Dani smiled at the compliment, but was unconvinced. "Luke, what do you really think about all these 'approaches' to preaching the gospel? I mean, isn't the simple thing just to give them the good news?"

Sixkiller shrugged his broad shoulders. "Oh, I don't know, Dani. It gets pretty silly sometimes." He plucked his mug of café au lait from the table. It looked like a doll's cup in his huge hand, and when he set it down, he added, "Everybody wants to tag the gospel with their hobby, like 'Fellowship of Christian Athletes.' There's even one 'ministry' called 'Karate for Christ.'" He scowled, his eyes glinting as he commented, "I guess they chop a guy down, then stick a tract between his teeth. Next thing it'll be 'Judo for Jesus' or something just about as silly."

"Did you ever see that group of weightlifters who visit churches? They break bricks with their bare hands and blow up hot water bottles." Dani put her chin on her hand, her eyes solemn with thought. "I think they give their testimonies afterward—but it seems odd to me. The best Christians I've met weren't the heroic football players or the stars of the court. Why do we have to try to 'improve' on what the Bible says about preaching the gospel?"

"It's the times, I guess. If it works to have famous jocks advertise Jockey shorts, some half-baked assistant pastor thinks we can peddle Jesus the same way." He looked disturbed, and said irritably, "Why do you bug me with these things, Ross? I'm just a brand-new Christian. People come to hear me give my testimony because I'm a hard-nosed New Orleans homicide detective. That's glamorous work—or they think it is. If I sold shoes for a living how many would show up to listen to me?"

"Paul was a tentmaker," Dani challenged. "He didn't do too badly, did he?"

Sixkiller was gloomy. "I've thought of all this, but so far no answers."

Dani leaned forward and took one of his big hands between hers. "You're doing a wonderful thing with your life, Luke. Not many men could go down into the Projects and tell that bunch about how Jesus can change their lives. God is blessing your testimony, so it's good."

He looked down at her hand, picked it up, and smiled. "That makes me feel better. You know how to make a man feel important, Dani." He tightened his grip on her hand, saying, "It could get to be a habit—"

For one moment Dani thought Sixkiller intended to propose—and she quickly pulled her hand free with a short laugh. "I've got to get back to work."

"Yeah—well, you're probably wondering why I brought you here," Sixkiller said. His dark eyes were fixed on her, and he seemed a little apprehensive. "You know about Eddie Prejean?"

"Prejean?" Dani nodded. "I followed the trial in the papers."

"He wants to talk to you."

Dani stared at Sixkiller. Eddie Prejean had been convicted of murdering his girlfriend, and after a relatively short trial, was sentenced to die. Capital punishment was back in favor, and Louisiana was trying to make up for lost time.

"What does he want with me?"

Sixkiller said evasively, "Don't know, but if you want to talk to him, it'll have to be soon. He's set to go in a week and a half."

"That soon?"

"Yeah, that's it." Sixkiller's eyes grew thoughtful. "I made the arrest, did you know that?"

"No, I didn't."

"No big deal. He was dead in the water, Dani. Didn't put up a fight, and kept saying all along he was innocent. Well, they all say that, I guess. But something about the whole thing bothered me. Still does."

"The governor was involved, wasn't he?"

"Sure, but not in a big way. He's a womanizer, which everybody knows. He was making a play for Prejean's girl, and Prejean killed her in a jealous rage."

"The evidence was pretty strong, as I remember."

"Open and shut. The girl, Cory Louvier, was beaten to death with a flashlight. The flashlight was found in Prejean's car, and samples of his skin and hair were found under the dead girl's fingernails. Jury was back in thirty minutes."

Dani frowned. "It doesn't seem long enough, Luke. I mean, the appeals take quite a while." Stop

"That's what bothers me, Dani. If Prejean had been from a minority, he'd have had half a dozen liberal groups fighting for him. But he had a lawyer who'd never argued before a jury—and none of the appeals went through. The judges who passed them by would have turned Hitler loose."

Dani stared at him. "You think something's wrong?"

"I got no evidence, Dani. But I've been to see Prejean twice." The big policeman's face was tense as he said slowly, "I think I know liars pretty well. I've listened to enough of them! All the evidence says Prejean's guilty. But when I listen to him, something inside me says he's not a liar."

"How'd he hear about me?"

"Been reading your press clippings, I guess. And I told him a little. Anyway, I saw him yesterday, and when I left, he asked me to come and see you." Luke hesitated, then said, "I'm afraid he's got the idea you can work some magic for him, Dani. I tried to tell him it's too late, but he asked me to do it. I—I figure I owe him a favor. Dead is a long time. And I was the one who picked him up."

Dani said at once, "I'll do it, Luke. Can you fix it with the warden?"

A look of relief came into Sixkiller's dark eyes. "Already fixed. You can get into death row anytime you want to."

Dani smiled at him. "Pretty sure of me, weren't you, Luke?"

"Yeah, I was." Sixkiller looked at the spires of the cathedral across the square, then back to her. "I'm not sure of much, kid, but you're one I don't ever doubt. Come on, I'll walk you back to your office."

Dani followed the blacktop road through twenty miles of thick, almost impenetrable, scrub oak and pine until she surfaced in the open country and saw the low buildings that made up Angola Penitentiary. Rain had fallen in slanting lines all the way, and the plum-colored sky was adorned with limp, dingy clouds that looked like decayed, old lace.

When she got to the front gate, she was admitted after a stony-faced guard gave her a short lecture on how to behave and a veiled threat of what would happen to her if she violated any of the regulations. He glanced then at his clipboard, saying reluctantly, "I got your name on my clipboard. I'll ride with you up to the Block."

Smelling of stale tobacco and sweat, he got into the front seat of the Cougar. He had the flat green eyes and heavy facial bones of North Louisiana hill people. "You must have some clout," he said, eyeing Dani carefully. "You a friend of the warden?"

"No, I don't know him."

The guard cocked his eye and punched her with his elbow. "Hey, you must be Eddie's main squeeze, right?"

Dani tried to move away from his persistent elbow. "I don't know him either."

That seemed to puzzle the guard, but he was the aggressive type, and as Dani followed his directions, she was engaged in avoiding him as he crowded closer, looking out at the huge, flat expanse of the prison farm at the same time. The main living area of the prison was a series of two-story, maximum-security dormitories contained within a wire fence and connected by breezeways and exercise yards. They were collectively called the Block, and they were as brilliantly lit as a football stadium in the rain. In the distance, she could see the surgically perfect fields of sugar cane and sweet potatoes and the crumbling ruins of the nineteenth-century camps silhouetted against the sun's red afterglow. The willows bent in the breeze along the Mississippi levee, under which, Dani had heard, lay many a murdered convict, buried in unmarked graves.

"You know the Red Hat House?"

Dani had moved as far as possible away from the man, so she turned and looked him in the eye. "Get on your own side of this seat or I'll report you to the warden."

"You don't know him!"

"We have a mutual friend named Layne Russell."

"Hey, no problem, lady!" The guard scooted back against the door on his own side at once and smiled nervously.

"What's the Red Hat House?"

"It's where they keep the chair," he said quickly, anxious to make amends. "They used to work the worst offenders down by the river there, and they made them wear striped jumpers and red-painted straw hats. Made good targets for the guards, you see? Then at night, they body searched them, then ran them into the Red Hat House and threw their clothes in after them. Wasn't no screens on the windows, so the mosquitoes would about eat them alive." Stop

Dani parked the car, and the guard said quickly, "I'll just go on back, lady. You go right in that door over there."

"Thank you," Dani said evenly. She entered, after a guard inside cleared her by radio with the front gate, moved down a long brilliantly lit breezeway between the recreation yards, and passed through another set of hydraulic locks and a dead space where two guards were playing cards at a table. Overhead a sign read *No guns beyond this point.* She was checked for identification, then one of the guards took her into the rec and dining halls where the trustees were waxing the gleaming floors. She followed the guard up some spiral iron steps to a small maximum-security corner, where he turned her over to another guard. This one pulled a single lever that slid back the cell door. Inside, a youngish man was lying on a bunk, staring up at the ceiling.

"Visitor for you, Prejean," the guard grunted, and as Dani stepped into the small cell, the man lifted himself and sat looking at her as the guard shut the door.

"You must be Dani Ross, I guess."

"Yes. Luke Sixkiller said you wanted to talk to me."

Prejean was a tall, wiry man of twenty-seven. He had black curly hair, brown eyes, and teeth that gleamed very white against his olive skin. He crushed the cigarette he had been smoking in the overflowing ashtray on the small table beside the bunk. "Didn't think you'd come," he said. His voice was soft and even, but his hands were unsteady. He motioned at the painted kitchen chair, saying, "Sit down, please." When Dani sat down, he said, "I appreciate your coming here."

Dani felt ill at ease. The young man seemed so alive, so healthy—yet in a few days he would be dead. She asked carefully, "Is there something I can do for you, Mr. Prejean?"

"Call me Eddie." Prejean pulled a battered package of Camels from his T-shirt pocket, stuck one between his lips, and lit it with a match. His movements were all quick and nervous, and when he tried to smile, he failed miserably. He puffed on the cigarette, then removed it with yellow-stained fingers. "I read about some of the cases you worked on," he said. "That story in the magazine section of the *Morning Advocate.*"

Dani shook her head decisively. "Most of that was hokum, Eddie. The woman needed a human interest story, so she thought an article about a woman private eye would do. She interviewed me, but I don't think she heard much of what I said." Dani smiled slightly, adding, "She read a lot of detective novels, and some of them got into her story. I'm not nearly so much of a hot dog as the story made me out to be."

Prejean listened carefully, then said, "Sixkiller thinks different."

"Oh—well, he's a friend of mine," Dani said lamely.

"Sixkiller's a pretty tough egg, and he don't have a lot of good to say about private cops. But he said you could handle about anything."

Dani asked, "What is it you want done, Eddie?"

Prejean stared at her, his dark eyes brooding, and there was a specter of fear over him. "I'm set to go in ten days, Miss Ross. And I didn't kill Cory." He rose from the bunk suddenly, turned, and faced the wall, leaning against it, pressing his head against his forearm.

He's scared to death—and too proud to let me see him cry, Dani thought. She waited until the tremors in his back ceased, then said gently, "I'd like to help you, Eddie, but this isn't a detective novel. You had a trial, and it would take something very solid to get a stay of execution. The governor's already turned you down, hasn't he?"

Prejean whirled and a streak of temper reddened his dark cheeks. "He's laughing about it—laughing!" He clenched his fists until the knuckles turned white, and, at that moment, he appeared to be capable of any violence. Then he took a deep breath and sat down. "You know my job—when I was outside?"

"No, I don't."

"I worked for DEQ—Department of Environmental Quality. I did more to clean up the pollution in Louisiana than any other man in the department." He allowed a grim smile to touch his lips. "And do you know who I had to fight tooth and nail to get that done?"

"The chemical companies, I suspect."

"No, I could handle them. It was our fearless leader, Governor Layne Russell, who gave me the worst time."

"Why would he do that?" Dani asked.

"Because the chemical people put him in office. Do you know how much they put into his campaign last election? Over a million dollars—and that's not counting what they slipped him under the table. Russell knows that I've got almost enough stuff to get him out of office next election. And he was after my girl—who turned him down. So there won't be any stay of execution, and no pardon."

Dani studied Prejean, trying to decide what she thought. She hated the idea of any human being dying in an electric chair, although she believed in capital punishment. The difficulty was, of course, that there was much unfairness and injustice in the process. "You can't put a million dollars in the chair," was a statement she'd heard, and she knew there was some bitter truth to it.

Eddie Prejean saw the doubt on Dani's face, and said slowly, "I got no right to ask you a favor, Miss Ross. Never even thought of it until Sixkiller came to see me and got to talking about you. He said if you'd been on my case, you'd have found some way to get at the truth. And he never told me to ask for help." He dropped his head, and was silent for a long, painful moment. "Well, thanks for coming. That's something most people wouldn't have done."

He looked so young and vulnerable that Dani felt a sudden pang of grief. *He's not much older than my brother,* she thought. *If Rob were here in this place, facing a terrible death—I know what I'd do!* She sat there struggling with her doubts, and could not get a clear direction. So deeply was she engaged in this inner struggle, she was not aware that Prejean was watching her with a faint gleam of hope in his dark eyes.

She began to pray, silently, and for several moments the thoughts that flickered through her mind were so confused that she could not even voice them to God. This had happened before, but she had learned that if she waited and kept calling on the name of Jesus, the wild thoughts would fade. Finally they did, and she asked simply, *Lord, if you want me to help this man, you'll have to give me some kind of assurance. I don't know your will—but I want to do whatever that will is.* Stop

Prejean watched, almost ceasing to breathe. He thought of Sixkiller's words about Dani Ross, *She's smart and can be tough, Eddie. She's also kind of a lady preacher—* The policeman's words had confused Prejean, but now as he watched the young woman struggle with her thoughts, he got a faint idea of what Sixkiller had been trying to say.

Finally, Dani looked up, and there was a peace on her face, an air of having come to a decision. "I'll help you all I can,

Eddie," she said quietly. "But you'd better understand that it's going to take more than any human being can do to get you out of this. You'll need God's help."

Eddie nodded slowly. "I—I don't know anything about God, Miss Ross. I'll just have to trust you, I guess."

Dani smiled and nodded. "That will do for now. But I'm going to pray that you'll find the One who can really unlock the prison for you." Then she said briskly, "All right, tell it to me, Eddie—all of it. And remember, if you lie, you're defeating your own chances. God has told me to help you, and I'll do that no matter what you've done." She paused, then held his eyes with a steady gaze. "Did you kill that girl?"

Eddie Prejean blinked, and then tears came into his eyes. "I loved her more than my own life, Miss Ross. No, I didn't kill her!"

Dani Ross studied the lean face in front of her, then nodded. "All right, let's find out who did."

3
A Visit to Baton Rouge

Never had Dani been so conscious of the passing of time as during the day after her meeting with Eddie Prejean. Every clock seemed to be saying, "TIME IS PASSING! TIME IS PASSING!" She had dreamed that night about Eddie Prejean, seeing his thin tense face, and finally had awakened hours before dawn. She went over and over his story, trying to piece it together, to find some sort of angle that would change the focus.

Finally she had risen and dialed Ben's number. He had answered at the second ring, his voice wary and cautious, "Yeah, who is it?"

"It's Dani. Did I wake you up?"

"No, I've been up for hours reading my old copies of the *Congressional Record*."

"Let's go get something to eat. Can you meet me at the Camellia Grill in half an hour?"

"Right. I'll be the one with red-rimmed, sleepy eyes."

Dani threw on a white blouse and a long purple skirt, slipped into a pair of alligator pumps, then hesitated. She gave the drawer of her nightstand a grim glance, then opened it, removed the .38, and slipped it into her matching alligator purse. She left the house quietly, although she knew that her mother would be awakened by the car starting. *Should have left a note,* she thought, but chose not to go back. *I'll call her from the office.*

It took her less than the half hour she'd allowed to get to the Camellia Grill. She spotted Savage's Hawk parked on the street as she approached the restaurant. She got out of the Cougar, locked it carefully, and went inside. There were no tables, just counters, and she went at once to seat herself beside Savage, saying only, "Hello, Ben." He was wearing a pair of faded Levi's, a white T-shirt covered by a black jacket, which didn't quite conceal the .44 he wore under his arm, and a pair of black Nike running shoes.

A small chef with a black face made blacker by the white chef's cap came over to them. "What can I get you folks?"

"Banana waffles and coffee for me," Ben nodded. He glanced at Dani who merely nodded. "Make it two, Leroy."

"Comin' right up!"

The cafe was fairly crowded; it was a favorite spot for those who enjoyed early breakfasts. Located on Carrollton Avenue, not far from Tulane, students especially came there often. Several of them were there busily downing the fluffy pancakes served by the corps of black cooks.

Dani waited until two cups of black, steaming coffee were set in front of them, and she took a cautious sip before she said, "Ben, I went to Angola yesterday—to see Eddie Prejean—"

As Dani spoke, Savage watched her face, taking in her words carefully. She was good at reviewing things, and he knew she was filling him in for a reason. The waffles came, and Dani interrupted her recitation long enough to cut hers up and baptize it in maple syrup. She ate slowly, pausing from time to time to think about her story. She had the sort of analytical mind, Savage understood, that would dissect every word and every action, so he ate his own breakfast, taking it all in without interruptions.

Finally she ended by saying, "That's it, Ben. What do you think?"

Savage pushed the last morsel of his waffle around in the pool of syrup with his fork, stabbed it, and put it into his mouth. He chewed it thoughtfully, then swallowed. Dani waited, knowing that he would be thinking over every angle.

"I think it's a waste of time," he said finally. "Execution is when—nine days?" Putting his fork down, he took a swig of coffee, then put the mug down and turned to face her. "You know as well as I do the odds against finding enough evidence to get a stay. Practically zero."

"I've got to try, Ben!"

"Why? Guys get burned pretty regular at Angola. What's different about this one?"

"Well, I think God is telling me to do something." She saw his eyebrow rise in a skeptical fashion, and looked directly into his eyes. "No, I haven't been hearing voices, if that's what you're thinking. But if you're even half serious about becoming a Christian, you'll have to accept the fact that God does lead people."

Savage saw that she was upset, and shook his head. "Sorry, Boss. Old habits die hard. Want to tell me about it? I'd like to help."

Dani's lips had grown tense, but now they softened, and she smiled. "Would you, Ben? Well, I realize it's hard for people who don't know God to understand things like this.

It's hard for me, too," she added. She gave her head a shake, causing her hair to sway over her collar. "I've been wrong about things like this. I may be wrong this time—but I'd rather make a mistake than miss God."

"Okay, let's go over it." Savage motioned for a refill of coffee, and when it came he tasted it slowly. "According to Prejean's story, he's got the goods on the DEQ and the governor—and he's gonna publish a book that'll blow them both out of the water." He swirled the ebony liquid around in the white mug thoughtfully, then added, "I don't think anyone can do that, Boss. It's been tried before, but Russell is a tough nut. He's slick and looks good, but he's been on the top of Louisiana politics for a long time. No man can do that unless he's a genius at covering up his tracks. I can name two or three guys who set out to nail him, and they're not around anymore—but Russell is."

"That's right, Ben," Dani nodded. "But even Louisiana voters get fed up eventually, and from what I can pick up, this will be the straw that breaks the camel's back. Eddie claims he's got proof that Russell's been bought by the chemical people—canceled checks and secret bank accounts—*and* one of the biggest wheels in the industry is willing to testify against Russell."

"He better not shout about it from the rooftop," Savage commented. "Some folks who tried that are feeding the fish in the Mississippi River. Well, what about the evidence against Prejean? I read the account in the papers. I'd vote him guilty on it myself."

"It's all circumstantial, Ben," Dani frowned. "Eddie claims that he got drunk and when he saw Russell making a play for his girl, he got mad. Some of Russell's goons put him out, and he says he went home and went to bed."

"That's not what the witnesses say," Savage objected. "According to one of them, he left with the girl."

"I don't believe it," Dani shrugged. "Eddie was positive about it."

"Anybody see him leave alone?"

"He was too drunk to notice, he said."

"Great! Well, how'd he get out in the country if he was too drunk to drive?"

Dani traced a pattern on the countertop, discouragement in her expression. She knew she was making a bad case, and it bothered her. She wanted Ben to believe her, and didn't know how to put the story to him. When Prejean had told it to her, something in his thin face and frantic eyes had convinced her, but now it seemed unlikely.

"He says he went to bed and passed out. He remembers that somebody woke him up—or tried to, but he can't remember. He thinks somebody gave him some drugs that really put him out of it, and he says he woke up in the car, sick, and with no idea what had happened."

"He didn't know the girl was dead?"

"No, he was definite on that." Dani turned to Savage, adding, "I know it sounds thin. But you should have been there when he was telling it, Ben. When he spoke about the dead girl, tears came into his eyes. I think he loved her."

They went over the evidence piece by piece, but the cafe filled up, and they had to leave. When they were outside, Ben said, "Let's take a ride on the trolley. That's a good place for a couple of private eyes to discuss a case."

They got on the streetcar, found a seat isolated from the other passengers, and talked quietly. There was something nostalgic about the sound of the trolley, and even as they talked, Dani noted the fine old mansions. They passed under the expressway, around Lee's Circle, then back toward Loyola and Tulane.

They were passing the Academy of the Sacred Heart when Dani finally said, "I don't know where to start, Ben."

"I do," Savage smiled. "Poke a stick down a hole and see if any rats come out."

Dani laughed, a relaxed sound, for the talk with Savage had brought relief to her. "Sounds like your most common method. Which particular holes do you recommend?"

"Any department of state government has a plentiful supply of rats," he shrugged. "Prejean worked for DEQ. I know a guy close to stuff at the top. I'll have a shot at that."

Dani frowned, saying, "That party where the girl was last seen—she had to leave there in a car. I'll take my little stick and poke down that hole."

Savage put his arm around her suddenly, and she knew that he was checking to see if she was wearing her .38. "It's in my bag," she said quickly.

Savage left his arm around her, but shook his head. "Hard to get a weapon out of that mess. Better wear it where you can clear it."

"You're hugging me, Ben," Dani accused.

"The trolley driver is getting suspicious. We've got to make him think we're lovers, or he'll be on to us." He turned to her, smiled, and suddenly kissed her lightly. Then he shrugged, saying, "It's a rotten job, but somebody's got to do it." Then he got up, saying, "Enough of your romantic nonsense, Ross—it's time to go to work."

They disembarked from the streetcar, got into their cars, and left the lovely old street. As Dani drove away, she thought, *He's a pretty good guy to have on your side, that fellow!*

Dani spent all morning in Baton Rouge. She talked to the hired help at the Leonard Hotel. She found several employees who had been on duty the night Cory Louvier had been killed, but they were all reluctant to talk to her. Dani was accustomed to that, for people in general didn't like to get involved with the police.

She finally got some useful information from one of the waiters, a small black man of about forty. His name was Leon Williams, and he seemed much more ready to speak of the party than any of the others.

"Why, I seen that girl, miss," he nodded, "and it didn't never once occur to me that she was gonna be daid 'fore mornin'—no, indeed." He sobered and added, "But ain't not a one of us knows when the Lord is gonna call us home. The book say, 'No man know the day nor hour of his death.'"

"Did she act afraid, Mr. Williams?"

"Oh, no, ma'am! She wuz happy as a lark." Williams coughed and added apologetically, "But she was drinkin' hard likker—lak folks do at parties like that. She was laughin' and dancin' and havin' a good time. Didn't have no idea, pore little thing, that she was goin' out to meet God 'fore sunup." He blinked and said with a sorrowful note in his voice, "Sho' hope she was ready 'fore she went."

"You're a Christian, Mr. Williams?"

"Why, I'm a preacher of the gospel, Miss Ross! Pastor of the Greater Golden Sunlight Tabernacle." When Dani informed him that she was a fellow believer, he smiled happily. "Ain't it good to serve the good Lord?"

From that moment, the small man eagerly gave his version of the events at the party. He had little enough to offer, but he did give one helpful hint. When Dani wanted to know more about the car Cory Louvier had left in, he nodded, saying, "You bettah talk to Bejay. He parks all the cars. I spect he kin help you."

"Miss, I'd like to have a word with you."

Dani looked up to see that a heavyset man with sandy hair

and a pair of hard blue eyes had come up behind her. She noted that a look of apprehension came to Williams's brown eyes, and she said, "Thank you very much, Mr. Williams." Then as the black man hurried away, she turned to look at the man who was watching her. "Yes?"

"What's your business, miss?"

"What's yours?" Dani asked at once.

"Mullins—security." He studied her, then said, "Maybe we better go to my office—if you don't mind."

"Not at all." Dani followed the big man to a small cubicle with no name on the door. He motioned to a chair, sat down behind the desk, then stated, "You've been questioning our employees."

Dani took her license from her purse, and handed it across the desk. "I didn't know there was a security force here, Mr. Mullins. If I had, I'd have come to you first."

Mullins stared at the card, then handed it back to her slowly. "I've heard of you." He took a cigar from his inner pocket, removed the cellophane, and lit it with a gold lighter. Dani was aware that he moved slowly and deliberately to test her, but she allowed nothing to show on her face.

"What's your interest in Eddie Prejean?"

"I haven't said I have any."

"You're poking around trying to find out about the night the bimbo got killed. Nobody but Prejean's interested in that."

"I can't reveal the name of my client."

"Yeah, I know all about that." Mullins expelled a cloud of smoke in Dani's direction. He grinned as she frowned and waved the smoke away. "Look, you got anything to ask our people, you clear it through me."

"Were you on duty the night the *young lady* was killed?"

"Sure, I was. Want to hear about it?"

"Very much."

Mullins shrugged his huge shoulders, leaned back, and put his hands behind his neck. "Just another government orgy," he grinned. "Those guys can't stand their jobs, so every once in awhile the big guys let them blow off steam."

"Is Governor Russell one of the 'big guys'?" Dani prodded.

"Don't be cute, Miss Ross! You know the governor's a swinger. He ain't never made no secret of it. People in this state, they like that. Shows he's a regular guy. Old tradition, goes all the way back to—"

Mullins rambled on, obviously enjoying himself. He didn't mind talking about Prejean. "The guy was so drunk he could hardly walk, and sore as a boil. Him and the girl had a row right in the middle of the dance floor. Which you already heard about, I guess."

"At the trial, one of the employees—a man named Givens—testified that Prejean and the girl left together. Did you see them leave?"

"Naw, but Givens did. He works in the parking lot. Go on, talk to him if you want," Mullins waved his ham-like hand in the air.

"I will. And I understand the governor was interested in the girl who was killed. Is that correct?"

Dani expected the big man to deny it, but Mullins smiled again. "Sure he was interested. She was a good-looking broad and on the make. The governor likes that—and so did about ten other studs at the party." He took the cigar from his mouth, ran his eyes up and down Dani's body, and nodded, "You might have a shot with Russell yourself. Want me to set it up?"

"Why, yes, if you would." Dani was amused at the startled look that leapt into Mullins's eyes, for he had expected another answer. She got to her feet, pulled a card out of her purse, and laid it on the desk. "That's my office number. Call me as soon as you've got me a date with the governor. You can tell him I'm looking into the death of Cory Louvier, and that I've got several questions he might like to answer privately rather than in front of some other gentlemen."

"Hey—!" Mullins struggled to his feet, his face red. "What you tryin' to pull?"

Dani smiled sweetly at him. "And I'll tell the governor how much help you've given me on this investigation."

She left the room at once, and was gratified to hear Mullins calling out, "You stay outta this hotel, you hear me—!"

Dani drove back to Mandeville, dark catching her before she was halfway home. Her headlights picked up the red eyes of a possum. As she swerved to miss the creature, she saw that it was a maternal situation, for several tiny ratlike babies clung to the scaly tail. "Better get home, Mama, or you'll wind up at the 'Roadkill Restaurant' as the main course," she muttered.

As the trees flowed by, she tried to block out the thoughts of Eddie Prejean and his problem. She'd discovered that if she concentrated too long and hard on a problem, she lost her ability to analyze it clearly. Her heart was with Eddie Prejean, but her head told her that he was guilty. *He loved her, and she didn't love him back—not enough, anyway. When a man like that sees he's losing the thing he loves best, he's capable of doing anything.* She traced that thought to its ultimate conclusion. *What would I do if I was about to lose my family or the man I loved?*

She thought then of how she'd reacted with blind rage when her father had been killed by a sleazy mobster, and shook her head in a faint gesture of despair. She resolutely turned her thoughts away from the case, and by the time she pulled into the driveway, she had regained some degree of ease in her mind.

She was pleased as she noted that the blue Hawk was in front of the house. She got out of the car and walked around to the back of the house where she found Savage giving a gymnastic lesson to Allison. The floodlights were on, and Dani stopped suddenly, standing in the shadows watching the pair.

Savage was wearing an old blue workout suit and a pair of scruffy Nikes. Allison wore a canary yellow tank top and a black scoop-neck unitard with legging stirrups. Savage was saying, ". . . a good one, but you forgot your toes."

"Oh, Ben, I can't remember *everything!*" Allison complained. Despite the cool night air, her brow glistened with sweat, and she looked tired.

Savage grinned at the girl, his face highlighted into sharp planes by the harsh floodlights. "You don't have to remember anything," he said. "There's no time to *remember*. It has to be automatic." He stopped smiling when he saw that Allison was frustrated. "Look, remember when you first started driving, how confusing it was?"

"Yes, I guess so."

"So many things to do—and all at once. Step on the clutch, pull the gear shift down, let up on the clutch and step on the gas at the same time," he shrugged. "And you'd get so busy with all the stuff going on with gears and things, you'd forget to watch where you were going. And if you left out a step, the car would die."

"I remember," Allison smiled ruefully. "I thought I'd never get it all put together."

"But you did," Savage nodded. "Now you don't get in a car and think, 'First I have to step on the clutch, now I have to pull the gearshift down, and now I have to give it some gas'—You just *do* them, and it's all smooth and easy. And you'll do the same with your gymnastic work, Sweetie. You won't have to think about pointing your toes—they'll just sort of point themselves because you've trained them to do it. Now, let's try it again—"

Dani stepped out of the darkness, saying, "After you get through with the lesson, Ben, come inside, will you?"

Allison frowned, "Oh, Dani, you always want to have Ben! I can't even have an old lesson!" She whirled and ran into the house, rebellion in the set of her back.

Dani started to go after her, but Savage said, "Make it up later, Boss."

"She's so—sensitive!" Dani shook her head. "She's either hanging on me or running away from me mad as a hornet."

"Hard time for her." Savage studied Dani, his dark eyes careful. "You're a little along those lines yourself, or haven't you noticed?"

Dani was startled, then a touch of anger came to her. She hated to think that she needed people, and said stiffly, "If I've been 'hanging on you,' I'm sorry!"

"It's okay, Boss," Savage nodded, his lips turned up in a grin. "I like to be hanged on. Why, you can help yourself right now if you feel the need."

His good humor drove the irritation out of Dani, and she smiled suddenly. "I may take you up on that if things don't get better." She moved closer to him, adding, "How does it feel to have three hysterical females dangling from your neck?"

"I like it. Makes me feel masterful." He studied her, then asked, "No luck in Baton Rouge?"

"Come on inside and I'll tell you about it."

They left the patio and, entering the house, found Ellen setting the table. Her stonewashed jeans and cranberry crushneck top gave her a youthful appearance. "Hi," she greeted Dani. "Go wash up. Supper is ready."

"Don't let Ben get at the boudin," Dani warned as she turned and left the kitchen. "He'll put it all away!"

Ellen smiled at Ben, then asked, "How did the lesson go?"

"Fine."

"You don't overburden anyone with excess information, do you, Ben?" Ellen picked up one of the boudin sausages and handed it to Ben. "See if it's good."

Savage bit the end off the sausage and a glow of pleasure touched his dark eyes. "Just right!" He chewed on the spicy meat thoughtfully, then added, "Allison's going to be fine, Ellen. Just takes time." He swallowed the morsel, then gave her a peculiar look. "Going to take time for you, too."

Ellen glanced up at him quickly, noted the concern in his eyes, and said quickly, "I'll be all right, Ben."

"You put up a pretty good front—but the nights are bad, aren't they?"

Caught off guard, Ellen stopped dead still, her hand going to her throat. The smile faded and grief that she kept carefully hidden surfaced, twisting her lips and dulling her eyes. She said nothing for a few moments, and the ticking of the clock in the hall was audible.

"Yes, Ben," she whispered finally. "The nights are pretty bad."

"Wish I could help."

Ellen lifted her eyes to meet his. "You really mean that, don't you? Well, you *are* a help, Ben."

"Not much," he muttered. "Not much anyone can do, is there? We can only go so far with someone who's had a loss—and then we have to fall back and let him go alone."

She was surprised at his perception, as she was from time to time, and said so. "You're so tough, it always catches me off guard when you let me have a little glimpse of what's underneath that hard shell you wear." She turned and picked up the bowl of shrimp remoulade, then turned to say, "You're *here*, Ben, and I'm aware of it all the time. So are the girls—and Rob, too."

Savage was uncomfortable, for he disliked being thanked. "Well, Ellen, I'll be around." He grinned crookedly, adding, "If you want to save some bucks, you can unload on me instead of a shrink."

She laughed, and he stood there, talking and listening to her until Dani and Allison came down. Savage caught Dani's glance and knew that she'd made up with the younger girl. "Did you let him have any boudin?" Dani demanded. "I don't need to ask, because you always let him do what he wants."

"Keep a man's stomach full and he'll behave," Ellen smiled. "Which is the extent of my wisdom, I guess. Let's eat."

Rob came in from the study, and the five of them sat down. Ellen bowed her head and asked the blessing. Everyone was totally aware of the loss in their house at that moment, for it had always been Dan Ross who'd asked the blessing.

But Ellen was smiling, and they plunged into the food at once. She'd made oysters Bienville, and both Rob and Ben ate as though a famine were coming to Louisiana. There were crawfish patties, too, which were Allison's favorite, and for dessert, there was a large platter of pig's ears—*les oreilles de cochon*, as the Cajuns called them—balls of dough fried in oil, dipped in cane syrup, and rolled in pecans.

After the meal, Ben and Rob washed the dishes. Then they all played Trivial Pursuit for two hours. Ben won by knowing which country lies directly south of Detroit, Michigan, and was insufferable about his victory.

"You people are ignorant of geography," he announced. "You should have grown up traveling with a circus, then you'd know something."

Finally the rest of the family went to bed, discreetly leaving Ben and Dani alone.

They sat in the study for a time, and Dani told him about her visit to the Leonard Hotel. Savage listened, then said, "I'll have a talk with Givens, and the preacher, too." He got up to leave, and she walked him to the front door. The moon was shedding a silver light over the drive, and she accompanied him to the Hawk. When he turned, she said, "Thanks, Ben."

"No charge." He hesitated, then said ,"I'd like to do more."

Dani knew his meaning, but said, "I have to have time, Ben—and so do you."

"Sure, I know."

Savage got into the car, slamming the door. The deep-throated roar of the big engine fragmented the silence. "I'll see you tomorrow," he said as the Hawk left the driveway, turning off onto the main road.

Dani stood there, listening to the fading sound of the car, then moved slowly back toward the house. When she reached the door, she paused, her hand on the knob, and for one moment she longed to turn and run away, to find someplace where there was no crisis. But there was no place on earth like that, she well understood—so she took a deep breath and stepped inside, closing the door firmly behind her.

4

Old Flame

Spanish Town was a tired section of Baton Rouge's inner city that lapped at the edges of the downtown area, running almost up to the steps of the Capitol. Savage drove along the narrow streets, noting that it had all the signs of a high-crime area: deteriorating housing, many young men with apparently nothing to do, and a lack of any elements of progress or improvement. Some of the houses had been fine specimens of southern architecture in the past, mansions gone to seed and cut up into miniature apartments or rooming houses. The paint was peeling from most of them, or had faded beyond hope of giving any color to the street.

Savage thought of a line of poetry he'd read: *Hope is a thing with feathers that perches in the soul.* As the words flashed across his mind, he looked at the graceless scene and muttered, "I guess not much hope perches around Spanish Town—"

He hated inner cities, and the sight of the area brought to mind bitter, harsh memories of the years he'd spent as a policeman in Colorado. He'd been a fine cop, but had spent most of his time fighting the system. It had rankled him that a sixteen-year-old black youngster from the slums could go to prison for smoking a joint, while a wealthy preppie could smoke all the dope he chose without fear of reprisal. It had been his refusal to see the difference between the two as far as arrests were concerned that had gotten him "released" from his job. He'd arrested the son of a state senator for dealing drugs, and had refused to heed the warnings that came at once. It had been a losing battle, of course. Within a few days the drug dealer was out of prison, and Savage was out of a job.

Savage saw several dealers plying their trade openly, but it was none of his business. He drove out of the area and parked his car in front of the Leonard Hotel. Getting out, he plugged the meter with two quarters, then crossed the street and entered the hotel. It was, he saw, an old building that had been kept up-to-date. He passed through the large lobby, admiring the fine chandeliers that were reflected in the glistening marble floors, ignored the desk clerk, and made his way into the parking area.

"Help you, sir?"

Savage found a small black man of no more than twenty standing beside a desk along the wall. He wore crimson trousers and a black jacket with *Leonard Hotel* written in gold script over the breast pocket. His hair was cut in a tribal pattern, and there was a shrewd look in his brown eyes as he waited.

"I'm looking for Clyde Givens."

"I'm Givens." The man's eyes grew more cautious as he studied Savage carefully. "You the law?"

Savage smiled at the quickness of the man. "Not anymore. What makes you think I'm the fuzz?"

"Most folks don't carry guns," Givens said quickly, adding, "mostly only cops and robbers. And you don't look like a robber." His speech was not southern, having none of the quality of Black English. There was something foreign about him, though Ben could not quite place it.

Savage took out his billfold and flashed a photocopy of his private investigator's license.

"Oh, you're private." Relief showed in Givens's eyes at once. "What can I do for you?"

"Like to ask you a few questions about Eddie Prejean." The question, Savage saw, brought an instant reaction. Givens's eyes dropped at once and his lips grew tighter. "Already told the law all I know, Mr. Savage. And I can't talk now, not on the job."

"How about I wait until your lunch break?"

"I don't want to talk about it." Givens shook his head, his voice adamant. "You go down to the station and get them to let you read my statement. It's all in there." He turned and walked quickly away, intercepting a new Buick Roadmaster that was nosing into the area.

Savage hesitated, but he had no leverage. If he had been a local cop, he could have gotten Givens to talk by threatening to have him arrested, but he had no authority. He could wait until the man got off, catch him alone and pressure him—but that wouldn't do, either.

Turning abruptly, he moved out of the parking area and went through the lobby into the dining room. It was four fifteen, too late for lunch and too early for dinner, so the tables were mostly empty. A pretty redhead in a green dress, with a badge that said *Hostess,* came to ask, "Smoking or non-smoking?"

"Non-smoking," Savage said, and followed her to a table beside the wall. "A waitress will be with you soon." She smiled, turned, and left. Almost at once a waitress was there, a young black woman wearing a starched white uniform. "Coffee?" she asked, handing him a menu.

"Yes, black." She left and Savage studied the menu briefly, then looked around the room. It was a large room, with ceilings at least fifteen feet high. High windows flanked one side, allowing light to fall across the room, and the curtains were a rich, mellow green. White linen tablecloths gave an immaculate look to the room, and the cup the waitress brought was real china.

"I'll have the gumbo." Handing her the menu, he asked, "Is Leon Williams working this afternoon?"

"Yes. That's him over there."

Savage followed her gesture and nodded. When she left, he studied the man. Dani had given him a description of Williams, and as he ate his meal, he kept his eye on the waiter. Not long after Ben finished his gumbo, Williams walked by. Savage got up and spoke to him, "Like to see you for a few minutes when you have time, Reverend."

Williams stopped and turned to him at once. "Have to be back in the kitchen, suh."

"That's fine."

Savage dropped a dollar on the table, picked up the check and paid it, then walked through the door where Williams had disappeared. He found the man waiting for him, and said, "Miss Ross talked to you yesterday, I think."

"Oh, the young lady," Williams nodded. "Yas, suh, she did."

"I work for her, Reverend," Savage said. "I've been trying to get some information from Givens about the night the young woman was murdered. He doesn't want to talk to me."

Williams nodded quickly, "He's real nervous 'bout all that. Don't like to talk to nobody."

"Why is that?"

"Well, fo' one thing, he's afraid he'll get sent back home. He's from Africa, you know."

"I didn't think he was from Louisiana."

"Goes to LSU—he's a real smart young man," Williams nodded. "Never did talk much, but ever since that killin', he's been tight as a clam, real nervous. I ax him about it, and he said if he got mixed up in any trouble, he'd get sent home."

"But he testified at the trial."

"Yas, suh, but not at first. He didn't say nothin' at all 'bout seein' that man leave with that young lady—not until the trial was 'bout over."

Instantly Ben was alert. "Why was that, Reverend?"

A cautious light came into the waiter's brown eyes. "Can't say, suh. But I kin say he didn't want to go to no courtroom."

"Nobody does," Savage said dryly. He stood there, not knowing what to say. Givens was sullen and it seemed pointless to pressure him. He'd sworn in court that Prejean and Cory Louvier had left together. If he changed his story, he'd be open to a perjury charge. A thought came to him, and he said, "Miss Ross said you mentioned somebody called Bejay."

"Well, I did say that—" Williams looked around quickly to be certain that the cook could not hear him, and lowering his voice, said, "Don't tell nobody I said that, please, suh."

"No, I won't. Who is Bejay?"

"He a bellhop here in the hotel."

"Why'd you tell Miss Ross to talk to him, Reverend?"

Williams looked like he was caught in a struggle, as though he wanted to say something but was not certain of the outcome. "I don't want nothin' to happen to Bejay, Mr. Savage—nor to Clyde neither." His large brown eyes were filled with apprehension, and he said quietly, "A black man—he ain't got much chance if he gits crossways with the law. All this civil rights stuff been goin' on fo' thirty years, but black folks ain't much better off."

"I don't want to get anybody in trouble," Savage said carefully. "All I want to do is try to help Eddie Prejean. If he killed the girl, he ought to pay for it. But Miss Ross thinks he's innocent."

"Whut do you think, Mr. Savage?"

"Don't know. But I'm going to try to find out."

"That Miss Ross, she's a Christian lady," Williams said thoughtfully. Then he asked suddenly, "You a Christian, Mr. Savage?"

The question took Savage off guard. He flushed and for one moment couldn't find a response. He'd been approached before and asked the same question, but somehow this time it was different. He stood there, trying to think clearly. Finally he shook his head. "No, I'm afraid not, Reverend."

He waited for Williams to begin to pressure him, but the small man just stood there quietly studying him. Finally Williams said softly, "It will come to you, Mr. Savage. I kin see the Lord is workin' on you. And when God gits aftah a man, sooner or later they gonna meet up. I'll be prayin' for you."

Savage felt a warm sensation at the words, and nodded. "I'd appreciate it, Reverend."

"Now—" Williams said, "Bejay's off right now. Fishin' in the Atchafalaya basin. Won't be back 'till next week. Mebbe you kin see him when he gits back."

"We don't have much time, Reverend," Savage said. "Can you tell me how to find him?"

Williams nodded. "I'll draw you a map—show you where his folks stay." He found a piece of paper and a stub of a pencil and drew a rough map. "Take this exit, go to Whiskey Bay," he said, "and you git a boat. Mebbe you better git a guide.

Don't do a man no good to git lost in them swamps." He drew the location of the Guidry shack, and handed it to Savage, who pocketed it.

"Thanks for your help—"

At that moment a door opened and a big man walked in, his hard blue eyes fixing at once on Savage. "What's your business here?" he demanded. Then, without waiting for an answer, he said roughly, "We don't allow anybody bothering our help. Come on—"

He took Savage's arm and gave it a rough jerk as he wheeled. Savage chopped down with the edge of his right hand, striking the big man's bicep. A slight gasp of pain came from the man's lips, and his hand fell away limply.

"Sorry I broke the rule," Savage said. "But I can get out without help." He studied the man, then added, "I guess you must be Mullins."

Anger had flared into the man's eyes, and he grated, "That's right. Who are you?"

"Ben Savage. I work for Miss Ross."

Instantly Mullins grew tense. "I don't need any big shot private eyes from New Orleans troubling the help. Now get out—and if you come back, you'll see just how little our local law is impressed by your license! And you, Williams, if you don't have enough to do, maybe we don't need you around here."

Savage said, "I didn't give him any choice, Mullins. Don't take it out on him."

Mullins glared at him, "This is your last warning, Savage. Don't come back to this hotel."

"Can't promise that," Savage said as he walked out of the kitchen. He heard Mullins, his voice ripe with anger, shouting at Leon Williams, and he regretted that he'd gotten the mild little man in trouble. *Hope he doesn't get fired over this,* he thought, and all the way to his car he tried to think of some way to help the preacher. But nothing came to him, and he gave up. For a moment he considered going on the hunt for Bejay Guidry, but it was too late for that, so he left the city and headed back to New Orleans. As he drove, he tried to make some sense out of the incident.

Mullins is pretty hard-nosed—but he's too touchy about this thing. Givens—he's not telling anything, but something's eating at him. Could be worried that he'll get sent back to Africa—but how could testifying in a case do that? And the Reverend knows something he can't tell me or Dani. That's why he's pointed us at Bejay Guidry. Got to get to that one quick. But he'll probably clam up, too.

He stopped at the grocery store and picked up a pound of turkey bacon and six cans of tuna, then drove straight to his apartment. Darkness cloaked the street in front of the building. As he locked the Studebaker, he hoped the hubcaps would still be there at dawn. *Not much of a market for 1963 Studebaker hubcaps,* he thought, but in New Orleans nothing was certain. A sixteen-year-old had been killed for a Saints jacket only the day before, and sneaker hijacking was big. Some of the new athletic shoes cost over a hundred dollars, and there were those in the Projects who would kill for the five dollars needed to buy a fix.

Turning toward the steps that led up to the landing, Savage's mind was on his encounter at the Leonard Hotel. He had the type of mind that zeroed in on a problem and moved through the ordinary duties of life in a mechanical fashion as he gnawed at the facts, much as a dog gnawed on an old bone.

The touch on his arm and the sudden voice that came out of the dark recess beside the door took him completely off guard. His reaction was totally automatic, a matter of nerve endings. Years of training and almost constant brushes with danger had created an alarm system that worked apart from his rational senses, and at the sudden touch, he dropped the sack of groceries he carried in his left hand and lashed out with a vicious chop that struck something soft. As the person who'd stepped beside him was driven backward, falling to the concrete, Savage whipped out the Colt Python he carried under his left arm and threw down on the dim figure.

A quick glance assured him that nobody else lurked in the shadows, and he released his breath. Kneeling down, he grabbed an arm, and at that same moment heard a gasping voice say, "Ben—"

The voice and the rounded arm Savage held was feminine, and he shoved the gun back into the holster, saying, "Are you hurt?"

"I—think so."

Savage bent forward, but in the darkness could not make out the woman's features. "We better get inside," he muttered, ashamed of his overreaction. He pulled her to her feet, and after opening the door, the two of them passed into the lighted foyer. He stared at her, and felt even worse, for the woman had apparently struck her head on the cement. "You've got a scrape on your cheek, Sunny," he said. "Come on—I'll put something on it."

The woman was trembling, but tried to smile. "Touchy, aren't you, Ben?" She was no more than twenty-five and had the classic face of a fashion model. Long blonde hair fell over the short blue jacket she was wearing, and her dark blue eyes reflected some of the fear and shock that had come to her. Reaching up with her left hand, she touched her right shoulder. "I'm going to have the grandmother of all bruises, I think."

"Come on." Savage walked with her down the hall and, taking a key from his pocket, unlocked the door. He reached in and threw the switch, then stepped back for the woman to enter. "Sit down. I'll get something for that scrape."

"All right, Ben."

Savage moved across the apartment, thinking of the last time he'd seen Sunny Sloan. They'd had a brief romance, which she had ended abruptly, and he'd seen her only on TV since. He'd always thought she'd dropped him because there had been some chance of their relationship getting serious— and Sunny Sloan lusted for a career, not for romance with a private detective. In a way, Ben had been relieved, for although he liked Sunny, she had become too immersed in show business for his taste. It was her ambition to become a news analyst for one of the big networks, and she had done well enough on one of the local New Orleans shows to draw some attention from CBS.

Returning from the bathroom with a bottle of antiseptic and some cotton balls, Ben sat down beside her, saying awkwardly, "I'm sorry."

Sunny smiled at him, and put her hand on his arm as he removed the top from the disinfectant. "I should have known better than to come out of the dark at you, but I'd forgotten how you react to things like that."

Savage soaked a cotton ball with the medicine and dabbed it on the spot on her cheek. "Not too bad, " he said. "You can cover it up with makeup before you go on camera."

"Good thing I don't have to cover my arm up with makeup." Sunny lifted her right arm, grimaced, then shrugged. "It'll be all right."

"If you've got a whirlpool, that'll help. Or soak in the tub with water as hot as you can take." Savage put the medicine down, leaned back and said, "What's going on, Sunny?"

"Do I need an excuse to drop by and see you, Ben? I never did before." A memory came to Sunny, and a smile turned her wide mouth upward. She was an attractive woman, and well aware of it. It was her stock in trade—or part of it at least. She resented with a white-hot intensity any suggestion that her success came as a result of her good looks. Once Savage had said, "You never see any ugly lady news analysts, do you?" and she walked out at once, leaving him alone at the restaurant where they were dining.

But Savage had grown to know her pretty well, and was aware that she hadn't stopped by on a friendly call. "Come on, Sunny," he shrugged. "You don't need a boyfriend to take you to the movies."

Sunny started to answer, but a muffled sound from the bedroom caught her attention. Startled, she cut her eyes toward Ben. "Who's that?"

"Jane."

The monosyllabic reply irritated Sunny. "I didn't know you had a—a friend. Maybe I ought to come back later."

"She'll be here when you do," Savage shrugged, then added, "unless I get rid of her."

"Oh? You might throw her out?" Sunny's lips grew tight, for the cavalier fashion of Savage's speech irked her. "You don't think she might get tired of you first?"

"She's got it good. I pay all the bills and all she does is loll around this place. If she wasn't so good-looking I'd have chucked her out long ago." He fixed his eyes on Sunny, adding, "You two have a lot in common."

"Really?" The tone was icy, and Sunny's back grew stiff. "I doubt that."

"Sure you do. Both good-looking females, and both so independent you'll never be able to please a man." Savage saw the anger in the woman's eyes, and got to his feet. "I'll introduce you."

Sunny stood up, saying, "Never mind, I'll just—"

But Savage had crossed the room and opened the door, saying, "Come out, Jane."

A beautiful, pure white Persian cat with large green eyes moved into the room, her gait arrogant and graceful. "This is Miss Sunny Sloan—this is Miss Jane Eyre," Savage said with a straight face. "You two get acquainted while I fix Miss Eyre's dinner."

Sunny laughed, her anger gone at once. "You're a case, Ben Savage!" she said. He had always had a dry sense of humor that attracted her, though it often had a bite. As Savage moved to the kitchen to open a can of tuna, Sunny sat down and patted the couch, but the cat merely stared at her, then yawned. When Savage came back with a small dish filled with tuna, she said, "I never saw such a stuck-up cat. Not your type at all, I'd think."

"No, she isn't." Savage put the dish down, then seated himself in a chair. "I like earthy women—just folks." He saw the remark struck Sunny, and grinned. "I called her Jane Eyre because she's so blasted independent. Guess I'll spend my life waiting on her."

Sunny looked at the beautiful cat, then sobered as she glanced at Savage. "I gave you a bad time, Ben."

"No problem."

"It really wasn't—not for you," Sunny nodded. "We'd have made a terrible pair if we'd gotten married."

"Probably." Savage leaned back, asking, "What's the problem, Sunny?"

Sunny offered a slight smile. "You know me too well, Ben. Well, here it is—I'm in some kind of danger."

"You mean someone's going to beat you up? That kind of danger?"

"Yes, that kind." She leaned toward him and shook her head.

"It sounds like something in a detective story—an old dime novel. At first I paid it no attention, but now I'm worried."

"Tell me."

"I've got a big chance to go up, Ben," Sunny said quickly. "For the last three months I've been working on a story about the petrochemical industry. And it's got some hackles up."

"I don't doubt it." Savage gave the woman a curious look. "Did you come because of the Prejean case?"

"Why, no, I didn't. Of course I know he was getting on the governor's nerves. As a matter of fact, I talked with him a couple of times—before he killed that girl." Sunny stared at him curiously. "What made you ask that?"

Savage thought quickly, then shrugged. "My boss is interested in him. We're doing a little poking around. He says he's got a book almost ready to print that's going to blow Russell out of the water."

"I heard that, Ben. That's why I went to talk with him." Sunny was excited. "He wouldn't tell me too much about what he had, but I was convinced he had something big."

"What about you, Sunny? Somebody making threats?"

"I've gotten two phone calls. It was the same man both times, and he says if I don't stop asking questions, I'm going to get hurt."

"You didn't know the voice?"

"No, I don't think so."

Savage thought for a moment, then asked, "You take it seriously? I mean, you TV people who stir things up, you must get hate mail."

"Oh, there's always someone who doesn't like what we say, but this is different." Sunny hesitated, then said, "I was nearly run down by a car this morning, Ben. And it wasn't accidental. Last night when I got the second call, I got mad, so I told him to bug off. He laughed and said, 'Hope your insurance is paid up.' I was a little worried, but not much. But when I left my apartment early this morning, I was almost run down."

"You see who it was?"

"N-no, not really." The memory of the thing made her nervous, and she said quickly, "I was crossing the street, and this car started up. I didn't pay much attention, but then I heard the engine roaring, and when I looked up, the car was racing toward me. I jumped back, but then he swerved right at me, Ben!" Her eyes opened wide, and she put her hands on her cheeks. "I was close to a lamppost, and I just scrambled behind it in time. If it hadn't been there, he'd have run me down."

"Might have been some wild kid," Savage suggested.

"No. I got a call this afternoon. The same man, and he said, 'Better watch yourself, Sunny. You're going to get run down sooner or later—unless you lay off that story.'"

Savage studied her carefully, then asked, "What are you going to do?"

Sunny bit her lip, then shook her head. Her long blonde hair swept her shoulders, and she said, "Ben, this is my big chance. It may be the only one I'll ever get."

"Won't do you much good to get on CBS if you're in traction."

"I know, but I thought—" Sunny hesitated. There had always been a competence in her, but now she was afraid. "I thought you might help me. The police can't do anything, but if you could just—"

Savage looked at her as her voice trailed off. "If somebody wants to get you bad enough, Sunny, they can't be stopped." He saw fear touch her eyes, and added, "Why don't we go talk to my boss?"

"Ben, I don't have a lot of money to spend."

Savage shrugged. "She's interested in this Prejean thing. Maybe we'll help each other. Dani and I both think Prejean's case had something to do with corruption in the capitol." He looked over toward the Persian who was licking her lips with a pink tongue, and smiled.

"Just what I need," he said. "To get hooked up with three liberated females!"

5

Sunny Sloan

A fine mist was falling over New Orleans, joining itself to a soupy fog that clung to the Mississippi. "It's like driving underwater," Dani complained as she drove through the narrow streets that led to the Quarter. Later, she knew, the sun would rise and burn the blanket of white fog and mist away, but that was no help now as she strained her eyes to see through the haze. A cab pulled out in front of her, abruptly ignoring a stop sign. She jammed on her brakes, thinking unkind thoughts about New Orleans cab drivers. It gave her some satisfaction when she saw a police car pull out, blue lights blinking, and she smiled grimly. "Do your duty, men," she urged.

Dani had skipped breakfast and was aware that she was hungry, so she turned toward Jackson Square, found a parking place easily at that early hour, and walked to the Cafe du Monde, beating the crowds of tourists that would gather later. As she ate an English muffin covered with butter and red raspberry jam, she read the front page and the editorial section of the *Times-Picayune*. The headlines were filled with evil tidings, as usual, and the editorial section set forth edicts on how to eliminate them—as well as dire prophecies as to what lay down the ominous road that comprised the future. She turned to the comics and read "Calvin and Hobbes," "The Far Side," "B.C.," and "The Wizard of Id," ignoring the pseudo strips that were added to fill up space. *More truth in "Calvin and Hobbes,"* she thought wryly, *than in the rest of the paper put together.*

The sun burned a slight opening through the watery haze and shouldered its way through. Dani sat for half an hour drinking several cups of *café au lait* as the Square came to life. The con artists came first, then their prey, the tourists from the Midwest aching to be taken. She watched as one of her favorites, C. L. Dinwiddie, transferred cash by some sort of mysterious alchemy from the pockets of the people who passed by into his own. C. L. sat in a wheelchair and played an ocarina, very badly out of time and tune, and cast his sad looks at those who passed by. He played hymns for people who looked churchy and rock-and-roll for the swingers. Dani had heard him go from "Amazing Grace" to the latest Michael Bolton hit without missing a beat—and had seen him fleece both sets of clients.

As Dani watched people drop bills into C. L.'s old hat, which he kept on his lap, she wondered what would happen if she would step beside the wheelchair and say to the people, "Hey, this is no cripple. He plays tennis every day of his life. And these duds are his working clothes. When he's off duty, he wears Girbauds and Tony Lama ostrich boots that cost two hundred and fifty bucks a boot!"

A smile crossed her lips as she thought, *They'd get mad at me if I told them the truth. People like to be fooled—they pay big money for it. And I guess C. L. is harmless enough.* Stop

And then a memory came floating into her mind, something Ben had said to her once when they'd been having a blazing argument about a case. Dani had forgotten what the argument was about, but she remembered that she'd been trying to steamroller Ben. He'd taken her arm and his dark eyes had riveted her as he'd said, *Boss, you've been educated beyond your capacity. You've spent a lot of time and effort trying to cover up the fact that you're a woman. Stop fooling yourself—or you'll pile up somewhere down the road!*

The coffee suddenly tasted bitter to Dani as she remembered how she'd yanked her arm away from his grasp, given him a scalding reply, and gone roaring off to do whatever it was that he was trying to prevent her from doing. And as she thought of it, she had a faint memory that he'd been right in the matter, and that she'd wound up with egg on her face in the middle of a large mess.

Dani pushed her cup away and rose, disturbed by her train of thought. As she left the Cafe du Monde, a notion came to her, and she walked across the square past the sidewalk artists and entered the cathedral. Barely noticing the few people that were inside, she slipped into a back pew, bowed her head, and began to pray. The quietness soaked into her spirit, and she didn't think it strange at all—coming into a Catholic church to pray. It was a habit she had, especially when traveling. She liked to stop and enter churches and pray for a brief time. This always left her refreshed. A friend had once asked, *Don't you feel out of place, praying in all kinds of different churches?* Dani had tried to explain that she went to talk to God, not to discuss doctrine, and that a Shaker meeting house, a Catholic cathedral, or a modern Baptist church were all the same to her.

For ten minutes she sat there quietly, her thoughts flutter-ing in her head like a captured bird inside a cage. She'd long envied those people who were, apparently, single-minded enough to simply drop all thoughts of worldly things and focus on God. Her mind was not of that sort, and she had learned that the best thing was to let the bird flutter around, bouncing all sorts of thoughts off her mind, knowing that sooner or later those wandering thoughts would grow faint and she would be able to concentrate on God.

The odor of old wood and melting candle wax filled the large space, and the silence was so profound that she could hear the faint sobs of a woman who knelt at the front, muf-fled and sad. Dani prayed, *Lord, help that woman—meet her needs and take away her grief. Give her your joy and your peace.*

She often prayed like that, for people she didn't know and would never know. *Help that old man—Give that little girl a good day at school—Lord, heal that woman of the cold that's worn her down—*

For some time she summoned up those dear to her—her mother, Allison, Rob. She didn't pray long for them—just a simple request for God to surround them, to keep them. Then she prayed for the country and its leadership—though this was hard for her. She did it in obedience to the Bible's injunc-tion, the clear command to pray for those in charge of gov-ernment. Finally, she put all out of her mind except God, and for some time sat there, thanking him for his gifts and bless-ings—and finally, just praising him for who he was.

Her father had taught her well, for he'd said often, *We ought to give thanks for our blessings, Dani. But those things aren't God. We ought to love God no matter how poor our circumstances—no matter how much we hurt. God made us to love him and to wor-ship him. Most people never really learn to do that—but as that's what heaven will be like, I want us to learn here so we'll be right at home there.*

Then Dani ceased to think at all, only sitting there as a peace flowed over her spirit. She knew it was not of her mind or of her emotions, but was a work of the Spirit of God. It was one of the fruits of the Spirit mentioned in Galatians, and had always been especially precious to Dani.

Finally she whispered, "Lord, what must I do about Ben?"

The question had been in her mind, buried not too deeply beneath her conscious thought patterns ever since he'd asked her to marry him. From time to time the matter would surface, catching her off guard, but she had been unable to pray about the matter until now.

"Do you want me to marry him?"

No answer came.

The quietness of the sanctuary cloaked her, and though she strained every spiritual sense in her heart—nothing.

A slight case of irritation came to Dani—a trace of the old Dani Ross she'd never lost, and she said crankily, "Well, do you want this for me or not?"

A black-robed priest came from a side room, walked across the front of the church, lit a candle, and then disappeared. The sobbing of the woman grew louder, and someone behind Dani coughed raggedly.

But still no answer came—not a word or a hint.

Dani clenched her fists, fighting down the impatience that rose in her and forcing herself to relax. When she had recovered her sense of peace, she smiled at her own foolishness. "I'm sorry, Lord. You know how I am—always wanting a quick answer. You'll just have to help me with this temper of mine." She sat there for a few seconds, then said, "Ben—or no Ben. Whatever you want, God, will suit me fine!"

She rose and left the cathedral, noting that the sun was

brighter than when she'd entered. A band of sparrows was quarreling and fighting over the remains of a muffalata some-one had dropped on the sidewalk, and she smiled at them, saying, "Take it easy, boys." Dani then got into her car and threaded the narrow, crowded streets back to Bourbon Street.

"Is it all right for Ben to come in, Miss Ross?"

Dani looked up from the stack of papers she was working on as Angie Park's voice came over the intercom. Flipping the switch on her desk, she said, "Yes, send him in." She leaned back, arching her back, wondering why the sudden formality. Savage usually came walking into her office as though it were his. But as he entered and she saw the woman with him, her attention sharpened.

"This is Sunny Sloan," Savage nodded. "Sunny, this is Miss Danielle Ross."

Dani rose, smiled, and put out her hand, saying, "I'm a fan of yours, Miss Sloan. I thought your special on the plight of the inner city was very well done."

"Oh—so nice of you to say that," Sunny beamed. She was wearing a close-fitting, two-piece knit outfit that showed off her figure admirably, and was obviously pleased by the recognition. "Sometimes I wonder if anybody ever sees anything I do."

Dani nodded toward a chair, saying, "Sit down, won't you? Would you like some coffee or tea?"

"Oh, nothing for me. Ben and I just had lunch."

Dani waited, curious as she studied the woman, and Ben said quickly, "I think you ought to hear what Sunny's run up against, Boss."

Then, as the young woman spoke rapidly, Dani leaned back and listened. She had an unusual ability to strain what people said, picking out the crucial facts and, at the same time, forming a judgment of the speaker. Sunny Sloan was a professional communicator, which made this more difficult. As was true with all her breed, she could make unimportant things sound *very* important, and was adept at swaying the minds and judgments of those she spoke to.

When Sunny ended by saying, ". . . and while I'm not usually a very nervous person, I have to admit I'm scared of what's happening—so I went to see Ben."

Dani stared at her, then glanced toward Savage. "Have you two known each other long?"

For the first time something stirred Sunny's smooth cheeks. Dani saw it instantly—just a flicker of the eyes and a quick protective tightening of the lips—and knew that she was about to hear a lie.

"Oh, I met him at a party some time back," Sunny nodded, and the professional smile was back. "Where was it, Ben—in the Garden District someplace?"

Savage glanced at Sunny with a sudden sharpness, but said nothing.

She's lying! The thought flashed through Dani's mind, but she allowed nothing to show in her face. Casually she looked toward Ben, but nothing showed on his craggy face. *He's stolid as an Indian—but they know each other,* she thought. Aloud she said, "What are you going to do, Sunny? May I call you that?"

"Oh, yes!" Sunny bit her lip, then shook her head, slight doubt reflected in her eyes. "I had some sort of idea about hiring a bodyguard, but that would be terribly expensive."

"Yes, it does cost quite a bit."

Sunny moved her shoulders slightly, as though put off by Dani's brief reply. She glanced at Savage, who gave her no help, then turned back to face Dani. "I've thought about it, and maybe we could work together."

"In what way?" Dani inquired.

"Well, you're interested in the Eddie Prejean case, aren't you?"

"Ben told you that?"

"Well, yes, he did." Sunny noted the sudden critical look that Dani gave Savage, and added quickly, "He told me after I'd mentioned that my story involved the DEQ—and perhaps even the upper layers of state government."

"You mean Governor Russell?"

"I think it could involve him—as well as others." Sunny's face became intense and she spoke forcefully, throwing herself into an attitude of persuasion. "Look, you want to dig up something that'll clear Eddie Prejean. I want to stay alive."

Dani looked at the young woman, then at Savage. "Well, Ben—" she said softly. "You're not saying much."

Savage looked uncomfortable, and his shoulders stirred restlessly. "It's up to you, but I think we might do some swapping. We've only got a few days before the execution—if Russell doesn't put it off."

"He won't do that!" Sunny said quickly. "He's a hard-liner on public execution—and he'll be especially anxious to dust off Eddie Prejean."

"Why is that?" Dani demanded.

"Because he's white," Sunny nodded. "The last eleven executions have been black men, and the howl is going up about prejudice in the judicial system. Russell's anxious to change the statistics on it."

Dani nodded, knowing this was true. She sat there thinking rapidly, then said, "I don't know how you can help much, Miss Sloan."

"I know state government, Dani," Sunny said quickly. "And I know the Department of Environmental Quality. I've put in a lot of hours with those two groups—and the proof that I've done it well is that someone is trying to shut me up.

After talking to Ben, I'm convinced it's all tied up with Eddie Prejean. They want to stop both of us from talking."

"Might be something in that, Boss," Ben observed. "I'm not much good with these government types. Way I see it, somebody needs to go see that witness who's hiding out in the swamp."

"Bejay Guidry?" Dani thought of her visit to the Leonard, then nodded. "I'd planned to go find him tomorrow." She hesitated, then added, "I thought we'd both go out there, Ben."

Sunny said quickly, "I don't want to seem pushy, Dani, but how about this—there are some people I think can help us in the DEQ. If I can get them away from the job, I think they'll talk. But I'm a little leery after getting nearly run down. If you'd let Ben go with me—?"

Dani considered the young woman, almost shook her head in a curt denial, but then thought again. "All right," she said. "Ben, you go with her, and I'll talk to Bejay."

Savage ducked his head, then lifted it. "Don't like for you to go poking around alone, Boss."

Dani smiled tersely. "As I remember, you're not at your best in a pirogue, Ben. Remember when you came to find me at the camp?" When she saw Savage redden, she added sweetly, "Ben fell into the water back in the bayou and bumped into an alligator—or what he thought was a gator. He nearly killed himself getting to shore. But it was just a log, wasn't it, Ben?"

Savage glared at her. "You never forget, do you? And there are worse things than gators running around."

Dani enjoyed his discomfort, and stood up. "I'll take my chances in the bayou. You try to get something we can use in the capitol."

"Oh, thank you, Dani!" Sunny got to her feet and took Ben's arm possessively. "Ben and I will work well together."

"I can see that," Dani said dryly, drawing a startled glance from Savage. "Let's meet tomorrow night—say at six o'clock."

"Where'll we rendezvous?" Savage asked.

"Ralph 'n Kacoo's will do," Dani answered. She nodded toward the young woman, saying, "Sunny, I need to speak privately with Ben. Would you mind waiting in the outer office?"

"Of course."

As soon as the woman was outside, Dani turned to face Savage, and there was a sharp bite in her tone as she demanded, "All right, let's have it."

"Have what?"

"Come on, Ben! That piece of fluff is lying."

Savage rarely showed embarrassment, but he did so now. "Yeah, she is—but I don't know why." He tried to grin, and said in a rather awed fashion, "You've got a built-in lie detector, Boss!"

"What were you two? Lovers?"

Savage blinked in surprise, and was slightly angered. "What difference does it make?" He peered at Dani more closely, and demanded, "Are you jealous?"

"Jealous?" Dani sniffed. "No, I'm not jealous. But I need to know what's going on. You're working for me, you know."

Savage was amused and said, "That's right, I am. And I forgot to give you last month's report on my love life. Sorry about that."

"Don't be a fool, Ben," Dani said sharply. "This thing could get bad, and I need to know this woman."

Savage shrugged, saying, "Sure, I guess that's right. We went out a few times. Don't know why she lied, though. Maybe she was afraid you wouldn't help her if you knew we'd been holding hands."

Dani wasn't satisfied with his reply and said so. "She's a

dish, Ben, but she's pretty tough. You don't get to the top in her business unless you're pretty hard."

"You think she's trying to pull something?"

Dani shook her head, but doubt was in her eyes. "I don't know. Just be careful, Ben."

"Yeah, you too, Boss," Savage said. He cocked his head to one side, then asked almost plaintively, "You're not even a *little* jealous? Just this much?" He held up his hand with his thumb and index finger about half an inch apart. "I'd be jealous if you were going to spend the day with that good-looking guy on Channel 4—the one with the spiffy hair job and the caps on his teeth."

Dani smiled, but shook her head. "No point my being jealous of her, Ben. She's going up in the world, our Sunny is. She wouldn't anchor herself with a small-time PI."

Savage nodded, a glint of admiration in his eyes. "You've read her pretty well, Boss."

"She dump you, Ben?"

"Like an old shoe."

"Well, you've got all day tomorrow. Turn on the old charm." Dani smiled and came to stand beside Savage. "Maybe she'll make you her paid escort. You can go to fancy parties with her and bring her things when she wants them."

"Like an organ grinder and his monkey, that it?" Savage had a slight grin on his face, but suddenly it vanished. "Thinking any about my offer, Dani?"

Dani stared at him uncertainly, then nodded. "It won't go away, Ben." She reached out and touched his cheek on an impulse. "I really *am* jealous of Miss Wonderful out there," she said softly. "Even if *I* don't get you, I want something better for you than her."

Savage took her hand, held it lightly, then nodded. "I wish

I had lots of flowery words," he said quietly. "Hard for me to say what I feel."

Dani stood there, enjoying the warmth of his hand surrounding hers, then said with an impish grin. "Write me a poem."

"I'll have to buy a greeting card and steal one. "

"I want it to rhyme. Moon—June—spoon—!"

"Don't they all?"

Dani pulled her hand back, saying, "Get out of here. I have work to do."

"Yeah—and don't forget, there are bad guys out there," Savage nodded as he turned to go. "Watch yourself."

When the door closed, Dani walked over and looked up at the picture of her Confederate ancestor. "What should I do, Colonel Ross?"

But the stern-eyed man who gazed down at her said nothing, and Dani sighed heavily, returning to her stack of papers.

6
Cabin in the Bayou

The buzz of a low-flying plane brought Dani out of a fitful sleep with an agonizing abruptness. She sat straight up, staring around her bedroom, her back arched and her eyes filled with the fading visions of early morning dreams. For a wedge of time that measured the vanishing dream with a Doppler effect, she sat there, her lips stretched wide and her neck pulled into tightened strings with the silent scream she held back. Then the outlines of her room—vague and shadowy like a ghostly edifice—sharpened and leaped into focus.

Throwing back the covers, she leaped out of the bed as though it were a snake pit, and quickly switched on the lamp beside her bed. The harsh light hurt her eyes and she shut them for a few seconds, then opened them into slits. Stripping off her nightgown as she moved toward the shower, she tossed it into a woven clothes hamper, then turned the cold water handle of the shower on full force. She put her hair under a shower cap, took a deep breath, and stepped under the cold spray. It took her breath away, and for a moment all she could do was stand there as her body rebelled against the cold.

The shock of the cold water drove away the immediacy of the rough awakening, and soon she began to add hot water. Slowly she tempered the needle-like spray, and soaped liberally, the delicious warmth running over her body. She lingered in the shower for ten minutes, then stepped out and dried herself with a fluffy yellow towel.

Only then did she move back into the bedroom and glance at the clock. It was only fifteen after four—too early, but she liked the cool, cobwebby hours of the morning. She brushed her heavy auburn hair, leaving it down over her shoulders. Thinking about the day's schedule, she put on light makeup and chose her clothing accordingly—a pair of stonewashed Levis, a long-sleeved blue-and-white checked cotton shirt, and a pair of thick-soled running shoes.

When she was dressed, she sat down, picked up her Bible, and read slowly for twenty minutes, plodding through a few chapters of the Book of Leviticus. She was reading the Bible all the way through, and after the thrilling adventures set forth in Genesis and Exodus, she found the long, involved prose of Leviticus tedious. She had reached the eleventh chapter and forced herself to read a list of animals that the ancient Jews were forbidden to eat—and was interested to see that they included catfish, pigs, and rabbits. She read in verse thirteen that the Jews were not to eat ". . . the eagle, and the ossifrage, and the ospray." She wondered vaguely what an ossifrage might be, then plodded on. The next few chapters gave detailed instructions on what an Israelite must do to get a case of leprosy diagnosed.

As Dani read doggedly on, she wondered why God had given such things as part of the Bible. She could understand why a nomadic people would need dietary laws and other instructions concerning various activities, but what did it all have to do with her? She had no answer, and read such parts of the Bible with hope, rather than with understanding. It was her conclusion that the Old Testament, with all its wealth of poetry, history, law, and prophecy was written to give the world a picture of the struggle of man. She remembered her father had once told her that his favorite book in the Bible was Genesis. Noting her surprise at this, he'd said, *If we didn't have that book, Dani, we wouldn't have the slightest notion about where we came from. We wouldn't know why the world is so devastated. And we wouldn't know about the great plan of redemption that God began to work with Abraham.*

Dani finally read a verse that leapt out at her: *For the life of the flesh is in the blood: and I have given it to you upon the altar to make an atonement for your souls: for it is the blood that maketh an atonement for the soul.*

That verse sent a sudden thrill along Dani's nerves—as verses did from time to time. She had a sense of the concept of blood—scarlet blood from thousands of slain animals. The Old Testament reeked with the blood of bulls and goats and birds. The priests slew them until it seemed a river of blood must flow over the altars of the temple! And as she thought of this, she remembered the verse in the New Testament that always awed her, leaving her weak and mystified by the enormity of its cosmic implication: *For this is my blood of the new testament, which is shed for the remission of sins.*

Dani closed the Bible, the verse ringing in her spirit, and said a brief prayer, "Thank you, Lord, for giving me this part of your Word. And this day may I remember that it is only by your blood that I am forgiven for all my sins."

She rose, strapped on her .38 with distaste, then plucked a long white nylon jacket and a white-billed cap to match out of her closet, and left the bedroom. The house was quiet, and she moved to the kitchen as softly as possible. It would be a long day, with food an uncertainty, so she began throwing a quick breakfast together. She was frying an egg when her mother came in wearing a chenille robe. "It's so early, Dani," she protested.

"I've got to go to Baton Rouge, Mom," Dani said. She flipped the egg over, studied it carefully, then slipped it onto a plate. "I'll be late. May have to stay over."

"What is it?" Ellen asked, and waited as Dani gave her a review of the details of the agency. Ellen listened avidly, and Dani went into more detail than she once would have. Her mother was alone now, cut off by the loss of her husband. Dani knew they had talked for long hours, Dan Ross sharing all the events of his busy life—but now there was a silence in Ellen Ross's life.

Ellen drank coffee as Dani ate, speaking quietly of the little things that now made up her life—the house, the grounds, Allison's problem with a teacher, her concern over Rob's apparent aimlessness. These things were not enough, Dani realized, and she tried to spend as much time as possible with her mother.

The two women lingered over coffee, Dani concealing her anxiety to be off. Ellen finally said, "You'd better go to work, Dani."

"I guess so, Mom. I'll be home tonight if I can, but it'll probably be around ten or so. Don't wait up for me."

Ellen's face was drawn, but a slight smile came to her lips. "I'll be awake," she said quietly.

Dani looked at her quickly, but said only, "I'll be having some free time in about two weeks. Why don't we go down to the Keys? Maybe we could get a little tan."

"Oh, that would be nice!"

Dani rose, and Ellen said at once, "I'll clean up, Dani. You go on."

"All right, Mom." Dani gave her mother a hug and kissed her on the cheek. "See you tonight."

Five minutes later she was driving the Cougar west toward Baton Rouge, thinking of how the death of her father had created such a vacuum in her mother's life. The loss had thrown them all into a numb shock that had faded only slightly. Every day, Dani thought of her father, missing him more than she had dreamed possible. What her mother was going through she could only imagine.

As she drove along the ribbon of highway that wound between tall trees, the lines of a poem by Emily Dickinson came to her:

> The bustle in a house
> The morning after death
> Is solemnest of industries
> Enacted upon earth.
>
> The sweeping up the heart,
> And putting love away
> We shall not want to use again
> Until eternity.

Putting love away, she thought suddenly. *I can never do that!* And she knew with an iron certainty that as long as she lived on planet Earth, she would think of her father. With one part of her heart, she knew that she would see him one day, when all her business on earth was done—but the world seemed hard and empty without him. She could put thoughts of him out of her mind for a time, but one little thing brought it all back. She had stepped on something in a corner of the den two days earlier, and bending over had found herself holding her father's Old Timer pocket knife. As her fingers had touched the rough bone surface, the sense of loss had swept over her, and she'd been unable to move as the tears overflowed, spilling down her cheeks.

Dani knew that the keen edge of grief would pass, but she felt vulnerable and, as she sped along the interstate, had to force her mind away from the thoughts of her father that brushed against her.

She reached Baton Rouge an hour later, winding around the city, which was just beginning to stir. Taking Interstate 10, she drove steadily until she came to the turnoff that Rev. Leon Williams had marked on the small map he'd drawn. She followed a twisting road that wound around the bayou, coming at last to the brink of a branch of the Atchafalaya River, and saw a bait shop with a large hand painted sign: BEAU-DREAU'S BAIT SHOP—NO CREDIT nailed on the side of one of the soaring cypress trees that rose out of the boggy ground.

Parking the Cougar on the small patch of gravel, she got out and went inside. It was a long, low building with a concrete minnow bay along one end and a counter that ran in front of some shelves at the other end. A short man wearing a dirty T-shirt that read *Don't Mess with Texas* looked up from where he sat in a cane-bottomed chair. He had a three-day crop of whiskers and could have been anywhere from thirty to sixty years old. When he spoke, it was with a thick Cajun accent. "Can I help you, me?" he asked.

"I want to rent a boat," Dani said.

"Oh, yes, we got four or five of dem," the man said agreeably. "You need some shiners, mebbe some crickets?"

"No, I'm not going fishing," Dani answered. "I'm going to Bejay Guidry's place. Do you know it?"

The man's sharp brown eyes lit with interest. "Oh, I know it, miss. My name's Simon Beaudreau. I know everybody around Whiskey Bay." He got to his feet and asked curiously, "You a friend of mah friend Bejay?"

"I never met him—but I need to talk to him."

Her remark interested the Cajun. He studied her carefully, as if she were a rather unusual specimen, then said, "You ain't no law, I don't think? No, you ain't none of that."

"Well, in a way, I am," Dani admitted. She usually didn't like to tell people so much, but she had the idea that Simon Beaudreau was an exception. "I'm a private investigator, Mr. Beaudreau."

The dark face of the Cajun was reposed, but there was a quick light in his dark eyes. "Must be about Eddie Prejean, no?"

Dani knew she'd guessed right—this was indeed a sharp man! "I hope you won't talk about it, Mr. Beaudreau, but you're right. I need to talk to Bejay about Eddie."

A fatalistic note was in the man's voice as he said, "Ain't nobody but the good Lord can help that sucker. He done got his tail in a crack, him!"

"Can you tell me how to get to Bejay's house?" Dani asked. She pulled out the map Leon Williams had sketched and, unfolding it, handed it to the stocky man. She saw that he was suspicious and suspected that it was part of his character rather than a personal thing.

Finally he said, "I draw you a better one. You git lost good if you don't be careful."

Dani stood there as he located a Red Horse tablet, carefully sharpened a stub of a short yellow pencil, then traced a surprisingly well-drawn map on the rough paper. "You follow dem white flags tied to saplings," he instructed. "Bejay's folks live way back in de bayou. And be a little careful when you gits close. Old man Guidry, he's a caution," Beaudreau warned. "Suspicious of everybody whose last name ain't Guidry. Las' month he took a shot at a hunter."

"He shot him?"

"Ah, no! He jus' shoot his hat off a little bit! It give the man to know he was serious."

Dani smiled nervously. "I'll go in waving a white flag."

"You come and I get you a good boat, me."

Dani followed Beaudreau out of the building and stopped beside a line of flat-bottomed boats anchored to cement blocks. "You know boats?" the short man inquired.

"Yes, I can handle one of these."

She got into one of the boats, opened the choke on the Evinrude, gave the rope a sharp pull, and grinned when the engine coughed once, then broke into a full-throated roar. "Got plenty of gas," Beaudreau nodded. "Tell old man Guidry I say for him to treat you right."

Dani backed the boat out into the deeper water, turned it smoothly around, and opened the throttle. She looked back to wave at the Cajun, who waved back with a smile.

The wind was chilly, and she shivered as it whipped around her. The lightweight, nylon jacket was not warm enough at this early hour, but it would be getting warmer soon. She guided the boat down the channel, enjoying the sensation of the throbbing engine and the water slapping the square end of the boat as it bounced up and down.

Half a mile downstream, she saw a fork in the river and swung the boat into a much smaller branch. The bayou began to close in, and soon the stream had lost itself in a swamp. Towering cypress closed off the sky as she slowed the boat to a crawl, dodging old logs that lay half submerged. It wasn't too difficult to follow the trail of small white rags, though some of them were weathered and difficult to see. She lost her way at one point, forcing her to backtrack until she picked it up again.

The swamp was silent except for the throbbing of the Evinrude, and she slowed the engine back until the boat was creeping along. White egrets rose from the glistening black water, and a coon peered at her from his perch on a limb, his eyes bright as buttons, as she passed beneath.

It grew warmer as the sun rose, and the green-gold morning light that fell through the canopy of limbs overhead made the glade seem like a sanctuary of some sort. Dani saw that the lily pads bloomed with purple flowers even this early in the year. She enjoyed the smell of the trees, the moss, the wet green lichens on the bark, and the sprays of crimson and yellow four-o'clocks that grew on the small islands.

She passed into a large, open body of water, and high up against the blue dome of the sky, a large brown pelican drifted by. Suddenly, his wings collapsed, and he plummeted like a small bomb into the water, erupting quickly with a fish dangling from his pouched beak.

She came upon the house suddenly. It was hidden from the open water by a small grove of trees and was set well back from the shore. She caught a glimpse of three boats anchored to cypress knees inside a small cove that hooked around like Cape Cod, and she turned toward it at once, shutting off the engine.

The silence that followed the sudden cessation of the Evinrude was complete, and as she glided in toward the shore, Dani spotted a five-foot gator up close to the cypress roots, his barnacled head and eyes just showing above the waterline like a brown rock. He would have been invisible to many, for he looked like just another half-sunken log.

The prow of the boat touched the shore, and Dani was mindful of the Cajun's warning. "Hello! Anybody home?" she called out. The metal prow slid in over the mud, and Dani got up and stepped ashore. As she lifted the concrete block from the bow and dropped it into the mud, a voice came from her left, startling her.

"You lost, lady?"

Dani turned quickly to see a tall young man standing in the shadow of a thick-bodied cypress tree. He wore a red and black checked shirt hanging over a pair of tattered jeans, and Dani thought she could see the outline of a pistol against his flat stomach.

"I'm looking for the Guidry place," Dani said carefully. She was aware of the .38 pressing against her spine, barely covered by the nylon jacket, but she was certain that this was the man she was looking for. Leon William had said, "Bejay, he looks like a cat." And there was definitely something feline about the young man who was watching her, Dani decided.

He was not effeminate, but catlike in the sense of watchfulness. He had round eyes, blue-gray in color, and a mass of glistening black curly hair that fell around his ears and almost touched the collar of his shirt. He was lithe and strong-looking, with powerful looking hands covered with small white scars.

"Which Guidry you looking for?" he asked, and looked over her shoulder out into the open waters. His eyes swept the scene, then came back to rest on her, wary as those of an animal.

"I'm Dani Ross—and I'm looking for Bejay Guidry."

"That right?" Guidry studied her, and a smile touched his thin lips. "That's me. What can I do for you?"

Dani hesitated. Now that she was here and had the man before her, she wasn't sure how to proceed. All she knew was that Leon Williams felt Guidry was aware of something that would help her.

"It's—a little complicated, Mr. Guidry," she said slowly. "Can I talk to you?"

"Come on," Guidry nodded. "I was just making breakfast. Been out running a trap line."

Dani hesitated, asking, "Is your father around?"

Guidry laughed, his teeth very white against his tanned skin. "No, he's gone to Lafayette. Ma went with him, so we can have a private breakfast. Come on inside."

Dani followed him across the open ground and stepped into the cabin when he paused and held the door open. The smell of frying meat and coffee was strong, and Guidry stepped over and picked up a frying pan. "How does bacon and eggs sound?"

"Oh, I've already eaten, but you go ahead. I could drink some coffee, though."

Guidry shrugged, and proceeded to put the skillet on the gas stove. He picked up the blackened coffeepot, poured what looked like tar into a cup, and handed it to her. He grinned when Dani sipped it and her eyes went large. "A little strong, I guess." He turned and took up the bacon, cracked two eggs and fried them, then put them on a plate and sat down. He began to eat, and the silence became oppressive to Dani.

"I know it seems strange, Mr. Guidry, my coming here like this, but I need some help."

"What kind of help?"

Dani was aware of the terse note in Guidry's voice, and knew that this was not going to be an easy matter. She had discovered that the best way to approach things with simple people was to just be simple. "I got a call from Eddie Prejean, Mr. Guidry—"

Bejay Guidry ate steadily, saying nothing as Dani related what had occurred at Angola. He seemed almost uninterested, and when she was finished, he leaned back and asked, "What's all this got to do with me?"

"You were working at the party the night the girl was murdered, weren't you?"

"Sure. You know that already. No other reason why you'd

come all the way out in the bayou to see me—unless it was because you heard I was so good-looking." He put his large hands around the coffee cup and saw that she was watching them. "I got those scars shuckin' oysters," he remarked. "Don't advise you to take it up for a profession."

"Mr. Guidry—"

"Bejay is good enough."

"Well—Bejay, then," Dani agreed. "I'll put it to you straight. I think there's something fishy about Eddie Prejean's trial."

Bejay smiled and leaned forward. Before Dani could move, he reached out and took her hand, holding it fast. She tried to withdraw it, but he was far too strong. He studied her hand, saying, "Smooth—and sexy, too." He looked across the table at her, asking, "You sure you didn't come out here because you heard something about me from the girls at Sally's place?"

Dani wrenched her hand free, and he laughed at her. "Do you know Eddie Prejean?" she asked.

"Met him once or twice. He fishes sometimes. Good guy, Eddie."

"He's going to die if I can't find some proof that he didn't kill that girl."

Guidry studied her carefully. "I hear lots of women go for prisoners. Some even marry guys in the slammer and wait for them till they get out. I hope you ain't fallen in love with Eddie. Be a short romance."

Dani took a deep breath, then tried again. "Clyde Givens swore he saw Cory Louvier leave the party with Eddie. But Eddie says Givens lied."

A fly buzzed around the table and Bejay brushed it away absentmindedly, then plucked up his coffee cup, his eyes fixed on Dani. "Sounds like you better talk to Clyde. He's the man putting Eddie in the hot seat."

"I think he's lying," Dani said quietly, then asked, "Did you see Eddie leave, Bejay?"

The young man showed nothing in his face, but his fingers tightened on the cup. Dani saw them splay out and turn white—and knew that Guidry had a secret.

"No, I didn't see him leave."

Dani sat there, not knowing what to say. She had no authority as a law enforcement officer—and even if she had, what could she have done? Vainly she tried to think of some way to get at the secret she was sure lay locked behind Bejay's smooth face, but could think of nothing.

Finally she said quietly, "Death's not such a big thing anymore, is it, Bejay?"

"What?" Bejay was startled, and stared at Dani with confusion making him blink.

"Every day somebody gets blown away in New Orleans—a corpse a day," Dani said, her voice even, and her eyes locked onto Guidry. "The cemetery's filling up. Cars with their lights on parading down the streets with the long black one in front."

"Hey—what is all this?"

"But they don't mean anything to you, do they, Bejay?"

"Listen, I don't go around offing people!"

"No, but you won't do anything to stop a man from dying either, will you?"

Bejay's forehead was glistening with sweat and his fingers were still white around the cup. "Get out of here!" he snapped. "Nobody sent for you."

"I'm going," Dani said, and rose to her feet. She moved to the door, but when she got there, she turned and said, "You ever visit Angola, Bejay? Drop in sometime and ask them to show you the electric chair. They like to show it off." Dani stared at the man, who had dropped his head, then said, "Eddie Prejean's a pretty good man, I think. He'll be sitting down in that chair in a few days. But that's nothing to you, is it, Bejay?"

"Get out before I bust you!" Guidry stood up, his face tight with anger. "I don't like to see nobody get burned—but what can I do?"

"You can tell the truth, Bejay!"

For one moment Dani was hopeful, for a strange expression had come to Guidry's face—something like relief, she thought. But then his lips drew across his face in a thin line. "You don't know what you're asking," he said, his voice hoarse. "I'd like to see the guy walk—but I ain't sticking my neck out and getting it chopped off. Now get out of here."

Dani considered the face of Guidry and knew she could do nothing. She said quietly, "I hope you sleep well, Bejay." Then she turned and walked out of the cabin. She walked slowly to the water, put the concrete block inside the boat, then started the engine and headed back.

He knows something, she thought, *but I can't make him speak out. I should have done it differently.*

Dani was depressed, and when she was paying for the boat, she could not hide it from Beaudreau. The stocky Cajun took the money, put it in a battered cash box on the counter, and said, "Well, come back, lady. Maybe you'll do better next time."

Dani looked at him, startled for a moment. But she saw that he was merely being nice. "No, I don't think so," she murmured. "Thank you and good-bye."

Simon watched her get into the Cougar and drive away, then remarked, "She didn't find nothin' good at Bejay's, I think." He studied the car as it disappeared around a curve, and scratched his nose. "I wish she wanted me to do something—I'd do it, me!" Then he turned regretfully and went back to sit in his worn cane-bottomed chair.

7

"The World's What It Is!"

Savage rang the doorbell of Sunny Sloan's apartment at exactly seven o'clock in the morning. He waited for what seemed a long time before the door opened a crack, only allowing him to see a pair of sleepy eyes peering out.

"Rise and shine, Sunny," he said cheerfully. "Time to get the show on the road."

The door closed, the safety chain rattled, and when the door swung back again, Savage entered to find Sunny dressed in a pair of rose-colored pajamas. "What time is it?" she muttered sleepily, batting her eyes against the sunlight.

"Crack of dawn," Savage replied. "I thought you wanted to get an early start."

Sunny stretched like a cat, her lush figure outlined against the sheen of the pajama top. She yawned, ruffled her hair, then shook her shoulders. "I was up late doing my homework on the gov," she said. Suddenly she seemed to be aware of her attire and said quickly, "Have a seat, Ben. I'll shower and be ready in fifteen minutes."

Savage shrugged as he slumped down on the couch beside the window and said, "You've changed your ways if that happens." Sunny disappeared through a door to his right, and he thumbed through the magazines scattered on the bleached walnut coffee table. Tossing aside copies of *Vogue*, *Harper's Bazaar*, and *Mademoiselle,* he grunted in disgust. "Not a single decent magazine—no *Popular Mechanics* or *American Car*. Not even a copy of *Dairy Goat Journal*!" He found a six-month-old copy of *People*, leaned back and studied it for ten minutes.

He found the contents interesting—as an anthropologist would find the civilization of an alien culture interesting. The pictures revealed some sort of sub-specie of beings, wearing strange clothing and with rather frightening hairdos. They came in black and white, but all seemed to have been born with the same expression—a congenital smile with lips glued back to expose artificially white teeth. *All look like descendants of a great white shark,* Savage mused. Their marital habits were rather obscure, most of them treating the institution of marriage as some sort of a game he remembered called "Kitty in the Corner," in which the participants would run from one person to another at a given signal.

Since the only movies Savage watched were those made before 1950—at which year he always insisted that moviemaking as an art form had died—he had seen almost none of the motion pictures mentioned. Most of the people seemed to be "celebrities" rather than people who had actually *done* something. That is, they were famous for being famous. *None of them*, he thought as he tossed the magazine aside, *built anything, wrote anything worth reading, made a movie worth seeing, or left a legacy that would benefit the world.* In an effort to be fair, he muttered, "But, then, neither have I."

He got up and walked around the room, studying the pictures. He was not a student of art, but reacted to paintings strongly, liking some and hating others. One of the pictures was a print of three men and one woman dressed in scarlet coats and riding horses that seemed eager to jump over fences. He studied the print, and despite admiring the fine drawing, wondered if people still did such things. He assumed they did in Virginia and England—but such a world was as alien to him as the far side of the moon. He could understand chasing an animal that could be eaten— but who would eat a fox? He suddenly recalled Oscar Wilde's definition of an English foxhunt: "The unspeakable in pursuit of the uneatable."

Moving over to another wall, he arrived at a small print that had a small brass plate on the bottom stating that it was Number 227 out of a limited edition of 1,000 prints. He studied the print, a photograph of a can of Campbell's soup against a pale beige background.

Just a can of soup.

For all of two minutes, Savage stared at the print, trying to feel something. He had the rather old notion that art was supposed to be moving to the spirit, and here someone had issued 1,000 pictures of a can of Campbell's soup.

Maybe the can is symbolic of man's destiny. No, it can't be that. I wonder if it's supposed to remind me of my mother? No—all it reminds me of is a can of Campbell's soup.

He shrugged and for one moment tried to compute how much the "artist" had been paid for taking the picture. *More than ten sixth grade teachers made in a year, probably .*

It was a depressing thought, and he moved to the third wall, pausing before a large print. It was not an original, and he'd seen a copy of it somewhere before, though he couldn't remember just where.

It was a picture set in the downtown area of a large city. A late-night scene, it featured a circular cafe with glass walls permitting people to see inside. The inside of the cafe was brilliantly illuminated—but it was the cold light of fluorescent tubes rather than a warm light of sun or candle or lamp. Outside, dark buildings lined the city street, standing ominously bulked together like alien monsters in a murky darkness.

There were four people in the picture, three of them customers and one who was a combination short-order cook and waiter. The cook was a handsome young man with blonde hair. He was bending over, looking at the couple who faced him, evidently saying something to them.

The couple sat facing the interior of the cafe, their backs to the dark street outside. They were well dressed and were looking straight ahead, instead of at each other. They seemed, in fact, not to be conscious of each other, though they obviously were either married or on a date. Their faces were expressionless, so that they seemed like mannequins rather than live human beings.

The third customer sat with his back to the viewer, his face hidden as he slumped over the counter. There was something ominous about him, a dangerous look that was heightened by the way he seemed to be watching the couple with some sort of feral interest.

There was an aura of death over the scene in the painting, and Savage was staring at it with distaste when Sunny came out of the bedroom. "Oh, do you like my new print?" she asked brightly.

"No, I don't." Savage turned away from the picture. "I'd take it down if I were you."

"Take it down?" Sunny was appalled at the suggestion, and

somewhat angered. "I just bought it. It'll be worth a lot of money someday. That's a *Hopper*."

"I don't care if it's a hopper, a jumper, or a leaper," Savage shrugged. "It's depressing. Look at the thing, Sunny—everybody in it is miserable. And if they leave that cafe they've got to go outside—and it's even more depressing out there. Looks like one of the Projects in New Orleans where we get corpses on a daily basis."

Sunny stared at Savage, then laughed. "I'd forgotten what a terrible critic you are, Ben. Edward Hopper is one of the finest artists America's come up with."

"Is he as good as the guy who took the picture of a soup can?" Ben inquired, motioning at the print with his chin. "That took real talent, didn't it?"

"You don't understand art!"

"Sunny, any twelve-year-old with a ten-dollar camera could take a picture of a soup can—and some of them could take a better one than that thing on your wall."

Sunny stiffened with outrage. "That's about all I need to hear, Ben! You don't know enough to talk about art. Let's go."

Savage stepped outside, waiting as she locked the door. As they walked out to his car, his eyes moved constantly along the street. As he opened the door, Sunny noticed he was watching a black Pontiac Trans Am that had started the engine a hundred yards away and was pulling away from the curb. She saw his hand slip inside his coat, and her eyes grew large. "Ben—!" she said quickly, but stopped when he ignored her.

The Pontiac passed them by, the driver, a harried-looking woman with a small child trying to help her drive, gave them a wan smile, and Savage's expression lightened. Sunny, realizing she'd been holding her breath, let it go and got hastily into the car. When Savage got in and drove away, she asked timidly, "Ben, did you really think someone in that car was out to get me?"

Savage turned his head, a small smile on his wide lips. "Didn't mean to scare you," he said. Then he shook his head. "Better to suspect everybody."

"Not a nice way to live, is it, Ben?"

"Well, it beats the alternative—which is to get killed."

His casual brutality shook her, and she sat there silently, thinking hard as he drove toward the interstate. "I'll be glad when this is over," she murmured. "I'd like to be able to get up without wondering if I'll be alive at sundown."

They were passing through one of the inner city housing additions called Desire Project. It was what remained of a dream someone had had to give decent housing to poor urban people. Once the paint had been as bright and gleaming as those bureaucratic hopes, but paint and dreams were now faded, peeling, and reeking of decay.

"Those people who live in Desire Project, Sunny," Savage remarked, "don't have any chance at what you call a 'normal' life. You told us all about it in that special you did on the horrors of urban decay, remember?"

Sunny shot him an angry glance, but he continued, "Guess it's one thing to do a story on a problem—and something else to have to live in the problem."

"I did all I could to call attention to the crime and vice that goes on here!"

"Sure, I know," Savage nodded. "That's what sociologists and reporters always do—point out the problems. But they never solve any of them, do they?"

"And what do *you* do to solve them, Mr. Savage?" Sunny demanded. She had thought of such things herself, but it angered her to have him point them out. "I don't see you mounted on a white horse, riding into the middle of the battle for right!"

"Guess I'll leave that for the Lone Ranger and Tonto," Savage nodded. He turned to her, studied her briefly, then cut his gaze back to the street. He drove up on Interstate 10 and headed west toward Baton Rouge before he said thoughtfully, "I think that's why that picture of the cafe bothers me, Sunny."

She thought about his remark, then asked in a puzzled voice, "What do you mean by that?"

"Guess I've gotten to the point where I believe the world's like that picture—a dark, frightening place where we dodge into a lighted spot for a few minutes, then have to go outside with the monsters sooner or later."

"The world's what it is," Sunny answered, disturbed by the cynical note in his words. He'd always been so easygoing, and tough enough to face whatever came. But now she saw that beneath Ben Savage's light manner lay a dark cynicism and fatalism that frightened her. "We can't change it—not really. The only thing we can do is make the best of it."

"Eat, drink, and be merry?" Savage asked, his lips curved upward in a humorless smile. "What kind of a stupid philosophy is that? Like that old beer commercial, 'You only get one trip around, so live it with all the gusto you can.'" Savage stepped on the gas and the Hawk lunged ahead, pushing Sunny back into the upholstery. "Got to be more to life than that."

"Maybe there isn't. Maybe what you see is what you get."

Savage didn't answer, but he shook his head stubbornly. Sunny moved around so her back was against the door and she faced him more squarely. She studied the rugged lines of his face, wondering about the source of the scar that rose out of his left eyebrow and wandered up his forehead to disappear into his thick black hair. She'd asked him once how he'd come by it, and he'd said in a curt voice, "Foolishness and misplaced confidence."

"Ben, what's the matter with you? You didn't used to be like this," she asked. "Are you in trouble or something?"

"No more than usual, I guess," Savage shrugged. "Just thinking more about things. When you're eighteen, you don't meditate much, do you? You just put your head down and run at any big ugly problem that jumps in front of you." Savage swerved skillfully, guiding the Hawk around an armadillo before continuing. "But those of us who survive that kind of youthful stupidity—well, we have to ask if there aren't some things that can't be whipped and that won't go away."

"What's got you scared, Ben?"

Savage held the steering wheel firmly, his eyes fixed on the distance as though he saw some sort of message written on the inverted bowl of the sky. "Dead is a long time, Sunny," he said finally. "I don't want to use up all my life and get to the end of it just in time to discover I've lived it wrong."

Sunny said no more, for she didn't understand this side of Savage. Finally they came to the city limits of Baton Rouge and she said, "Take the Bluebonnet exit, Ben." Half a mile later, he left Interstate 10 and followed her instructions to cross underneath the overpass. On the right was a pink building with green letters across the front that said *Ralph 'n Kacoo's*. "We'll meet Dani there tonight," Savage observed. "Where we going?"

"Right up there," Sunny nodded. "To that big building with the glass front."

Savage was surprised. "I thought that was part of the Bible college." He gestured at the sign that blazoned the name of a famous TV evangelist who had suffered a moral lapse.

"It was built to be a part of it, but after the trouble, DEQ leased it," Sunny shrugged. "Made a lot of people mad when the decision was made to move the DEQ to this place. They claimed a ministry has no business renting out office space. Look, there's the parking lot right over there."

Savage pulled into a parking lot that was packed, and ended up by pulling the Studebaker up on a strip of lawn. "Probably get hauled off," he observed as they got out. He looked up at the gleaming glass front of the building which was seven stories high, whistled, and said, "Some building!"

They walked through the glass doors, and as they went up on the elevator Sunny said, "I've spent a little time cultivating this lady, Ben. She's kind of anti-men." She hesitated, then added, "Behave yourself, will you?"

"I promise not to punch her out."

"I'm not kidding, Ben. She can help us—but she's on the razor's edge. If she says too much, she's out of a job."

The door opened, and Sunny led him down a broad hallway with bright new green tile to an office that had six names on the door. "That's her—Adelaide Lawson," Sunny said. They stepped inside a large room cut up into small cubicles, each manned by a worker. Sunny ignored them and went to a room with a frosted glass door with an inscription in black script: Assistant Coordinator.

Sunny tapped on the door, and when a woman's voice said, "Come in," she opened the door and stepped inside. Savage followed her and shut the door behind him. Glancing around, he saw that the office was very small, with one window that looked out on a large warehouse across a field. The woman sitting at the desk was small, thin, and intense. She was, he decided, no more than thirty-five, but she had the look of an older woman. She had small eyes, made up to look larger, and dyed black hair. The roots were lighter than the jet black of the rest of the hair, he saw, and there was an angry light in her eyes.

"I asked you not to come here," she snapped, then turned her eyes on Savage. "And who is this?"

Sunny said apologetically, "Addie, I'm sorry! But I've been having some threats, and had to have some protection. This is Ben Savage."

Addie Lawson stared at Savage as if he had crawled out from under a rock, and then dismissed him. "What do you want?"

Sunny turned on her full powers of persuasion, but it took ten minutes for her to get the woman into a talking mood. Finally Addie relaxed, and even behaved civilly toward Savage. Sunny played her skillfully, saying, "Ben, it's awful what's been done to Addie!" She turned toward Savage so that the woman could not see the left side of her face and winked at him. "She was absolutely *robbed* of her rights."

"I'm sorry to hear that, Ms. Lawson," Ben said, putting regret into his voice, and trying to look as humble as possible. "What happened?"

He had asked the right question, for the answer boiled out of Addie like a fiery explosion. It appeared that she had been scheduled to become head of her department—a position that *everyone* agreed she deserved! But the governor had fallen for that little tramp straight out of a barroom—and had given *her* the job!

"Why, I can't believe that!" Ben said, letting amazement wash over his face. "Even the governor couldn't get by with something that raw!"

"Oh, he did it through his stooges, like he gets all his dirty work done. He got Phil Herndon to do the actual hiring." Hatred sharpened Addie's features, and she gave one short, bitter burst of laughter. "Can you imagine what that floozie did in that position?"

"But did she have any training in geology or environmental control?" Ben asked quickly, pouring gas on the flames that roared out of the woman.

"Training!" Addie stared at him scornfully, her black eyes glittering. "The only training she had was rolling drunks in a bar!"

Sunny spoke up sympathetically, "Ben, it was terrible! And Addie here had to do all that girl's work in addition to her own! Isn't that right, Addie?"

Savage sat there, getting a clear picture, and wondering how much validity there would be to the woman's testimony. She obviously hated men, hated the governor, and hated Cory Louvier. Finally he heard Sunny set the hook by saying, "Addie, you've got to help us. The only way you're ever going to get your rights is if this thing blows up in Russell's face."

At once apprehension made the woman blink. "You don't understand state government, Sunny," she said, lowering her voice. "The first rule—and the last rule—is: 'Don't make waves.'" A haggard look came into her eyes, and she seemed older and very tired. "No matter how bad things are—no matter if the director puts his muddleheaded nephew in charge of the whole operation—you don't talk about it, *especially* to the press!"

Sunny said at once, "All this is privileged information, Addie. I've promised you that. We need to *know* the truth. If you'll help us, we'll leave your name out of it."

Finally Addie agreed. "It's a cheap story," she said tersely. "The governor's always been a skirt-chaser. He saw this girl, Cory, in a bar. I think she was ostensibly a waitress of some kind, but she did more than that! Anyway, Russell went bananas over her. But she was smarter than most of the chippies he bundles with," she admitted. "She held him off—which was the way to get him. She kept him dangling until he got her this job. . . ."

Finally, after the woman had run down, Sunny said, "We'll keep this under wraps—your part of it, Addie. Can you give us some names? People who can give us more on this?"

"It wouldn't do any good to give you names of people in the department," Addie frowned. "They won't talk. But you can get an earful from one man who's no longer with DEQ. His name is Baxter Rogers." She wrote a number down on a pad, tore it off, and handed it to Sunny. "He'll tell you what I've said is true. And he'd be happy if you put the truth about this injustice on page one!"

"Thanks, Addie," Sunny smiled. She got to her feet, saying, "I'll look forward to the day when I come into an office that says Department Chairman on it—and find you inside."

"Well, I want to do my duty," Addie said primly. "Just don't let my name come into it."

When they left the office, Ben asked, "What's all that about, Sunny? She hates the governor—and I guess it's true about his messing around with the Louvier girl, but what good is it?"

"Not much," Sunny admitted. "Not in a courtroom, anyway. But you've been a policeman, Ben. You know how it is when you don't have much; you just keep on digging. Maybe this man Rogers will have something."

"That's the way it works, all right. What now?"

"I've got a contact in accounting. He knows something, but like Addie says, it could cost his job if he speaks up."

"Might not be too good to approach him on the job," Savage observed.

"He's got a private office. Nobody will see us. And this place is so busy nobody seems to notice much what's going on in the next office."

"I'll bet they do," Savage countered. "This kind of place is like a school of sharks. They look for blood, then go for it."

But Sunny insisted, so they spent the next hour moving

around the building. She talked to several people, but it all seemed like wasted effort to Savage. Finally, she said, "Let's go uptown, Ben. There's a reporter there who might have something for us."

"Okay."

They were in the middle of the hall, and started down toward the elevator. When they were fifteen feet away, the door opened and two men got off. At once Savage reached out and seized Sunny's arm.

"What—!" she protested, but then she saw the men and her face grew pale.

One of the men was huge, about six feet four and weighing at least 230 pounds. He had the look of a power lifter, with a thick neck and arms that stretched the seams of his brown suit. "Come along, you two," he said. He reached out to take Sunny's arm, and Ben at once shoved the beefy hand aside. "Back off," he said, not taking his eyes off the two.

The big man blinked, a little shocked that anyone would challenge him. He had thinning blonde hair and small eyes, set a little too close together. His eyelids pulled down, and he cursed Ben, then put his hand out again.

This time Ben pulled the Colt from the holster so quickly that neither man could move and slashed it down on the huge forearm.

"What—!"

"Just hold it right there, friend!" The big man's companion had let his hand dip inside his coat reaching for a gun. He was much smaller, looking almost frail beside the other's bulk, and his gray eyes went blank as he stared into the muzzle of the revolver that Savage put on him.

"You're making a mistake," the smaller man said evenly. He was not afraid of the gun in Savage's hand, but he carefully lowered the hand that had been inside his coat.

"You've already made yours," Savage remarked. "Who are you?"

"Police officers," the gray-eyed man said softly. "Baton Rouge Police Department. Now, let's have the gun."

Savage stared at the hand the smaller man held out, but said, "Let's have some ID."

"Sure." The smaller man reached carefully into his pocket, pulled out a leather covered badge and held it up for Ben's inspection. "I'm Detective Catlow and this is Detective Oakie. Show him your buzzer, Lou."

Oakie, his eyes burning, slowly pulled out his ID, held it up, and said, "All right, let's have the gun."

Savage reversed the weapon, put his gaze on Oakie, then handed the Colt to Catlow. "Next time," he said, "show some procedure. You ought to know better than to approach a man without—"

He heard Sunny cry wildly, "Look out, Ben—!"

He knew that Oakie was making a move, but it was too late, for something struck him on the head, sending a million lights flashing before his eyes. He never knew when he hit the floor.

"A real tough guy!" Oakie said, looking down at the motionless form of Savage, and stroking the leather covered sap in his big hand.

"He wasn't doing a thing!" Sunny cried angrily. "I'll report you to the chief."

Oakie put the sap away, then turned his smallish eyes on her. "Report what, Sunny? That he was resisting arrest?" He looked at his partner, saying, "We had to take him, didn't we, Lieutenant Catlow? He had a gun in his hand, and we had to use force."

Catlow looked down at the Colt he'd taken from Savage,

then lifted his eyes. He stared at Oakie and nodded. "Yes, we had to do it."

"Come on, I'll drag him to the car," Oakie said. "You bring the woman." He pushed the elevator button, and when the door opened, he said, "Everybody out!" Three startled women scrambled out of the elevator, their eyes wide. Oakie reached down and gripped Ben's wrists in one huge hand and dragged him inside.

"Let's go, Miss Sloan," Catlow said quietly. Sunny obeyed, her mind reeling with shock. She looked down at the lolling head of Savage, and saw the thin line of scarlet that ran from the cut in his scalp, then she stared into the eyes of Detective Lou Oakie.

Oakie said gently, "I'm being easy on him, Sunny. Ordinarily, I'd drag a tough hombre like this down the steps by his ankles." He grinned at her, and when the elevator stopped, he said, "Everybody out." A small, prim-looking man in an expensive-looking suit stared at Oakie, dragging the limp body of Savage as if he were a bag of leaves. Oakie smiled at the small man, saying cheerfully, "Have a good day, you hear?"

8

Under
Lock and Key

The cell had no toilet or running water and contained only an iron bench bolted to one wall. The bars of the door had been painted white, but were peeling now, except where they were gummed up with thick, dried gobs of hardened, yellow pigment.

Savage sat down carefully on the bench, trying not to move his head too suddenly. The guard, an older man with bushy white hair and ebony skin, shook his head. "They give you anything for that in the infirmary?"

"Couple of Tylenol."

"Well, they didn't take no stitches. But you got a pretty bad lump there." He studied Savage with eyes that had seen just about everything and asked curiously, "You really throw down on Oakie and Catlow?"

Savage nodded—and was immediately sorry. The simple

act sent a white hot ice pick through his head, and he closed his eyes quickly. "Could I have a drink of water?"

"Sure." The guard moved away, his leather soles scuffing on the concrete floor. Savage sat very still on the side of the bunk, allowing the pain to recede. When it was mostly gone, he looked down at his shirt, studying the dried blood that had changed from scarlet to a cruddy shade of brown. He'd come out of it in the police car, and had said nothing through all the process that followed. He'd been fingerprinted, photographed, then taken to the infirmary where a young intern had washed the cut on his head, saying, "No need for stitches. You'll be all right when the swelling goes down."

"Here you go—"

Savage lifted his eyes to see the guard holding out a large, green plastic glass through the bars. He stood up, keeping his head carefully balanced, and stepped over to take the glass. It was tepid, but he drank it thirstily. He handed the glass back, saying, "Thanks. That was good."

The guard took the glass and paused outside the cell. "Wasn't too smart, pulling a gun on two detectives. They'll nail you with resisting arrest."

Savage sat down carefully. He knew it would do no good to explain, so he made no effort. "How long will I be in this holding cell?"

"Not too long. Soon as the papers come, I'll move you down the hall. You can lie down there. You want another drink, just call me."

"Sure—and thanks."

The cell was quiet, and Savage was glad it wasn't packed with the usual group of drunks. All he needed was to be jostled around! He leaned back against the concrete wall, put his head back, and thought about what had happened. He was aware that it could have been worse. Oakie could have put a bullet in him—probably would have if Sunny hadn't been there. He tried to think of some other good aspect of the mess, but failed.

The concrete was rough and scraped his head, so he sat up and peered around the room. He'd seen double for a short time after he came out of unconsciousness, but he was relieved to see that his perspective was all right.

Looking around, he noted that the walls were grimy and filled with graffiti of the coarsest sort. He'd read once that someone had removed a wall from one of the toilets in a bus station rest room and had entered it in a contest for modern art.

"This one would probably win first prize," Savage muttered, scanning the "art" that ranged from the obscene to the obscene.

The heat was off, and there was a clammy coldness in the cell. The air was filled with the odors that were part of every jail he'd ever been in—sweat, urine, disinfectant, old food—and fear. The fear, he knew, could not be tested in a laboratory, but it was always there. When a man is locked up, he's going to be afraid. All except those who've been locked up so long or so often that being a prisoner has become the norm. Despite himself, Savage felt tendrils of fear crawl along his nerves.

He stood up, clasping the damp bars and staring down the hall. He could see a table at the end of it, and the guard that had given him the water was seated, reading a paper. He was still thirsty, but decided not to ask for another glass of water. He was good at waiting, but only in certain circumstances. On a stakeout, he could sit in a car outside a building for long hours—but that was different. He could always quit and walk away from the job. Maybe that was it, why fear kept creeping up when you were blocked off from all that you loved in the world by a steel door and people who would shoot you if you tried to walk.

The time crept by, broken by the sounds of slamming steel doors and the faint sound of a radio playing country music somewhere in the bowels of the jail. He had no watch, and this made it worse. *Probably better not to have one,* he thought. *I'd be looking at it every two minutes.*

Finally, he heard the guard scuffing down the hall and looked up. "Time to go," the guard stated.

"Go where?"

"A regular cell. Got cots in it. You can lay down."

Savage followed the guard to the steel door, stepped through it, and the two of them moved along a wide hall. They had to pass through another steel door that was activated by a very fat guard who resented their intrusion on his cultural life. He was studying a dog-eared copy of *Penthouse* as the two came to stand before his desk.

"Hate to interrupt, Simms, " the black guard grinned. "But when you get through with your lechery, would you mind opening the door?"

Simms glared at him, cursed, then stared at Savage. "This the big bad cop-hater?"

"Just open the door, Simms."

But it was the corridor of power for the fat guard. He had small eyes the color of walnuts that gleamed beneath his low brow. "I'd like to have you in the interrogating room for about five minutes," he whispered. The thought pleased him and his pouting mouth drew into a smirk. "Yeah, I think I could make a believer out of you—"

"Come on, Simms! Open the door!"

Simms reluctantly threw a switch and the lock clicked loudly. Savage's guard pushed it open, and the two walked through. "Guy has to hassle every prisoner comes through," he grumbled.

"Some are like that." Savage smiled as the guard paused in front of a large cell. "You're not, though. Thanks for everything."

The black man smiled. "You just put your trust in Jesus, brother. If it wasn't for him, I'd be just like Simms." He shut the door and glanced at the sleeping man on one of the two bunks. "When you go to interrogation, don't stir up Oakie. He's got a mean streak."

"Thanks for the tip."

"Yeah, well, I hope it works out for you."

As the guard left, Savage turned to survey the room. It was about twenty feet square and the walls were lined with bunks covered with gray blankets. In the center was a wooden table surrounded by three chairs. A toilet was stationed in one corner, flanked by a sink. The smell of bodies and the toilet dominated the room, and as Savage walked toward an empty bunk, one of the prisoners spoke to him. "Hey, dude, what's happening?"

Savage sat down on the bunk and looked up at the speaker. He was one of five men, and was by far the largest. Wearing only a pair of jockey shorts, he had a neck like a linebacker and shoulders so wide they looked almost grotesque. "Not much," Savage murmured.

"What you busted for?" the big man demanded. He was very pale, his body the shade of milk. But muscles ridged his stomach, and with every move there was a rippling of smooth flesh.

"Resisting arrest—and assaulting a police officer."

As Savage had known it would, this statement created intense interest in the big man and in the rest of the prisoners.

"Hey, that straight?" A smile creased the brutal lips of the big man, and he said, "I hope you cooled him, man!"

"No, I got cooled." Savage touched the lump on his head and summoned a grin. "All I found out was that the sap he carried was harder than my head."

"Who was it?" A skinny young man, no more than eighteen asked.

"Names were Oakie and Catlow."

A mutter went up from the group, and the big man cursed with delight, saying, "I wish you'd offed that big gorilla, Oakie!" He added, "I'm Al Rankin—that's Jimmy, Dutch, Franco, and Peaches."

Savage murmured, "Glad to meet you gentlemen." He blinked at the pain that had returned and said, "Guess I'll try to lie down and wear out this headache."

Jimmy, the skinny young man, said, "Sure. I got some aspirin." He went to his bunk, rummaged through a bag, and came up with a bottle. He stopped at the sink long enough to get a cup and fill it with tap water.

Savage took the tablets, downing them in one gulp. "Thanks. That'll help." He lay down carefully, and when the hulking Rankin said, "I wanna hear about what happened with you and Oakie—" all Ben could do was mutter a faint agreement.

Savage slept many hours despite the sounds around him. The noise level in any jail is loud and ceaseless, and this jail was like any other. Doors clanged, shoes thudded on stairs, cleaning crews scraped buckets across the cement floors, showers hissed and spattered from somewhere, radios tuned to a dozen different stations issued their cacophony, and inmates shouted to other inmates in adjoining cells.

All of this flowed over Savage, but he awakened only once, long enough to eat. He was not hungry, but Jimmy urged him until he struggled up to eat some of the pork chops, greens, and cornbread. He drank the iced tea thirstily, and then sat on his bunk for a time. Rankin was gone, and Jimmy said, "Be careful about Al. He's hot-tempered."

"Don't think I'm able to give him a problem."

"Yeah, he beat a guy pretty bad day before yesterday."

Something in the young man's voice caught Savage's attention. "He hassling you, Jimmy?"

"Well—" A shamed light came into the blue eyes of the youthful prisoner. "I guess he is, a little. Always making jokes about how I look."

There was more to it than that, Savage understood, and he said, "Maybe you could get them to change you to another cell."

Anger flashed in the boy's eyes. "They think it's funny!"

Savage knew then how it was, but was powerless to do anything. "Tough," he murmured. "But things pass. Hang in there, Jimmy."

His words seemed to encourage Jimmy, and he smiled shyly.

"What are you in for?" Savage asked curiously.

"DWI—third offense."

That meant, Savage knew, that Jimmy would be doing a little time. "Won't be more than three or four months," he said. "You can handle it."

"I guess so. But I'll tell you one thing," Jimmy said vehemently. "I like to drink—but it ain't worth *this*!" He waved his hand around with his jaw set tight. "When I get out, I'm off the booze, Ben. It just ain't worth it!"

"I think you're right, Jimmy. Stay away from it."

The two talked quietly, and then the other men came back from the exercise room. Rankin came over and put his hand on Jimmy's neck, "Hey, Savage, you messin' around with my buddy?"

Jimmy's face turned scarlet, and he tried to pull away, but

the massive hand held him fast. "Aw, don't be bashful, kid! I'm your friend."

Savage said mildly, "Let him go, Rankin."

Rankin blinked in astonishment. "What'd you say?"

"I said let him go."

A rush of red blood swept over Rankin's blunt face. He dropped his grip on Jimmy's arm and squared himself before Savage. "You tellin' *me* what to do, Savage?"

"Sure, I am."

The cell had grown totally quiet, the men staring at Savage as though he had lost his mind. Ben got up, looking almost frail against the bulk of the massive Rankin. He held up his hand, saying, "Look at the edge on my hand."

Rankin stared at the hard ridge that ran along the little finger down to the heel of Savage's hand. A sneer came to his lips. "You some kind of karate nut? I eat 'em alive." He lifted a massive fist in a threatening gesture, saying, "Why, you little—"

But the threat was never finished. Savage whipped his arm around so quickly that his hand was a blur, and in one motion drove the hardened edge against the muscular throat of the big man. The blow made a meaty sound, and Rankin staggered backward, clutching at his throat. He was gagging, and his eyes bulged wildly as he tried to speak. As the other inmates watched with astonishment, Savage moved closer to Rankin.

"I didn't hit to kill that time, Rankin," he said, and there was something in his still face and burning eyes that held the big man still. He was coughing and gagging, trying to breathe. The pain was worse than anything he'd ever known, and he stared at Savage who said, "Next time I'll give you a *real* chop. It'll smash your trachea—and you'll choke to death. Or maybe I'll do this—"

Again the motion was too swift for Rankin to dodge. Savage struck the nose of the big man with the heel of his hand, catching the nose underneath and driving it upward. The force of it drove Rankin's head back, and the intense pain brought a hoarse roar from the big man. He stood there, unable to speak, his eyes filled with confusion.

"That was a love tap," Savage said. "If I have to do it again, I can drive the bones of your nose up into your brain." He stepped closer to Rankin, adding, "You're a pretty tough fellow, Al. I know you could flatten me with one punch—but if you do, make it a good one. Because no matter how you beat me up, you have to sleep. And all I need is one good shot to break every bone in your throat and stop your clock."

Rankin was gagging and it was with difficulty that Savage made out the words. "You want to see a doctor? Sure, I'll call the guard."

When the guard came to stare inside, he demanded, "What's going on?"

"Rankin's had an accident," Savage said. "He wants to go to the infirmary."

"What happened?"

"He hurt his gully-gully," Savage said blandly.

The guard stared at him, then opened the door, saying, "Come on, Rankin." As he shut the door, he grinned slightly. "Watch your buns, Savage."

"Yeah."

When Savage turned around, the other men looked at him with awe in their eyes. Jimmy whispered, "Gosh, Ben—I never saw anything like that!"

"He'll nail you for sure, soon as he gets able," said one of the inmates, a long, lean man with black hair.

"Hit the Rankins hard enough, and they don't come back," Savage shrugged. He wanted to tell Jimmy it was better to get beaten to a pulp than live in fear. Anything was better than fear. But he knew it wasn't the right time for a lecture, so he lay down on the bunk, aware that the others were staring at him.

An hour later, the same guard that had taken Rankin to the infirmary came to unlock the cell. "Come on, Savage. Interrogation room."

"What about Rankin?" the skinny inmate demanded.

The guard shook his head. "Had something broke in his throat. They sent him over to Baton Rouge General for surgery."

"He say how it happened?" Jimmy asked quickly.

"Said he tripped and hit his throat on the table." A slight grin touched his lips. "You guys better watch out for all these dangerous tables in here."

Savage followed him down the hall, then down two flights of stairs. "In here." The guard opened a door, and Savage stepped inside a fairly large room with several chairs and a desk over to one side. Oakie was sitting in a chair which he'd tilted back against the wall. He grinned wickedly at Ben, saying, "Hey, here's the famous cop-shooter, Riley."

Catlow was standing beside the window, peering out at the construction that was going on. He turned and shook his head. "Well, the Highway Department found a street they'd forgotten." He glared at Savage as if it were his fault, then shook his head, saying sourly, "They'll never be satisfied as long as we've got *one* lousy street that's not blocked off with their little orange barrels!"

Oakie grunted, "Sit down, Savage. Got a few questions for you." He heaved himself out of his chair and came to stand in front of Savage. "Give me some good answers, and we'll be nice and let you go. Give us a problem, and we'll keep you in the slammer for a long time."

"Aw, come on, Lou, don't be so hard-nosed." Catlow shrugged and said, "Savage, we checked you out. For a PI you're not so bad. Just give us a few answers and you can go."

Savage stared at the two. "I think you've been seeing too many old cop movies," he remarked. "The old 'good guy and bad guy' routine went out with *Dragnet*."

Oakie's face turned red instantly. "Don't play games with me, Savage!"

Savage turned to Catlow. "Now, it's your turn. You're supposed to take the big bad cop off my back. Then I'll be grateful to you. Then you can send Oakie out of the room and I'll tell you what you want to know, because you've saved me from the bad cop."

Oakie cursed, but Catlow smiled, his thin lips turning up at the edges. "Be quiet, Lou." He studied Savage carefully, his gray eyes sharp and calm. "Okay, so you know the drill. You gotta know that we can give you a bad time if you don't cooperate."

"Sure you can." Savage had decided that it was Catlow who was the brains of the pair. There was a lazy air about the man, but Savage had seen men like Catlow before. Ignoring Oakie, he faced the small officer. "What do you want to know?"

"What you were doing with Sunny Sloan in the DEQ building."

"Aw, come on, Catlow," Savage shrugged. "You know that already. She told you exactly what we were doing there."

"I'd like to hear your version of it."

Savage saw no harm in sharing part of what he knew, so he went through the story. He told the pair about the threats the reporter had received, and ended by saying, ". . . so I just tagged along to be sure she didn't get popped. And when you two stepped off the elevator, it never occurred to me that you were the law. If you'd said 'police,' that would have made things a whole lot easier."

Oakie sneered, his eyes pulled down to slits. "You'll have a time proving that in a court—that we didn't show IDs."

Savage asked curiously, "Who called you guys?"

Catlow shrugged. "One of the secretaries you and the dame interviewed. She called Phil Herndon, and he called us."

"Herndon? He's the governor's little helper, isn't he?"

"Yeah. And he told us to see that you stopped hassling the help over at DEQ. Said if you wanted any information you should see him."

"I'll bet he's already had a visitor," Savage remarked. "The Sloan woman's probably camped on his desk."

"No, she's been seeing the mayor and the chief," Catlow frowned.

Savage suddenly grinned. "Make things a little hot for them?"

Oakie burst out, "I'd like to—"

"Shut up, Lou!" Catlow glowered at his partner, and Oakie flinched. "You got us into all this with your stupid sap!" He turned to Savage, and there was a light of amusement in his eyes, though he allowed nothing to show on his face. "The media folks, they've got quite a punch," he remarked. "I think the powers that be would just as soon not have a 'Special Report on Police Brutality' appear on Channel Two."

"What about me?"

"You're outta here," Catlow said.

"When?"

"They've got your stuff ready now."

Savage nodded, then remembered something. "Got a favor to ask."

"Favor!" Oakie burst out. "You've got more brass than—"

"What favor?" Catlow asked, eying Savage cautiously.

"Kid named Jimmy in my cell—he's being hassled by a big thug named Rankin. Be nice if you get the kid out of there."

"Didn't know you were a Boy Scout, Savage," Catlow did smile then. "I'll take care of it."

"Thanks."

Catlow turned and walked to the door. He called for the guard, but as Savage reached him, he said, "Don't come back here, Savage. The climate of Baton Rouge is dangerous to your health."

Savage paused, then nodded, "I'll take it up with my doctors. Thanks for the tip, Catlow."

Savage left the room, and as he followed the guard down the hall, he heard the sharp voice of Catlow cutting the cursing of Oakie short. He was mildly surprised that he had gotten out of it so easily. Pulling a gun on a police officer wasn't a little thing.

He thought of the kindness of the black guard, and his words: *You just put your trust in Jesus, brother.* The memory stirred him strangely, and he had a sudden sense of longing for something that seemed to elude him.

9

Sisterly Advice

The old State Capitol Building of Louisiana stood as a beautiful edifice while the new one rose above it in stark contrast. The old structure, built of pink marble, displayed all the classic lines of past centuries, while the new, a tall, gray structure, had nothing to recommend it except height. Huey P. Long, the fabled governor who ruled the state with an iron hand in the twenties and thirties, decided that Louisiana would have the tallest state capitol building in the union and forced the legislature to squeeze the people for the funds to build it.

As is true with most dictators, the taste of the Kingfish was execrable, and he left the monument to bad taste sticking up in the air so that the first thing one saw when crossing the Mississippi River was the drab building.

Inside, the capitol appeared no more artistic than any other modern building. The first floor had a semblance of taste, with dark marble floors and a spacious lobby. But as one went upward, floor after floor yielded nothing but hallways dissecting rooms filled with utilitarian and tasteless office furniture. Like a huge beehive, people moved endlessly around and through the passageways, bound on meaningless errands that would produce nothing but mountains of paper—which would either be shredded at once, or filed and shredded a few years later.

On a tour, one citizen looked around with admiration at the activity of the building and said, "Boy, they're sure an active bunch, ain't they?" His guide looked around and said scornfully, "Look—the most active chicken in the barnyard is the hen that's just got her neck wrung!"

But if nothing significant happened in most of the rooms, there was one office on the tenth floor that occasionally became the scene of some activity that actually produced action. Governor Layne Russell had created an inner sanctum out of part of that floor, and from time to time he called his hirelings together to do some fine tuning on his machine.

The noon sun pooled its yellow light on the floor of the office, which was covered by a Persian rug that cost enough to feed a Korean village for a month. It was a sensuous piece of work, thick and soft, with an intricate design woven into endless patterns. These patterns curled and arched in such a way that they sometimes seemed to move.

Governor Layne Russell sat in the black leather chair behind the huge rosewood desk that had at one time belonged to Andrew Jackson. He had furnished the room with the finest of antiques and paintings—using state money, of course. He already had placed them, in his mind, in the fine home he was building in the Garden District of New Orleans.

That would come later, of course, for one of the two senators was stepping down in just one year—and who but Layne Russell could fill his shoes? And after that—who could say. Huey P. Long scared the pants off presidents in his day, and there was no reason that a modern version of the Kingfish couldn't do the same.

The governor leaned back in his chair, puffing nervously on a cigar. He finally ground it out and tossed it into a gleaming brass cuspidore—one that had been spat in by no less a notable than Ulysses S. Grant. Russell thought of Grant, of his greatness as a soldier—and his absolute impotence in the office of President of the United States. Russell was a history major—though a lawyer by degree—and had learned to avoid pitfalls by studying those who'd fallen from high places.

Grant could fight wars, but he didn't have political savvy enough to be a justice of the peace, Russell mused. *His trouble was always picking the wrong man for any job.*

Russell locked his fingers, the four-carat diamond on his right hand glittering, and allowed his mind to run over the government of the state. He could call the names of thousands of men and women, never forgetting a face. When he stopped a farmer on the streets of Bunkie and said, "Why, Albert Miles—I haven't seen you for five years. How's that boy of yours doing in vet school?" well, that man would vote early and often for Layne Russell!

"Yes, sir!" Albert Miles would say with pride to his friends, "some politicians are stuck up, but not Layne Russell! He's a man of the people, he is!"

Russell had built his machine on minority votes, and despite the fact that he never improved the plight of these people in the state, they somehow thought he was their only hope. How he did this was a mystery. He dressed like the millionaire that he was, drove the finest cars, and spent almost no time with any minority group—except just before elections. But in every poll, his name led all the rest where minorities were concerned.

The strangest thing of all about Russell's success in office lay in the fact that he was a crook. He had been indicted several times for theft, though never convicted. A governor who holds the power of an absolute monarch is extremely difficult to convict.

And the people of Louisiana—a majority of them, at least—seemed blind to the fact that Russell was a crook. During his last campaign, he ran a close race with Mason Henderson, a former High Dragon of the Klan.

During that hard fought battle, the slogan of Governor Layne Russell that appeared on hundreds and thousands of bumper stickers was: *Vote for the crook! (as opposed to the racist, of course!)*

Russell sailed into office with a respectable margin, which seemed to prove that people of the state wanted crooks in office more than they wanted racists.

A soft tap on the door pulled Russell's thoughts around, and he said, "Come in."

The man who entered was in his early forties. He was overweight and tried to hide this fact by wearing tight clothes. Nobody had ever explained to him that it was *loose-fitting* garments that disguised spare tires and that tight knit shirts advertised the bulk. He had brown hair, receding somewhat, and a pair of muddy brown eyes that looked worried.

"Sorry to be late, Governor," he said, sliding into the chair in front of Russell's desk. "Had to run over to Monroe and get that mess the mayor made cleaned up."

Russell stared at the man without comment—which proved to be somewhat unnerving for the visitor. Phil Herndon had made a career out of pleasing Layne Russell, and one frown from the governor was like a falling barometer to a seaman. He was an intelligent man, but had missed making a great career. Early in life he'd been sure of being a leader in state government, but time had passed, and he'd spent himself getting other men elected to office. He was one of those men whose time never comes, or comes too late. Now as he sat nervously before Russell, he tried hard to cover the fear that welled up inside his gut.

"Phil, we're in trouble."

Russell was, perhaps, the most handsome man in the state. Tall, tanned, and with silver hair always in place, he could have been an actor on the stage. He knew how to charm the socks off people, but there was a carnivore lurking beneath his suave exterior—and no man knew this better than Phil Herndon! He'd seen too many men sliced up politically and dumped in the obscurity of political limbo to doubt it.

"What's wrong?" Herndon asked, trying unsuccessfully to keep the fear out of his voice.

"You know—or ought to know." Russell got to his feet, crossed the room, and poured himself a drink. Turning quickly, he shook his head, displeasure on his lips and in his eyes. "It's the mess you made with that detective from New Orleans."

"Savage?" Relief washed over Herndon's rounded face. "Hey, it's cool, Gov. We put the skids under him."

Russell glared at Herndon, and anger crackled in his tone. "Skids? All you did was stir up a hornet's nest, you stupid idiot!"

"Hey, I don't—"

"If I hadn't stepped in, that woman reporter from New Orleans would have had the thing plastered all over the front page of the *Advocate*!"

"But you told me—"

"I told you to put a damper on the Prejean thing." Russell leaned back, thinking hard. "It's only a few days until Prejean's execution. Once that's over, the Sloan woman can't get anywhere. Nobody cares enough about a dead con to make waves."

"She can't dig anything up, Layne."

Russell stared at him with contempt. He had to have tools like Phil Herndon, but he grew easily disgusted with their incompetence. *This clown doesn't know what a fine line we're walking,* he thought. *If the truth ever got out about that woman's death, we'd both be fed to the crocodiles!*

"Phil, we're in trouble on this," he said slowly. "I know you think we're covered, but one slip and we're dead in the water. Now, you did a good job that night," he nodded. "I owe you for that. And you know the attorney general's job is going to be up for grabs next year. You handle this thing right, and I'll help you get it."

Herndon's head came up, and his eyes brightened with excitement. "You mean it, Layne?"

"Sure. You keep this thing from hurting us, and you're in." Then a hard light came to Russell's eyes. "But if you blow it, Phil, it's all over. You'll be selling insurance instead of being attorney general!"

"I'll handle it, Layne!" Herndon got to his feet, and hope brightened his eyes. "Don't worry about a thing. I'm going to stay right on top of it."

After Herndon left the office, he went to a public phone booth and closed the door behind him. Picking up the receiver, he dialed a number. When a voice answered, he said quickly, "Johnny? This is Phil. Gotta talk to you. Meet me at Banyon's." He listened as the voice posed a question, then said carefully, "It could come to that, Johnny. We'll do what we can to keep it easy—but if that doesn't work—it might have to be a contract job. We'll talk about it." He hung up and stepped out of the booth. A look of satisfaction came to his face.

"Attorney general!" he said to himself.

Then the smile faded, and a look of grim determination came into his brown eyes. "Nobody's going to stand in my way," he muttered, then walked with a new sense of purpose as he left the building.

When Dani came into the kitchen, she found her younger sister sitting at the dinette table staring out the window.

"Mom's sleeping late, I guess. You're up early, aren't you?" Dani said brightly. "What's the occasion?"

"I just couldn't sleep."

The brevity of the reply caught Dani's attention, and she considered Allison's expression thoughtfully. *She's worried about something. I know that look.* She moved to the counter, put four spoonfuls of coffee into the Mr. Coffee machine, added water, and threw the switch. "How about if I make us an omelet?"

"I'm not hungry."

"You will be when I get this masterpiece done," Dani said. She was not particularly hungry herself, but making breakfast would provide a good opportunity to talk to Allison.

As she gathered the contents for the omelet, she talked casually about unimportant things. When the omelet was done, she slid it onto a blue and white plate, then brought it to the table. "Here, you'll just *have* to eat half of this. If I eat it all, it'll go right to fat."

Sitting down she bowed her head and prayed briefly, then began to cut the omelet with a fork. "We haven't had much time to talk, have we, Sweetie? What's happening with you?"

Allison was cutting her half of the omelet into rectangular portions, but her mind was not on it. She said offhandedly, "Oh, nothing, I guess."

"Come on, now—I know that look," Dani said. "What's bothering you?"

Allison's blue eyes were fixed on her plate, but when she lifted them and looked across the table, Dani knew the girl was troubled. "Oh, Dani, I get so mixed up sometimes!"

"Well, join the club," Dani nodded. "Wish I could tell you that it'd all go away, that when you get older you'll have perfect control over everything—but you know that's not so." She sipped her coffee, then shook her head. "You've seen your big sister muddling around too much to believe that." She leaned forward, her eyes intent, saying, "Come on, Sweetie— what's the problem?"

Allison was wearing a pair of pajamas with a cuddly bear on the front, and her hair fell about her face as it had done when she was younger. *She looks about ten years old,* Dani thought suddenly. She was a sensitive girl, this younger sister of hers, more than she herself had been—which was saying a lot.

"There's this boy at school," Allison said in a subdued voice. "He's the most popular boy in the whole school, Dani. And he likes me!"

When Allison paused, Dani said quickly, "Well, who wouldn't like *you,* Allison Ross?"

"I could give you a list," Allison replied with a trace of bitterness.

"What does *that* mean? You've always had good friends."

"Oh, sure—*girl* friends," Allison shot back. "But I've never had a real boyfriend."

"And here you are at the creaky old age of sixteen!"

Allison said, "Oh, don't make fun of me, Dani!"

"I'm not making fun, Sweetie," Dani said quickly. "Do you think I can't remember what it's like growing up?" She laughed shortly, adding, "Whenever I hear people talking about the 'golden days of youth,' I want to throw up!"

"Really, Dani?"

"Sure. I can remember very few days of my 'golden youth' when I wasn't scared or embarrassed."

"What were you afraid of?"

"Oh, lots of things," Dani smiled briefly. "Afraid that I'd grow up to be too tall. Afraid that my face would *never* clear up. Terrified that no boy would ever like me enough to go on a date."

Allison had forgotten the omelet. She leaned forward, wonder in her eyes. "I didn't know you were like that!"

"I think all girls are like that," Dani answered. "Even beauty queens. I read a story once about them. The writer said every one of them he interviewed had one thing in common—they were all unhappy about the way they looked."

Allison sat there, thinking, and Dani knew that she was trying to get up enough nerve to tell the real problem. Finally she said, "Well—his name is Mark Gordon. And he goes with lots of girls, Dani. We worked together on a science project when the semester started."

"He make any moves on you?"

Allison stared at her sister, then flushed rosily. "He tried to kiss me once—" then added quickly, "But I wouldn't let him."

"Good-looking, I'll bet."

"A dream—an absolute dream!" Allison's cheeks glowed for a moment, then she looked down. "I think he's going to ask me to go to a party, Dani."

"Well, that's fine, isn't it?"

"I guess so—but he may ask Megan Loy."

"Oh, fuzz! You can beat out any old girl named Megan!"

But Allison didn't respond to Dani's mild teasing. She twisted her fingers together, obviously longing to say more, but somehow couldn't get it out. Dani thought carefully, then said, "Let me make a guess about Megan Loy. I guess she's pretty wild."

Allison's head shot up, her eyes wide with astonishment. "How'd you know that? Did somebody tell you about her?"

"No, Allison, but I'm a private detective, you know. When you said that Mark went with lots of girls, that he tried to kiss you, and that he might go with Megan, I put it all together and made a deduction." Dani sipped her coffee thoughtfully, then said, "What I guess is that you're bumping into modern morality. The boys want sex, and they'll go with the girls who'll provide that. So you're trying to decide if you're willing to go the way of the crowd in order to get Mark Gordon."

"I—I don't want to be that kind of girl—like Megan Loy," Allison whispered. "All the kids make jokes about her. But—"

When Allison halted abruptly, Dani said quickly, "It was no different for me, so don't think this is something new, Allison. I was blind with adoration for a boy named Ted Brickell when I was about your age. And I had to make the same kind of decision."

"But wasn't it hard?"

"It's always hard to do the right thing—always!" Dani shook her head and her lips grew tight. "This isn't a modern thing, Allison. It's been going on a long time. Do you remember the story of Joseph?"

"Most of it, I guess."

"When I was mooning over Ted Brickell—and just about ready to pay the price he was asking—Dad asked me to read the story of Joseph. I don't know how he found out I was about to do the wrong thing, because I never told a soul. But he must have known," she added, "because he just said one day that he'd like me to read Genesis 39. I did—and it made all the difference."

"What does it say? I can't remember that chapter."

"Well, Joseph had been sold into slavery by his brothers, and he was a slave in the house of an officer of Pharaoh, named Potiphar. But God blessed him greatly—so much so that he actually ruled over the whole house of Potiphar."

"I remember," Allison said slowly. "Potiphar's wife tried to seduce Joseph, didn't she?"

"Yes, she did."

"The first time I read that," Allison said, "I was shocked. I didn't think anything so—so sexy would be in the Bible!"

"The Bible is a book about men and women," Dani responded. "And one of the proofs that it's true is that it never overlooks the flaws of mankind. If the Bible were written by men, and not given by the Spirit of God, quite a bit of it would have been left out, because we don't like to record our faults."

Allison nodded slowly. "I remember now. Potiphar's wife took hold of his coat and tried to pull him into bed, but Joseph just tore out of there and left his coat in her hand."

"That's what happened. And you'll remember that Joseph paid a pretty high price."

"Yes, the woman told her husband that Joseph had tried to rape her. As a result, Potiphar had him put in prison." Allison frowned, saying, "That must have been awful for Joseph, being put in prison for something he didn't even do!"

"It was tough," Dani agreed, "but I can think of something that would have been worse."

"What could be worse than being put in jail for something you didn't even do?"

"Remember the story of Joseph after he was thrown in prison?"

"He interpreted Pharaoh's dream and became the most important man in Egypt, next to the Pharaoh."

"That's right. And because of this, he was able to save his

family back in Judah from starving when a famine came. But suppose he'd given in to Potiphar's wife. It would have been easy, wouldn't it? But if he had, he'd never have been in prison, and he'd never have been Pharaoh's second in command. He'd have died a slave in Egypt, and his family back home would have suffered."

Allison's face was thoughtful. She looked at Dani with a faint smile. "I guess it's not so important that I go to that party with Mark Gordon."

Dani got up and walked around the table. "I think you're super cool, Allison Ross!" She leaned over and gave the girl a hard hug, then kissed her on the cheek. Allison grabbed her and held her for a long moment. When she finally released her, she said, "It's good to have a sister—especially one who's a detective and can deduce stuff!"

Dani laughed, hugging her again, then stood up. "I'm late. You can have the whole omelet."

"Okay."

Dani started to leave, but the phone rang at that moment. She picked it up and said, "Hello?"

Ben's voice came to her, "Hey, Boss, glad I caught you."

"What's up, Ben?"

"Sunny thought somebody was trying to get into her place. She called me, so I went over and checked it out."

"When did all this happen?"

"Oh, about three this morning. I didn't find anything, but Sunny was pretty scared, so I hung around to run the monsters off."

Dani asked tightly, "You're still there? You've been at her apartment since three this morning?"

"Yeah."

"Well, if you can tear yourself away, come to the office!"

Dani slammed the phone down harder than necessary, and

was suddenly aware that Allison was staring at her. She found her face growing warm, and said inanely, "That was Ben."

Allison asked, "Are you jealous?"

"Me?"

"You're the only one here besides me."

"Oh, don't be silly, Allison!"

"I've seen Sunny Sloan. She's a real dish."

"She's on television. It's part of her trade to look nice."

"She's a yummy."

"She's a *what*?"

"A yummy. When guys look at some girls they say, 'She's a yummy.'"

Dani felt Allison's gaze and became more uncomfortable. "I don't think it's wise for one of my employees to be with a client all night."

"You didn't say anything when Ben had to stay with that woman in Yazoo City," Allison said relentlessly. "But she was sixty-two years old and fat."

"The circumstances were—different," Dani said, faltering. "I've got to run," she blurted out.

"Do you love Ben?"

Dani stared at her sister, knowing that she was going to have to be honest. She'd taught Allison all her life that honesty was the foundation of all true relationships, and now she was going to have to measure up.

"Allison—I don't know the answer to that," she said carefully. "Ben's so different from any other man I've known. We were thrown together in that silo and had to learn to trust each other to stay alive. He saved my life, and that's something I'll always be grateful to him for." She hesitated, then faced Allison, saying, "He's kissed me a few times—and I have to say that I felt something—more than I should, I guess."

"He loves you, Dani," Allison said quietly. "I can see it in his eyes when he looks at you."

Dani felt trapped, and finally said, "If Ben were a Christian, I'd marry him, I think. But we're not one on that—and to me it would be wrong to try to put my life with a man unless we agreed on the most important thing of all."

Suddenly, Dani felt tears begin to gather, and said quickly, "We'll talk some more when I get home, okay?"

"Okay. And Dani—thanks!"

Allison sat at the table long after Dani left, and when her mother finally came in and asked what she'd been doing, she said, "Oh, just talking to Dani about stuff."

10

Witness
on Death Row

By the time Dani got to her office, she had attained an exterior semblance of peace, but the sight of Sunny threatened to ignite her temper. *Put a cap on it, Ross*, she told herself sternly when the sight of the reporter sitting gracefully on her couch giving Ben a dose of white teeth and big eyes stirred the embers.

"Sorry to be late," she apologized briefly. Slipping out of her jacket, she walked to her desk, taking Sunny's outfit in with one glance—a herringbone-patterned suit, the long jacket coming almost to the hem of the slim skirt. It was an outfit that should have made a woman look brisk and efficient, but it somehow emphasized the sleek sensuality of Sunny Sloan.

She'd look sexy in a pair of carpenter's overalls! Dani thought, but resolutely forced herself to say, "I guess you had a rough night, Sunny."

"I was petrified," Sunny said at once. She looked up at Ben, who was lounging with his back against the wall, and came up with a smile measured in incandescent units. "Ben must hate it—having to watch over hysterical women all night long."

"Goes with the territory," Savage shrugged.

"Did someone try to break in?" Dani asked.

"I thought I heard someone trying the door," Sunny answered. "But I was too afraid to look and see. All I could think of was Ben."

Dani had the impulse to ask if she'd ever heard of the New Orleans Police Department, but resisted it nobly. "Well, I'm glad it was a false alarm." She looked at the papers on her desk, then shrugged. "Work's piled up. I'm going to have to wade through this."

"Sunny thought we might go back to Baton Rouge," Savage offered. "Some of those DEQ people know something."

"That's probably true," Dani nodded. "Check back with me, Sunny, as soon as you get back."

Sunny said, "Dani, I don't think it's safe for me to go alone. I think we've stirred up so much muddy water that whoever's out to shut me up will try to get me. Couldn't Ben go along?"

Sunny Sloan was not a small woman. Actually, she was Dani's own height of five feet eight inches. But somehow, when she looked up at Savage for support, she seemed to make herself seem very small and vulnerable. She had a mobile face and complete control of her body in the way of dancers and gymnasts, so what Savage saw was a small, helpless, very young woman with an appealing face asking him for help.

"Might be a good idea, Boss," he said, blandly unaware of Dani's hard stare as he fell into the web. "Some pretty rough cookies out there."

"I don't want you over there, Ben," Dani said instantly. "The police are sore as boils because you were set free. If they caught you inside the city limits, they'd find some excuse to jail you— or to give you a lump to match the one you've already got."

Savage looked at Sunny, and felt pity for the poor girl who was staring at him in an appealing fashion. Dani was a worrying sort of woman, he reasoned, and had to be handled firmly. His jaw assumed the rather tight look that came when he was prepared to be stubborn, and he said with a rather insufferable air, "Oh, I'll be all right, Boss. But we've got to take care of Sunny."

Dani had run into this side of Savage's character many times. From the first he'd treated her, at times, like a naughty little girl who needed the firm handling of a strong, understanding male. Nothing in him infuriated her so much as this "I'm big strong Daddy—and you're my willful, cute little girl" attitude.

She stood there with anger rising in her, and wanted to scream at him, *Wake up, Ben! She's twisting you around her little pinkie!* But she managed to say quietly—though her lips were somewhat tight—"Sunny, would you mind stepping outside for a moment. Ben and I have some confidential business to discuss. You understand."

"Oh, certainly," Sunny said. She rose from her chair, and Dani noted that Savage didn't miss her progress out of the office.

"Ben, I've got an agency to run," Dani said as soon as the door closed. "I know you want to tag along with Tinker Bell, but I don't think she's in much danger."

Savage was relaxed, his back against the wall, but his dark eyes were alert as he studied his employer.

"I have a couple of days off coming. I could take them and tag along."

"There's no point in that, Ben," Dani insisted. She was angry and it always disturbed her to lose control. But Ben Savage could be so provoking! "It's not like she's going into the inner city in the middle of the night. She'll be all right."

"What if she's not?" Savage rubbed the scar over his eyebrow, and then came away from the wall, pausing before her. "Look, I know you're jealous, but—"

"Jealous!" Dani slammed her pen down on the desk, and glaring up at him grated out, "You are the most egotistical man I've ever known!"

"Why are you so mad?" Savage demanded. "You think I don't know what's going on inside you? From the minute I told you I'd spent the night in Sunny's apartment you've been like a bomb with a short fuse." He leaned over, putting his fingers on her desk, adding, "Why would it be so hard for you to admit that you're jealous? When you were letting that long-haired guy from the D.A.'s office take you out, I was jealous, wasn't I?"

"That's different! I wasn't spending time in his apartment in the middle of the night!"

The argument grew hotter, and once when it reached a crescendo, Sunny Sloan looked at Angie Park and asked nervously, "Do they shout at each other like that a lot?"

"Only when they're upset," Angie responded. She ripped a sheet of paper out of her typewriter, looked over her shoulder, and raised one eyebrow. "This one is a pip. Did you do anything to set it off?"

"Why, no!" Sunny smiled slightly, her eyes half-lidded. "I think Miss Ross resents me."

Inside the inner office, Ben was making exactly that point. "Look, Dani, there's nothing between me and Sunny. And I don't agree with you about the danger she might be in. There's guys in Baton Rouge who'd take her out for a glass of beer."

He made one final appeal, "Look, what if you let her go alone—and she gets killed. You'd have a hard time living that one down, wouldn't you?"

Dani was weary of the argument. She nodded, saying, "All right, Ben. You're going to go with her whatever I say. Go on and do it then."

Savage was disturbed. He hated arguments with Dani, and even though he had won his point, there was something in the set of Dani's shoulders and the tightness of her lips that told him it had been a costly victory.

"I'll be glad when this mess is over," he said morosely. "I don't like to fight with you."

He turned and walked out of the office without saying anything else, closing the door with just a fraction more force than necessary. "Come on, Sunny," he said glumly. "Let's get going."

Sunny said brightly, "Oh, Ben, I'm glad she let you go with me."

Angie waited for a signal from Dani on the intercom, but nothing came. Two hours later, Dani came out, her coat on and her purse in her hand. "I've taken care of the papers, Angie." She had a dissatisfied look on her face and her tone was not lively. "I'm going to Angola to see Eddie Prejean."

"Will you be back this afternoon?"

"I don't know yet. I'll call you if I have to go anyplace else."

After Dani left the office, Angie shook her head. She'd never seen Dani so disturbed, and it bothered her. She fixed a cup of coffee, and when Al Overmile came in to ask for Dani, she said, "Out for the morning." She sipped the coffee thoughtfully, thinking hard, then with a worried look on her face, added, "I'm worried about her, Al."

Overmile's meaty face took on a look of surprise. "The agency's doing good, isn't it? More cases than we can handle."

"The agency's doing fine—but the Boss Lady is stumbling a little."

Angola had not improved since Dani's last visit. As she parked her car and made her way toward the section where Eddie Prejean was kept, she sensed again the aura of gloom and desperation that hung over the prison like an invisible shroud. She had always been skeptical of stories of how a place could take on the nature of its inhabitants, though there had to be *something* to it. She had been in homes that reeked of the anger of couples, and in homes that had radiated peace, which she had attributed to the character of a loving family.

But something about Angola—an almost palpable pressure—seemed to press against her as she crossed the yard. She thought of the thousands of men cooped up with all the frustration, fear, and rage that could come to an imprisoned human being and knew that the canopy of gloom that pressed against her was not her imagination. She wondered what it would be like to be put in such a terrible place, to hear the key click in the steel locks and know that every aspect of her life was in the hands of others. She shivered as fear laid a frigid frost on her nerves, and she tried to put on a better face as a guard led her to Prejean's cell.

"Hello, Eddie," she said as brightly as she could. "How are you?" The inanity of the question struck her, and she shook her head, her lips pressed together tightly. "Excuse me. Stupid question."

"It's okay, Miss Ross." Eddie was thinner, it seemed to her—at least the bones of his face seemed more prominent than when Dani had seen him last. "One of the guards always says as he goes off duty, 'Have a good day, Eddie.'"

"I hate that expression," Dani responded. "Those words mean absolutely nothing."

Eddie motioned to the chair beside the cot. "I guess lots of words are like that," he said quietly. "If we stopped using them, it would cut down on most conversations quite a bit." He leaned against the wall and studied her carefully. "Not good news," he murmured.

Dani was startled, but realized at once that he was intelligent enough to pick up on her lack of spirit. "No, not really," she said slowly. "I'll tell you what I've done, then we can go from there."

Prejean's face was still, his brown eyes half hooded as Dani quickly sketched what she had been doing. There was a shadow on him, Dani saw, that was growing darker. Even as she spoke, part of her mind was ranging ahead—despite her will—thinking, *In a few days, he'll be dead if something doesn't change. His blood won't be rich and red. He'll be cold and stiff, cut off from whatever life might have had for him.*

She broke off finally, shaking her head wearily. "I'm sorry I don't have better news, Eddie."

"I didn't really expect it, Miss Ross."

Dani looked at him quickly, and said with a sudden burst of emotion, "Don't give up, Eddie!"

Prejean held her gaze, but there was no light in his dark eyes. "No sense wasting more of your time on me, Miss Ross," he said quietly. His tone before had been keen and edged, but now he let the words fall without life in them. "If there was a chance—something I could do, I'd do it. But the dice are loaded." Cynicism and doubt ran deeply through his words, and bitterness curled the edges of his lips. "Don't know why I ever expected anything else. The big fish eat the little fish— and the little fish eat mud."

Dani yearned to give the young man some sort of comfort, but found it almost impossible to find something to say. "I know it looks dark, Eddie, but we've got to *try!*"

Prejean stared at her for a moment, then cocked his head to one side. "Why are you so anxious to help me?" he asked. "You don't even know me."

"I don't think you're guilty," Dani said. She looked down at her hands, searching for the right words. She'd always disliked Christians who poured Scriptures down the throat of those who were in an impossible situation. It had seemed somehow unfeeling, as though the believer was saying, "Look, I can't do anything for you, so let's read the Bible instead."

Dani knew the power of the Bible to bring comfort, but she understood as well that a person had to be open, willing to *receive* what God had to say. A temptation came to avoid using the Bible, but she knew deep down that there was nothing else for Eddie Prejean.

"Eddie," she said quietly, "I don't know what you think about God, but I believe that he loves every one of us. I know," she said quickly, holding up her hand as he started to interrupt, "you're going to say that it sure doesn't *look* like it. And I can't answer all the questions people ask. Why does an innocent baby die in a fire if God loves him? Why does a young woman die of cancer at the age of twenty-five, when her life is just beginning? How could a loving God let such terrible things happen?"

When she paused, Eddie said, "Well—how *could* he?"

Dani wanted to give this man hope, and she prayed intently for wisdom, for the right thing to say. "Eddie, the world you see is not the world God purposed." She took the small Bible she'd bought from the Christian bookstore and opened it. She spoke quickly of the fall of man, reading verses from the Book of Genesis. As simply as she could, she explained that the world had been lost by sin, but that Jesus came to win it back, by his blood and by his death.

Eddie listened carefully, then asked, "Why didn't God make Adam and Eve so they *couldn't* sin?"

"Adam and Eve were made in the likeness of God, Eddie," Dani said quickly. "Not that they looked like God physically—but they had spirits that responded to God. No other part of creation has that quality. No matter how intelligent some animals might be, they can never know God in their spirits. But along with their spirits, Adam and Eve were given free wills. They were free to choose. If they hadn't been created like that, Eddie," Dani said urgently, "they would have been robots. And God wanted his creatures to love him voluntarily."

Eddie was interested. He came and sat down on the cot, thinking hard. "I guess I can see that." He stroked his cheek with a thin hand, adding with a slight smile. "Wouldn't be much fun having a bunch of puppets around, would it?" A thought came to him, and he added, "I saw that Disney picture, *Pinocchio*, when I was a kid. It was about this old guy who wanted a son. I forget how it happened, but he made one of his puppets come to life."

"And at the end of the movie Pinocchio became a *real* boy," Dani said eagerly. "And as a real boy, he could give the old man love and devotion—and that's all that God wants from us, Eddie. I've read the Bible through many times, and despite all the things theologians say, all God wants is for us to love him!"

Eddie seemed intrigued by the earnestness in Dani's tone and in the flush that had come to her cheeks. "You really believe that, don't you?"

"Yes!"

Eddie said wistfully, "I'm glad you do—and I wish I could."

"Can I tell you how I found God, Eddie?" Dani asked quickly. When he nodded, she sat for half an hour, telling him about her life. She was unaware of the surroundings, so intense was her desire to see Eddie Prejean come to know Jesus Christ.

Finally she finished, saying, ". . . and so from the moment I asked Jesus Christ to come into my life, Eddie, everything's been different. And it's not just for me—it's for everybody."

"Are you saying if I get saved, I'll get out of this place?"

"No, I'm not saying that. Many of God's people have been put to death. I may die on my way home from here. The Bible says, 'As it is appointed to man once to die—but after this the judgment.' God wants you to love him for eternity, Eddie, not just for a little time on earth. I'm praying that we'll get you free, but if you were set free from the charges that are against you in court here, what about the judgment when you stand before God?" Dani took a deep breath and whispered, "Eddie, you may not understand this, but if I had to choose between the two, I'd rather see you become a Christian and be executed, than to see you set free and go out to meet God unprepared in thirty or forty years!"

Eddie looked down at his hands as she spoke, and when she began to speak of the death of Jesus, he grew tense. Dani had seen this before. It didn't disturb people to talk about God, but the name of Jesus had the power to stir people. Some it offended, but others heard it with a hope that nothing else could bring.

Finally Dani said, "Eddie, the last thing in the world I want to do is to force someone to become a believer. I don't think that's even possible. All I can say is, I had no peace until I found Jesus Christ. And now he's with me every day. Oh, I still have problems. My father was murdered recently by a hood—and what I wanted to do was *hate* the man who killed him. If I had done that, I'd have become a bitter woman filled with hatred. But Jesus is in me, so through his power I was able to forgive my father's murderer. Day by day I have to give up what *I* want, because when I became a Christian, I gave all my 'rights' to Jesus."

"That sounds hard!"

"Not as hard as becoming bitter," Dani countered. "Not as hard as becoming a drug addict. Not as hard as dying and being cut off from the love of God forever."

For the next few minutes, Eddie threw questions at Dani— harder questions than her professors had ever given her. But she knew that they were not malicious questions, for Eddie suddenly had become alive, his face quick with interest. Finally he paused, then asked, "Can I borrow that Bible?"

"I brought it for you, Eddie," Dani said at once. "Are you ready to give your life to God?"

"No," he said bluntly. He turned the Bible over in his hands, staring at it. "I've always been a guy who wanted to know what he's getting into. Never was able to jump into things without thinking it over." A shadow crossed his face, and he added, "I don't have much time, but I want to read about Jesus. I don't know anything, really. But I've got twenty hours a day to read." He tried to smile, and failed. "I hope what you're saying is right, Miss Ross. Guy in my situation, he needs something solid."

Dani saw that it was not time to press Eddie, so she said, "We all do, Eddie. I'll pray for you to find the Lord." Then she took a deep breath, and said, "And I haven't given up on getting you out of here." She smiled at him, wanting to give him some hope. "I'm a very stubborn woman, Eddie. I hate to lose! So now, give me everything you can think of. Give me an angle. Who can I see? What can I turn over? Eddie, sometimes it's a very small thing that breaks a case—so tell me again, and don't leave anything out."

Eddie was willing, and for the next hour he spoke steadily. Finally he put his hand on his forehead, saying, "That's all I can remember, Miss Ross—except about the ring. I'd almost forgotten that."

"What ring?"

"A big ruby ring that Cory had gotten. Had to be from a rich man—which meant Russell. I told her he'd want payment, but she just laughed and told me she could handle him. She wore it all the time, never taking it off, but it wasn't on her finger when she—when they found her."

"What did it look like?"

"Big, maybe two carats or more. And the band was like a golden snake, even had two small rubies for eyes." He dropped his hand and met her eyes. "Anything in it for you?"

Dani had listened intently, trying to pick up on something that might help. She picked up her purse, saying, "I'm going to go back to where you were found, Eddie. Go over the area with a fine-tooth comb. Then I'll go talk to Cory's family." She put her hand out and took his firmly. "I'll see you soon, Eddie. Don't give up!"

Prejean held her hand, his eyes fixed on hers. "Thanks for coming, and thanks for not giving up." He dropped her hand and riffled the leaves of the small Bible. "I'll read this. Gotta be something in it if it makes folks like you, Dani!"

Dani left the prison, got into the Cougar, and drove out of the parking lot. She knew that nothing had changed—at least not insofar as Eddie Prejean's fate was concerned. The date of the execution was moving inexorably closer. She had no new evidence to take to the courts. The governor was *not* going to give a stay or a pardon.

All seemed dark and gloomy, yet in her heart she felt that *something* had changed. Nothing she could talk about to anyone. It was one of those very private, intimate certainties that came to her from time to time. She had no name for it, yet it was a sort of peace that forced all doubts and fears to flee. It was as if a light had gone on in a dark room, forcing all the darkness to flee.

As she drove down the narrow highway, Dani wondered what God was up to. She felt more keenly alive and aware than she had since she'd first taken the Prejean case. The burden lifted. She wished she could always have the sense of rightness that enveloped her, the certainty that no matter how dark the way, or how hopeless the circumstances, all was in strong hands. Hands so strong that she could rest from worry and care.

It was a good feeling, and it made the trip to Angola seem right. As she drove along, she began to sing, the joy spilling out of her. She was happy and filled with joy. She broke off singing long enough to say, "Thank you, Lord, for being God!"

11

An Unexpected Treasure

No one had put up a marker to identify the spot where Cory Louvier's body had been found. As Dani drove carefully along the abandoned logging road, she tried to keep one eye on the map, while at the same time looking for one of the landmarks she'd been given by a reluctant sergeant at the Baton Rouge police station.

Taking her eyes off the road, she dropped one front wheel into a cavernous rut left by a logging truck, the blow snapping her jaw shut with a distinct click. She gunned the engine and the Cougar roared, shattering the silence of the grove. A flock of doves flew up, their long slender bodies and delicate necks outlined against the cool blue of the sky. Gaining control of the bucking car, Dani wound around between stands of second growth pine and scrub oak. At one point, a deer crossing in front of her gave one startled look, then exploded into that most graceful of all motions as it seemed to alternate between an earthbound run and a floating glide that quickly took it out of sight.

The road narrowed until the Cougar had to squeeze through the scraping branches, and Dani wondered who would back up if she encountered another vehicle. But none came, and finally she reached one of the landmarks the sergeant had given her.

A rough wooden bridge spanned a small creek, and on a tree beside the small structure, a peeling sign hung by one corner from a thick sweet gum tree. The metal sign was so badly peppered with bullet holes that it took Dani a few moments to decipher the words—*No Hunting!*

Dani eyed the bridge nervously, for the bulk of the boards that made up the structure had warped so badly that the ends had wrenched the spikes free. On the far side of the bridge, she saw that the road forked, and remembering the instruction she'd received, "Take the right fork, the one less travelled," brought the line by Frost to her mind: *Two roads diverged in a yellow wood. . . . I took the one less travelled by.*

Carefully she eased the Cougar over the bridge and was relieved when she reached the other side. Just as the rear tires rolled off the rough planks, she caught a glimpse of movement to her left. Instantly she turned her head, leaned forward, and reached back for the .38 she wore.

But she relaxed at once, for what she had seen was a young boy, no more then ten or twelve years old. He was sitting on the stump of what had been a huge tree, watching her carefully. He held a long cane pole, and a red and white cork bobbed rhythmically in the dark water to the beat of the small stream.

Dani hesitated, then stopped the car. Cutting off the engine, she got out and walked to the side of the road, then spoke casually. "Catching any fish?"

The boy was very dark of skin, and had the blackest possible hair. He was not, it seemed, much of a talker, for instead of answering Dani, he reached down and pulled up a cord stringer that held ten or twelve fat sunfish.

"My, that's a nice stringer!" Dani exclaimed. "What bait are you using—worms?"

"Crickets, mostly." The dark eyes were curious, and after a moment's pause, the boy added, "The little 'uns steal the worms. When you get a bite on a cricket, it's usually a keeper."

At that instant, the colorful cork disappeared with a sudden *plôp*! The boy's head swiveled quickly, and he gave the pole a sharp twitch to sink the hook. The line ran frantically across the water, jerking spasmodically. The youthful fisherman, however, played the fish skillfully, his face intent and filled with pleasure. He let the fish run, then lifted the pole sharply. A flash of red and gold and green flickered from the huge redear sunfish. With an easy movement, the boy swung the fish toward him, caught it with one hand, expertly avoiding the sharp fins, and dropped the pole. Carefully, he took the hook out, then reached down and pulled up the bulging stringer. As he slipped the fish onto the stringer and lowered it back into the water, he nodded with satisfaction. "That 'un was a real pole bender!"

"Sure was," Dani nodded. "You've got a nice mess of fish. How does your mother cook them?"

"Ma's dead," the boy announced. "Me and Pa, we cook this kind whole. Give 'em a good coat of cornmeal and drop 'em in hot grease." He seemed to be in no hurry to resume fishing, and turned to face Dani. He was, Dani thought, probably a Cajun. "You lost?" he asked curiously.

"No, I'm not lost," Dani smiled. "Well—maybe a little. Did you ever hear of Daniel Boone?"

"Course I did!"

"Somebody asked him once if he'd ever been lost. He said, 'No—but I was pretty confused once for three days.'" Dani shook her head, smiling. "I'm looking for a place, but I'm not sure where it is. Do you know this road?"

"Sure. Me and Pa live just half a mile from here." He studied her, then asked, "You looking for the place where the lady was killed?"

Dani was surprised. "Yes. How'd you know that?"

"Lots of people came down here right after it happened. Police and reporters, mostly. Some people came just to see it."

"Can you tell me where it is?"

"I guess so." He hesitated, then added, "My name is Tommy Cohoon."

"I'm Dani Ross."

"You a reporter?"

"No, Tommy. I'm a private detective."

The dark eyes widened, then grew careful. "For real?"

"For real."

The boy got to his feet and walked over to stand closer. He wore only a pair of faded jeans and a thin blue cotton shirt despite the cool air. "I'll show you where it happened," he volunteered.

"I'd appreciate that, Tommy. But what about your fish?"

"Aw, nobody's gonna bother them fish," he shrugged. He was a handsome boy with a thin face and fine features. "Do you have a gun like the detectives on TV?"

"Sure do." Dani had long ago discovered that children always asked this question. She thought it was unhealthy, the interest they had in weapons, but had more or less given up trying to fight the trend. Reaching behind her, she pulled the .38 from the holster at the small of her back, and held it up for Tommy to see.

As she had expected, his eyes fixed on it with an intensity

she had not seen in him. "Gosh!" he whispered. "Can you shoot it?"

Dani was enjoying the small moment of triumph. "Well, I've had a good teacher, Tommy, but I'm still learning."

Tommy looked around at the landscape, then spotted something. "Can you hit that beer can over there?"

Dani spotted a silver beer can on the bank of the stream, caught in some weeds. "I don't know, Tommy," she said. She had fired the .38 regularly when she'd first gotten it. Then after being forced to shoot a man in defense of one of her clients, she'd hated the sight of the weapon. But as months had passed, the guilt had slowly faded. Now she looked at the gun, thinking of how hard it had been even to wear it for a time.

As much to prove to herself that the gun was no longer a threat as to please the boy, she swung the muzzle up, gripping the .38 with both hands as Ben had taught her. When the sight leveled on the silver can, she squeezed the trigger. The glade was filled, it seemed, with the explosion, and the .38 kicked back in her hand. She smelled the acrid odor of burning gunpowder, then saw the can flying out of the water. It hit the bank and rolled a few feet. She could see the jagged hole the slug had torn through the thin metal.

"Gosh!" Tommy breathed as he stared at the can. Turning his face toward her, he said in awe, "You really *can* shoot!"

"Oh, I'm just fair, Tommy," Dani disclaimed. "You should see my friend, Ben Savage, shoot."

But Tommy had seen enough. He watched her put the .38 away, then said, "I wish I had a gun and could shoot like that!"

It was a sore point with Dani, for she basically didn't like guns, and she was totally convinced that the fixation that most young boys had for guns was not healthy. However, she muffled her impulse to give the boy a lecture on the danger of firearms. *He wouldn't listen anyway—not after I've shown off like a real member of the Gunlover's Association!*

"Why don't you get in the car, Tommy?" she asked. "I don't want to get lost in these woods."

"Sure!"

Dani smiled as the boy scrambled up on the road, then plopped himself down beside her. She thought vaguely of a lecture about taking rides from strangers, but abandoned that one at once. She started the car, and as they bounced along the corduroy road, she drew the boy out. He was, she discovered, a very bright young man indeed. His grammar was rough, but his speech itself was spiced with Cajun expressions that made it richer than most. She thought of Emerson's essay on language, in which he said that country people speak a much richer speech than city dwellers.

Tommy told her about the finding of the girl who'd been killed, and Dani perceived that it had been the highlight of his life. Nothing like that happened in the backwoods where the boy lived, and she discovered that he'd been on the site almost as soon as the police. She also found out that he'd almost taken up residence on the scene during the investigation.

Tommy told the story of how he'd seen the police cars come down the road early in the afternoon. His dark eyes glowed as he related how he'd followed them and watched them find the car. He described how they'd gone over it, and how more cars had come. Then he said, "They tried to keep folks away, but I hid in the woods and watched. Climbed a big ol' pin oak, me! And I seen 'em when they dug her up!"

Dani felt a wave of revulsion as the boy described the grisly details of the recovery of Cory Louvier's body. She knew that young people had an active interest in death, that they were driven by an avid curiosity—and now she listened carefully.

The boy was matter of fact about the episode, giving the details without any sign of disgust.

Just as he was ending his tale, he said, "There—that's where the car was. Right by that big ol' cypress."

Dani stopped beside what seemed to be the backwaters of a swamp on one side of the road. The area Tommy pointed out, as they got out of the car and walked around, was part of the road apparently used by loggers as a spot to pile the logs for loading onto the trucks. The logging, evidently, had taken place some years ago, for saplings had taken root and were now shoulder high in the area. The ground was rutted still, for in damp weather, the trucks and dozers had torn the earth into small canyons. But time and weather had done much to level the ground, so that now a car could get through in dry weather.

"This is it," Tommy announced. He led Dani to a spot underneath twin cypress trees, and turned to face her as he pointed at the ground. "The car was right here—but it was wet then, so it was stuck. They had to git a wrecker in to winch it out and haul it off."

Dani stared at the spot, but had no idea what to do next. *I wish Ben or Luke were here,* she thought suddenly. *They'd know what to look for.*

She was aware that Tommy was watching her expectantly, and knew she had to do something. "Think I'll just look around, Tommy."

"Looking for clues?"

"Yes." Dani walked around the site, glad that she'd changed into jeans and a soft cotton shirt at a rest room. She'd exchanged her high heels for low quartered walking shoes, and thought how ridiculous she'd have looked trying to walk around in the mud. Cigarette butts and empty soft drink cans littered the ground, but what use were they? As she walked aimlessly around, she stopped from time to time to pick up a paper, more to convince Tommy that she was a detective than for any legitimate reason.

Finally she could see no reason to bluff any longer, but at that moment Tommy said, "Wanna see where they found her?"

Dani did not *want* to see that particular spot, but nodded. "Is it far?"

"Nah—just over in that thicket."

Dani followed the boy through saplings, getting scratched by some briars in the process. Once Tommy pushed a branch forward, and when he released it, it caught her full in the face. With one eye weeping, she pushed her way through the thicket, coming to stand beside Tommy, who waved his hand dramatically at a small open spot. "That's it—right there. See the hole? She was right in there."

A grisly vision of the young woman's body rose in Dani's mind. She tried to avoid it, but staring down at the slight depression, she could not completely ignore the facts of the homicide. Aware that Tommy was watching, she shook her head. "I guess the police looked at everything pretty closely."

"Oh, yeah, they messed around here a long time," Tommy nodded.

Dani went through the motions of looking around, but soon said, "Well, I guess that's it, Tommy."

When the two of them were clear of the thicket, she said, "Hop in. I'll take you back to your fishing hole."

On the return trip, Dani was depressed. The trip had been fruitless and she had no idea why she'd come in the first place. What could she have been thinking she'd do that the police hadn't?

Tommy asked suddenly as they approached the bridge, "Do you have any little boys?"

Dani laughed. "No, I don't, Tommy. But one day I hope I'll have two or three—just like you!"

She stopped the car, but he didn't get out. "Well, thanks for your time," Dani smiled. "Hope you catch lots more fish."

Tommy sat still, and Dani was puzzled by the expression on his face. He looked troubled, and she asked, "What's the matter, Tommy?"

"Well—" The boy squirmed in his seat, his head down as he stared at the floor. He halted his speech, and finally lifted his head to give her a troubled look. "I think I done a bad thing—and I'm afraid I'll go to jail if I tell."

Startled, Dani blinked at the boy, then said, "Oh, Tommy, I'm sure you haven't done anything so very bad."

"I didn't mean to," he said quickly. He bit his lower lip, and Dani had the wisdom to say nothing. She saw that he was in the throes of making a hard decision and felt that pressure could only confuse him. She sat patiently, wondering what the boy could be hiding.

Finally, Tommy came to a decision. "Miss Ross, will you not tell on me if I tell you something?"

Dani wanted to assure him, but had learned that honesty is best with children—or with anyone, for that matter! Carefully she said, "I can't quite promise that without knowing what it is, Tommy. It might be something I'd have to tell—for your own good, maybe." She saw his lips grow tight, then put her hand on his shoulder, which was tense as a board. "But I'll help you all I can. No matter what it is, I'll stand by you, Tommy."

His dark eyes came up to meet hers, and she saw the relief come into his face. "Well, all right," he said. "You'll have to go to my house."

"All right. You tell me the way."

She put the fish in the trunk and he hid the pole behind a tall pine tree, then they both got back into the car. All the way, as Dani drove slowly toward the almost invisible fork that Tommy pointed out, she wondered what the boy was so troubled about. She spoke about the woods, getting him to talk so that he wouldn't let fear make him change his mind.

The house was set back under some tall pines—a weather-beaten cabin that had never known a drop of paint. Dani stopped the Cougar, and when they were walking up to the house, she asked, "Is your father here?"

"No, he's working."

"Why aren't you in school, Tommy?"

He gave her a short look, then answered, "I'm sick. Pa said I needed to stay in for a couple of days."

Dani wondered about that but said nothing. Tommy didn't go into the house. Instead, he took the worn path that led around to the back, stopping in front of a line of rabbit hutches. "These are my rabbits," he announced. "I raise 'em and sell 'em to people."

"Do you? That's nice to have a job like that." Dani stuck her finger between the wire of one of the hutches, and at once a fat white doe with startling pink eyes hopped to take a taste of it. She rubbed the silky fur, and said in an admiring tone, "What's this one's name?"

"Marie. I named her after the woman who invented radium. It was in my schoolbook."

Dani scratched the doe's ears, then turned to face Tommy. "What is it you want to show me, Tommy?"

The boy hesitated, teetering on the brink of a decision. Dani saw the doubt in his eyes, but could not do anything to prove her good faith. Finally Tommy seemed to surrender. "It's over here," he said. Dani watched as he opened one of the cages containing a small black rabbit. He reached past the animal into what seemed to be a sleeping compartment and came out with a box in his hand.

He closed the door of the cage, then held the box carefully as he faced Dani. "This is my treasure box," he said. "It's my secret place. I figure nobody will ever figure to look out here in the hutches for anything."

"That's very wise, Tommy," Dani said, her eyes on the box. It was a cigar box, she noted, tied with a red string. She watched as he untied it, then slowly opened the box. Dani got a glimpse of some bills and silver, some glass marbles, and a small notebook.

Tommy reached inside and took something out. He closed the box, then held his hand out. "I found this out where the lady was killed," he whispered.

Dani felt a sudden lurch in her breast, as if her heart had skipped a beat. She knew that sometimes cases were broken by such small things as this—though not often. She reached out and took the item the boy was holding, then stared at it.

It was a gold cigarette lighter, she saw, but it was like none she'd ever seen before. She held it up carefully, noting that it was shaped like a rifle shell. She didn't know enough to be able to name the caliber, but Ben would know, or Luke. She could tell that it was too large to be used in a pistol or an automatic.

"It's got writin' on it," Tommy volunteered.

"I see that."

"It says, 'To Skip—from Lila'—and it's got some numbers, too."

Dani read the numbers 5-24-91 written in curling script around the base of the shell. The inscription was carefully done, not an amateur job, she realized. She flipped the top to one side, and instantly a flame glowed.

"It's pretty neat," Tommy observed. "My pa, he's got a cigarette lighter, but you have to roll the little wheel with your finger to make it light."

Dani clicked the top back into place, muffling the flame, then studied the lighter. It was a beautiful piece of work—but whose was it?

"Tell me about this, Tommy."

"Well, I seen them when they was bringing the dead woman out, and I wanted to see where she'd been buried. So I snuck in while they was puttin' her into the truck. They were all going to do that, so I moved real quiet through the bushes—and I seen the hole they'd dug her out of."

"What about this?" Dani asked.

Tommy dropped his eyes and dug into the ground with the toe of his worn sneaker. "I found it," he muttered.

"Tommy—where!"

He glanced up, struck by her tone, and looked scared. "It—it was right there, close to the hole. It was kinda hid by some weeds, but it wasn't far from the hole."

"Did anybody see you?"

"No!" He shook his head quickly, then added, "I heard them comin' back, so I run off."

Dani stood there, staring at the lighter, thinking hard. *It's possible one of the officers might have dropped it,* she thought. *But it could have been the killer. I'll have to find out who made it—*

"Will I have to go to jail, Miss Ross?"

Dani had been so excited and deep in thought that she had forgotten Tommy. She saw the fear in his eyes and impulsively moved forward and put her arm around his shoulder. "No, Tommy, you won't go to jail." His shoulders felt thin, and he was still afraid, she knew.

"I'll be sure that nothing like that happens," she said.

"You promise?"

"Yes, I promise." Dani saw the relief wash over his face, and added quickly, "It may be that you'll have to tell the police or a judge. But I'll be right there with you, telling them how it was."

Tommy gulped and expelled a deep breath. "I ain't slept good since I took it. I wanted to give it to the police—but I was too scared."

Dani smiled at him sympathetically. "We all get scared when we don't do the right thing, Tommy."

"You, too?" The boy was shocked at this confession. "Really?"

"Yes, really."

Her confession seemed to give Tommy some relief, and he nodded. "I feel better now. Sure am glad you came along!"

"I'm glad, too, Tommy. Now, I'm going to take this with me, all right?"

"Sure. You gonna see if it's a clue about who killed that lady?"

"Yes, I am. And when I find out, I'll come back and tell you about it."

"Will you for sure?"

"For sure! And then you might have to tell about how you found it."

"But you'll tell them about it, won't you?"

"Yes, I'll be right there. Now, don't talk about this to anyone, all right, Tommy?"

"No, I won't, honest!"

Dani took out her handkerchief, wrapped the lighter carefully in it, then said, "I'll be going now. Thank you for trusting me, Tommy."

She left then—remembering to take the fish out of the trunk. On the way back, as the Cougar bucked and plunged over the ruts, she was thinking of what a difference this might make to Eddie Prejean.

When she reached the main highway, she stepped on the gas. *Got to find out who made this lighter. It looks like a custom job. Can't be too many of them around. And if I can find a "Skip" or a "Lila"— that'll be enough to force the Governor to postpone the execution!*

And she was thanking God—for boys that fished beside the road!

12

Two Tough Men

Downtown Baton Rouge, Dani thought as she plugged a parking meter with three quarters, *is one of the most beautiful and tasteful inner cities in America.* Huge live oaks lined many of the streets, lending a gracious air to the scene.

But as she walked down the sidewalk toward the police station, she thought, *Too bad there's nobody here to enjoy the downtown. They've all gone to Cortana Mall.* It was a regret to her, for she disliked malls and liked the variety of businesses found downtown. But Americans had voted malls in and downtowns out—and no city in America had succeeded in reversing the trend. *Not much use traveling across the country—it's all the same, no matter if you're in Conway, Arkansas, or New York City: JC Penney, Sears Roebuck, and B. J. Dalton's Bookseller are in the mall.*

She spoke to Sergeant Williams, who'd given her directions earlier, asking to see one of the detectives who'd handled the Cory Louvier case.

Williams, a short, heavyset man of forty with a new set of false teeth that were not seated so far, grunted, "Lieutenant Catlow—second floor."

Dani located the lieutenant by pushing open a door marked *Detectives* and found Catlow sitting at a green metal desk in one of the small offices, across from another officer. Both men looked up when Dani walked in. When she asked, "Lieutenant Catlow?" the smaller officer nodded. "I'm Catlow."

"My name is Dani Ross."

Instantly the room grew tense, or in any event, the larger man began to bluster. "You the PI from New Orleans Savage works for?"

"Yes, I am."

"I'm Lou Oakie," the big man said, his eyes narrowing. "You come to cry over your baby boy's getting his lumps?"

"No, I'm here about another matter," Dani said evenly. Ignoring Oakie, she turned to the smaller man, saying, "Lieutenant Catlow, you handled the Cory Louvier case?"

"Yeah, I was on it."

"Could you give me a few minutes?"

Catlow's sleepy gray eyes sharpened. "Sure. Have a seat."

As Dani sat down, Oakie got up and came over to stand at Catlow's desk. "What's a good-looking dame like you doing hiring a wimp like Savage for?" He let his eyes run over Dani, grinned, and added, "You might even get a real man like me if you play your cards right."

"Lou, go over to Baker and run that guy Mattox down. Get a statement from him—but no rough stuff."

Anger brought a flush to Oakie's face, and Dani thought he was going to give the smaller officer trouble—but when Catlow lifted his eyes and fixed them on Oakie, the big detective muttered, "Okay!" He grabbed his coat and left the office, slamming the door behind him.

"Cup of coffee?" Catlow asked, and when Dani nodded, he got up and poured two cups from the Mr. Coffee machine—one of the first models ever made, Dani guessed. The result was better than she expected, for the coffee was not too strong and was not laced with chicory. When she commented on this, Catlow grinned slightly. "Can't stand that stuff," he commented. Leaning back, he considered Dani for a moment, then asked, "What's your interest in the Louvier case, Miss Ross?"

Dani gave him a straightforward account of how she'd gotten involved with Eddie Prejean, leaving out nothing. She omitted only Tommy Cohoon's part in the investigation, and finally shrugged, saying, "It's getting pretty late, Lieutenant. If anyone's going to help Prejean, it'll have to be soon."

Catlow asked idly, "Nobody's paying you for this?"

"No. This is on my own."

"You do a lot of charity work?"

Dani felt uncomfortable under Catlow's careful eyes. "Well—I've never done anything like this before." When he said nothing, she added defensively, "I like the young man, Lieutenant. I felt that there was at least a possibility that he might be innocent."

"Never met a guilty man in the slammer," Catlow grunted. He sipped his coffee thoughtfully, then observed, "They all scream that they're innocent. Of if they were caught standing over the body with a smoking gun, they say the devil made them do it—or that they were temporarily insane—or that their mama didn't get them a bicycle." There seemed to be more fatigue than anger in Catlow, as though he'd given up any attempts to make sense out of the world.

"I know, Lieutenant," Dani nodded. "I run into it all the time. There's not much justice, is there?"

"Not a lot."

Dani hesitated, then smiled with a trace of embarrassment. She made an attractive picture to the policeman, who was accustomed to facing much cruder types in the chair across from his desk. He was a cynical man, having lost his innocence in Vietnam, and had not recovered much faith in his years with the department. He'd dealt with many PI's and had found most of them to be of average honesty and competence—but there was something about the young woman who faced him that he couldn't find a pigeonhole for. She didn't fit any of the categories he'd arranged in his mind, and he said, "I get the feeling you're not telling me everything. You in love with this Prejean guy?"

"Oh, no! I'd never met him before he sent for me." Dani hesitated, not sure if she should speak the truth, then decided that it would do no harm. "I suppose you'll think this is pretty wild, Lieutenant—" she lifted her clear gray-green eyes to meet his, then added, "I feel that God wants me to help Eddie Prejean."

Catlow's sleepy eyes opened wide, for he had expected anything but this. He'd had his moments with would-be messiahs, none of them pleasant. He sipped his coffee to gain time, then said, "Well, I guess Eddie's going to need help from God if he stays out of the chair." It was an observation made to create time for him to think, to consider the woman more carefully, and when she made no other remark, he said, "You really think God's told you to help Prejean?"

Dani wanted very much to make the policeman understand. She had always felt uncomfortable when someone said to her, "God told me to do this." Now she longed to make Catlow understand, but felt inadequate for the job. "I know how it sounds, Lieutenant," she said quietly, her hands folded in her lap. The sun from the window struck tiny reddish gleams from her hair, some of which turned gold as she moved her head.

"I never heard a voice," she murmured. "I've never heard anything from God that could be caught on a tape recorder. That's what makes this thing so hard to explain." She cocked her head to one side and smiled. "I don't suppose you're an Emily Dickinson fan? No? Well, she has this little poem that sort of sums it up:

> I never saw a moor,
> I never saw the sea,
> Yet know I what the heather is
> And what a wave must be.
>
> I never spoke with God,
> Or visited in Heaven—
> Yet certain am I of the spot
> As though a chart were given!

Catlow moved his head slightly, nodding in approval. "Now that's a good poem. Even an illiterate cop like me can understand it!"

Dani was encouraged by this. "It is fine, isn't it? I just think that we were made by God, and it would be strange if after making us, he didn't let himself be heard from at times."

Catlow said unexpectedly, "My old man was a Baptist preacher."

Surprised, Dani stared at him. "Really?"

"Yeah. Poor as a church mouse," Catlow nodded. He picked up a Bic pen, balancing it thoughtfully on the tip of his index finger, then said with a frown, "When I got to be big enough, I decided he was the world's biggest flop.

Always talking about God—how good he was. And here we ate white gravy and stale bread for weeks at a time! Made no sense to me, so I got out as soon as I was sixteen. Then the army, and I saw enough in Nam to kill off any ideas of God's mercy."

He tossed the pen down, rose in a sudden movement, and went to stand at the window, his back to her. When he spoke, there was a strange note in his voice, one that Dani couldn't quite identify. "Yeah, I had it all figured out. I'm a pretty smart fellow, Miss Ross. None of that God stuff for me. I wanted more than white gravy and stale bread."

Dani made no answer, for she'd learned long ago that it was impossible to argue a man into believing in God. The thing was not a matter of intellect, but of the spirit. Academic methods could build a bridge, but they could not change a person's heart.

Catlow swung around, his mouth twisted in an expression of sadness. "Yeah, I had it all figured out. But the thing was— I've never come up against a guy as good as my old man." He slumped down in his chair, took a swig of the black coffee, then looked at Dani with sadness clouding his eyes. "He wasn't smart, but he never broke his word in his life. He never had much, but he worked his tail off to do the best he could for us kids and Mom. And when he died, he went out smiling and praising God."

"He sounds like a fine man," Dani said quietly. "Like my own father."

Catlow moved restlessly, then said, "And he always said things like, 'The Lord wants us to move to Mississippi'—stuff like that. I never believed it for a minute—not then." He put the cup down, locked his thin fingers together, and stared at them, adding softly, "I've thought a lot about my old man lately. Maybe I'm the sucker, not him."

"We get a different view of things as we get older—some of us, anyway," Dani said sympathetically.

"Yeah, I guess so." Catlow tried to smile, then said, "So God's told you to help Prejean. What can I do?"

"Did you ever hear of anyone connected with the case named 'Skip' or 'Lila'?"

"No."

"Did the ruby ring Cory always wore ever turn up?"

Catlow's eyes narrowed in thought, then he shook his head. "Doesn't ring a bell."

Dani took the cigarette lighter out of her purse and handed it to Catlow. "Have you ever seen this before?"

Catlow took the lighter, examining it carefully. "No. I've never seen it. Pretty fancy lighter." He struck a light, studied the yellow flame, then clicked it shut. "I take it this has something to do with the murdered woman?"

"I—I can't be sure, Lieutenant," Dani said, "but could you find out if any of the police officers who were at the site where the victim was found had a lighter like this?"

Catlow frowned, two lines making vertical creases between his eyebrows. "Hard to escape the conclusion that this came from that area. But we scoured that ground with a fine-tooth comb. I went over a lot of it myself. How'd you come by it?"

"I can't say at this time," Dani answered. "It involves another person."

"We could call a thing like this withholding evidence."

"If we can find out that none of your people had such a thing," Dani said quickly, "there's a good chance it belonged to the murderer. And if necessary, my witness will step forward and testify."

Catlow studied Dani carefully for a long moment. The only sound in the room was the humming of the electric clock on a walnut shelf affixed to the wall. Dani knew that Catlow had the right to throw her out—or to give her problems about concealing evidence. She found herself breathing shallowly, and her lips felt dry.

"Okay, I'll ask around," Catlow said brusquely, then grinned as a look of relief washed across Dani's face. "Had you worried, didn't I?"

"Yes, you did. I know I'm on shaky ground, Lieutenant."

"Call me Riley," he nodded. He leaned back in his chair, his thin face thoughtful and relaxed. "I asked myself what my old man would have done, and it didn't take too long to figure that one out." He stared at the lighter, then said, "I doubt it belongs to any of our guys. You got any thoughts about tracing it?"

"It's a special job, maybe one of a kind," Dani answered. "It looks like it was made from a real shell."

Catlow nodded. "Yeah, it's a Winchester thirty aught six, 180 grain powder, probably. Big enough for a deer or even a bear, I guess."

"A woman gives a man a lighter made from a bullet used for hunting," Dani murmured. "Our man may be a hunter."

"You big-time PI's are pretty sharp," Catlow nodded with a grin. Then he sobered, adding, "Like hunting for a needle in a haystack if this thing isn't made by a regular manufacturer. I can find out about that with a few calls—but I'm pretty sure it's a one-time thing."

"I'll go to a few stores," Dani said. "Maybe some of them will be able to tell us something about the engraving, or maybe they'll know who does specialty work like this on lighters."

"Better bring it back and leave it here—or at least put it in a safe place."

Dani smiled and got to her feet. Putting out her hand she

said, "I'm very grateful for your father, Riley. He did me a big favor."

The policeman stared at her. "You think he might know about stuff like this?"

Dani felt the pressure of his hand and returned it. "We are not unseen, Riley. I feel that very strongly. And somehow I think you're going to do something with your life that's going to make your father shout with joy."

Catlow released her hand and stood there, an odd expression on his face. "I'd like that a lot," he murmured quietly. "I didn't give him much to shout about when he was around. Be good if I could make up for that a little bit."

Dani left the station, happier than she had been for several days. The way ahead was still rocky and dark, but it always started some little bells ringing when she saw someone start a pilgrimage toward God—and she felt certain that Riley Catlow was making those initial steps that would bring him to Christ.

She found a phone book, wrote down five addresses of jewelers, the ones with the biggest ads in the yellow pages who also were specialists in inscriptions, and went out to her car. It was two-thirty, and by the time she'd covered three of the stores, she was discouraged. The jewelers had all been polite, but she thought wryly, *Whoever saw an impolite jeweler.* And they had been no help at all.

She got lost finding the next shop, and was not encouraged to find that, despite the large ad, Blanchard's Jewelry Store was a small, rather dingy shop on Government Street. That particular street was in the twilight years of business—having some fine stores, but also having many empty buildings with *For Sale or Lease* signs posted on the windows. She almost passed it by, then decided it would take too long to go to the next address.

As she parked the Cougar, she spotted a group of young men grouped in front of a used furniture store next to Blanchard's. Carefully she locked the car, and, ignoring the whistles and raw invitations that came from the group, entered the store.

There were no other customers, and for one moment she thought there was no one at all in the store. Then a tall, thin man with only a rim of white hair around a rosy scalp stood up from behind a counter at the rear. He stared at her one-eyed, with a jeweler's eyepiece fixed to the other eye. Slowly he rose, and in so doing reminded Dani of one of the blue herons she saw at the beach or in the bayous. He had the same stoop-shoulders and thin neck, and when he moved, he even moved his head forward and back as they did. She expected him to remove the eyepiece, but he kept it in place, staring at her with one black eye.

"What can I do for you?" he asked, his voice as thin and reedy as his body.

Dani removed the lighter from her purse and handed it to him. "I'm trying to find out something about this," she said.

Mr. Blanchard—for Dani assumed he was the owner—took it with a hand that seemed filled with bony fingers. They matched the rest of him—the long legs and arms, the face, the neck—all were longer than seemed necessary. She watched while he examined the lighter. He finally looked up and asked, "You want to sell it?"

"Oh, no," she responded. "I need to find out who made it and who did the inscription."

The black eye fixed on her. There was something frightening about being stared at by one eye—especially since the eye was held wide open so that it seemed to be reflecting some sort of fear or terror in the owner.

Why doesn't he take that thing out of his eye? Dani thought nervously. But he made no move to do so. He seemed to be turned to stone, as he was not moving, and his eye didn't blink.

Finally he spoke. "You police?"

"I'm a private detective. Dani Ross from New Orleans." She dug her ID from her purse, and the staring eye fixed on it. "I can't tell you why I need to know something about the lighter," she said. "But it could help a man who's in a terrible predicament if I could find out who made this lighter."

Blanchard's head remained motionless, but his staring eye rotated until it focused on Dani's face. It stopped, remaining fixed, and a long silence followed. It ran on so long that Dani almost took the lighter and left the store. That eye was awful!

Then the old man slowly lifted his left hand and removed the eyepiece. The eye that came into view matched the other, for it was as wide and staring as was its fellow.

"I try to stay clear of police cases," he said. "I also try to avoid doctors and lawyers. No good ever came of any of them."

Dani was nonplused. "Well, that's one way to look at it, Mr. Blanchard," she said. "But some of us can't manage that." She had a thought and took a trial shot. "I don't suppose you could help in any case. I've been to several of the biggest stores in town. None of the jewelers could help a bit. I suppose it's too much to ask. Nobody could know obscure things like that."

The staring eyes grew even wider—which Dani would have said was impossible. "You are young, and therefore have a right to be wrong," he pronounced in a haughty tone. His nose was long and sharp, and when he elevated it in a gesture of disdain, it made quite a sight. "There are some—" he hesitated, then pronounced the word with obvious disgust, "—some *shopkeepers* in this city who call themselves professionals. I personally would not trust them to fix a pin on a cheap brooch, much less repair a watch or give an opinion on a fine stone."

A thread of hope ran through Dani. "Are you saying that you *can* tell me something about this lighter, Mr. Blanchard?"

The tall man looked down his nose at her, then swung around saying, "Follow me!"

Dani stepped behind the counter and followed as Blanchard led her down to where the room abruptly turned left. He flicked a switch, and a double rank of fluorescents threw their light over glass cases that ran around the wall. Blanchard waved his long fingers in a kingly gesture. "Look!" he said in his high-pitched voice.

Dani moved forward and saw that one case was filled with nothing but pocket watches—most of them, she knew, were old railroad watches, mostly Hamiltons and Elgins. "What a beautiful collection!" she breathed, and suddenly pointed at one of the watches. "My uncle had one exactly like that. He was an engineer on the Missouri Pacific."

"Then he had a fine watch," Blanchard nodded, his tone more agreeable. He was pleased with Dani's obvious appreciation of his collection and took time to point out several of his prize watches that had won international competitions.

Then he said, "I think you will find this collection even more interesting, Miss Ross."

Dani turned and walked to one case at least ten feet long, and looking inside, caught her breath. "Mr. Blanchard—!" she exclaimed, then could say no more, for the case was literally packed with cigarette lighters of all sorts.

"Well, Miss Ross," Blanchard chortled. "Perhaps now you think that there's at least *one* man in this city who knows a little something about cigarette lighters?"

"Mr. Blanchard—!" Dani turned to face the tall man, open

175

admiration showing on her face. "I apologize deeply! I was never more wrong in my life. Please forgive me!"

Dani's obvious admiration brought a smile to the long lips of the jeweler. He rationed it carefully—as though he were only permitted one each day—then waved his thin fingers. "I accept your apology. Now, let me tell you a little bit about lighters in general, and then we will see about this one of yours. . . ."

Thirty minutes later Mr. Blanchard had told Dani *much* more about lighters than she wanted to know! With relief, she heard him say, "Now, let's talk about this piece." He held up the lighter, stared at it, then said, "Not factory made. I know all the production models, and this one is not made in any factory."

"In this country, you mean?"

"I mean in the world." Dani ducked under his scornful glance, half expecting him to add, *"Or anywhere else, for that matter!"*

"This is an American shell," Blanchard continued, "so why would anyone take an American shell to Germany to have a lighter made from it?"

"Is it hard to make a lighter, Mr. Blanchard?"

"A cheap one, no. This one—very difficult." He held the lighter up, put his eyepiece in, and studied it. Once again he forgot to remove the eyepiece as he looked at her. "Let me show you how delicate it is. You've had it apart?"

"Oh, no!"

"Ah, then I will show you. Come with me."

For the next ten minutes Dani watched as the nimble fingers of the jeweler disassembled the lighter, showing her how the fuel cell had to be specially made, turned on a lathe to exact dimensions. Using a bright steel probe, he pushed the moving parts of the lighter back and forth, showing her how each piece had to be exactly dimensioned and made on a fine scale. And then it had to be gold-plated, which was difficult in itself.

Dani watched all this, then asked, "Are there many men who can make a lighter like this?"

"Oh, yes, there are many who *can*—" Blanchard nodded, but when he saw the disappointment on Dani's face, he hastened to add, "but only a few who do it on a regular basis. It is very tedious, and most workers simply recommend one of these."

"Can you give me their names, Mr. Blanchard?"

"Of course. I know them all. We meet at shows from time to time." He looked at her carefully, then removed the eyepiece. "This man you speak of—he's in serious trouble?"

"He's going to die if I can't help him," Dani said simply. "And right now, this lighter is the only piece of evidence I have."

"I see." Blanchard slowly rotated the lighter. Finally he said, "Come by tomorrow. I will call the men who might have done this."

"Oh, Mr. Blanchard!" Dani reached out, and the old man took her hand with a startled look in his wild eyes. "I can't ever thank you enough!"

The old man seemed disturbed at being thanked. He pulled his hand away in an embarrassed movement, saying, "What thanks? I make a few calls—no big thing."

"Yes, it is," Dani insisted gently. "May the Lord bless you!"

This statement seemed to disturb the old man even more than her handshake and her thanks.

"Now, don't drag God into this!" he cried, holding up a bony hand. "I don't believe in him!"

Dani shook her head. "Well, he believes in *you*, Mr. Blanchard!"

She left the shop, and when the young men accosted her with a new chorus of crude remarks, she laughed, and waved at them, calling out, "Jesus loves you!"

The group fell silent, and as Dani pulled out and drove away, one of them said, "Aw, what a waste! A good-looking chick like that, off on some kind of religious kick!"

13

Annie's Place

After trying to call home for the third time to tell her mother she'd be in late, Dani gave up. *Mom probably took Allison to a movie,* she thought. Retrieving the quarter, she tried her office, but it was five-thirty, and she got no answer. Fishing the quarter out again, she left the phone and got into her car.

She'd stopped at a gas station on Siegen Lane to fill up the tank and use the phone out front. Yellow dozers and backhoes were ripping up the broad street in large chunks, making so much noise that she probably couldn't have made herself heard over the phone. *Baton Rouge doesn't have a whole street in the entire system,* she thought with disgust. In crisscrossing the town she'd seen so many orange barrels marking out street construction that she'd muttered, "I'm going to get a bad case of orange jaundice out of this!"

Now as she drove away, headed for the tavern operated by Cory Louvier's mother, she had to thread her way through dozers, sawhorses with yellow lines, and orange barrels by the hundreds, it seemed. She'd mentioned the thing to the woman taking the money for gas, but the woman had merely shrugged wearily, saying, "I think they've got a crew out looking for streets to tear up. And they never finish one—just get it tore up then go tear up another one!"

Traffic was heavy over the Mississippi River bridge, and weariness pulled at her as she finally headed west on Interstate 10. She knew the country to the South, around New Iberia, with its canebrakes thick and green and bayous crowded with lily pads. It was a beautiful country, dotted with egrets nesting in the sand and herons breaking from their feeding places, gliding on gilded wings along the corridors of live oaks.

She'd fished those backwaters, and as she sped along past Grosse Tete and the exit to Butte La Rose she wished suddenly that she could do exactly that—drop the case and fish in the rich brown waters that lay to her left. Once used by Jean Lafitte's collection of brigands and slavers, the marshland was currently utilized by a modern group of pirates that made Lafitte's crew seem almost angelic by contrast. These "modern pirates" were smugglers of marijuana and heroin who thought nothing of wiping out whole families for the change in their pockets. They often hijacked boats to use in their drug runs, killing the owners and sinking the boats when they were no longer useful.

By the time Dani was a few miles out of Lafayette, dark was closing in. She pulled off at the Breaux Bridge exit and found Annie's Place with no difficulty, for it was located exactly where Riley Catlow had told her—almost in the shadow of a tall rice dryer, the tallest structure for miles.

Annie's Place was one of the thousands of small taverns that seemed to spring up like mushrooms in southern

Louisiana—every town having at least one, no matter how small the population. To call them "taverns" was to lend a dignity to them that they did not possess, "beer joints" being a more accurate description. Annie's Place was a small concrete building set well off the highway. As far as Dani could tell by the yellow lights that outlined the door and the sign over it, it was painted a leprous gray. Annie evidently was convinced that beauty of decor was unnecessary to entice customers, for the place lacked grace of any sort.

Pushing through the front door and stepping inside, Dani saw at once that Annie had not wasted money on expensive decorations inside either. A long bar ran along the side wall for the length of the building. It was held up by customers, most of them dressed in cowboy outfits—jeans, fancy shirts, and ostrich skin boots. The room was not entirely dark, but it was gloomy enough that Dani had to squint carefully as she made her way across the floor. Tables were scattered randomly over half the floor, and on the other half, couples were doing Cajun shuffles to the stereo. Dani could never quite understand the words of Cajun songs—perhaps because like country western "artists," Cajun entertainers all seemed to have nasal problems.

She bumped into a chair, and the occupant at once stood up and took her arm. "Hey now, Baby, how about it?"

"Later maybe." Dani managed to retrieve her arm from the man's grasp, and arrive safely at the bar.

A young woman with the long ringlet hairstyle and a peekaboo blouse came to stand in front of her. "What'll it be?" she asked in a lazy voice. There was a sensuous quality in the girl, who was no more than eighteen, Dani guessed. She was pretty, but hardness had already begun to creep into the planes of her face and had put a glint in her dark eyes.

"I'd like to talk to Annie Louvier," Dani said.

"She ain't here," the girl said. "Went into Lafayette."

"Are you expecting her back soon?"

"Yeah, she don't never stay gone long." The girl shrugged, then demanded, "You want some beer?"

The smell of hot food came to Dani, and she glanced over the girl's head to see a window, and beyond that, a man standing over a grill. "Could I get something to eat?"

"What'll you have?"

Dani saw no refinements such as a menu, and said, "If you have any shrimp or boudin, I'll have that—and a large Coke."

Without turning around, the girl yelled out, "Jake, shrimp and boudin!" Then she nodded carelessly toward three booths along the far wall. "You can wait over there. I'll bring your food when it's done."

"Thank you."

Dani made her way to the booths, found one that was empty, and for the next few minutes was occupied in declining offers from men to join her. It took some effort, for a simple "no" seemed to be too complicated for them to grasp. Finally she said, "I'm expecting a friend," and even this was not enough, for most of her would-be suitors went to great lengths to explain how she'd be missing a blessing if she didn't have a drink and a dance with them.

One of them, a tall, good-looking man in his mid-twenties, went right to the heart of the matter. He ambled over with a can of Miller's in his hand, stood over her, and asked, "You married, honey?"

"No."

A confident grin came to the man's lips. "Got a main squeeze?"

"Well—no, not really."

A smile came to the man's broad lips. He pushed his black Stetson back on his head, leaned forward, and whispered,

"Honey, this is yore lucky day! I'm Dax Fontenot—I'm the bouncer here."

He evidently expected Dani to be impressed with his position and was a hard man to convince that she had no interest in him. Dani energetically fended off his offers to show her a good time, and when the waitress came, she said, "Have to give you a rain check, I'm afraid."

The waitress laid a heaping plate of fried shrimp and boudin in front of Dani with a beer schooner filled with ice and Coke. "Be seven dollars," she announced.

Dani fished a ten out of her purse, and handed it over, saying, "Keep the change."

"Yeah, thanks." The waitress looked up, peered across the room, then said, "There's Annie—you want I should tell her you wanna see her?"

"If you would. My name's Dani Ross."

In the murky darkness, Dani didn't see the sudden interest that leapt into the girl's dark eyes. "I'll tell her," she said quickly. Leaving the table, she made her way across the floor, dodging hands expertly, and said to the woman who'd come to stand behind the bar, "Annie, woman to see you. Name's Dani Ross. Over there in the last booth."

"All right."

The girl watched as Annie moved to the booth, then picked up the phone and dialed a number. When she got an answer, she said, "Skip—this is Lila . . . Yeah, I miss you too . . . sure, I'll be ready. Hey, Skip, you asked me to be on the lookout for anybody who came around asking about Cory? Well, one just came in—at least I think so. It's the woman from Baton Rouge you tole me about—Dani Ross." She listened carefully, then said, "Yeah, Skip, Dax is here . . . what?" Her eyes widened, and she shook her head. "That's trouble, Skip!" The man's voice crackled, and the girl finally said, "I'll tell him—

but I'm out of it if it's trouble. And listen, bring that perfume you promised to get me from Maison Blanche—that Passion stuff." She hung up the phone, studied the pair in the booth, then a call for more beer caught her attention and she turned to the cooler.

"You want to see me?"

Dani nodded, saying, "If you have a few minutes—" She put her fork down, adding, "I hate to bother you at your place of business—"

"What is it you want?"

Annie Louvier, the mother of the murdered girl, was about fifty. She had very black hair with no sign of gray, and her eyes were black as well. She was attractive in a hard fashion, her trade having formed her. She gave Dani her full attention, her lips tight with suspicion.

"I know it sounds—well, trite," Dani said slowly. "But I'm sorry about your daughter."

"You didn't know Cory."

"No, but I always feel bad about things like that."

Annie's hard black eyes didn't mellow. "I done my crying, Miss Ross. Now, what are you doing in my place?"

"I'm a private—"

"I know who you are. That guy Savage, the one who got into trouble with the law, he works for you."

Dani blinked in surprise. *How did she know about that? It wasn't that big in the papers.* It alerted her, for if Annie Louvier was keeping score on such things, she might know something that would help.

Dani gambled then, for she knew that this woman could not be influenced by other methods. "I don't think it was Eddie Prejean who killed your daughter," she said. Carefully she watched for a reaction in the woman, but saw only a glint of suspicion growing in the dark eyes that were fixed on her.

"You got any proof of that?"

"Well, not really—"

"You go to the trial?"

"No, I didn't."

"Then what makes you think he didn't do it?"

"I talked with him, Mrs. Louvier." Dani felt the weakness of that statement, but had no other choice than to forge ahead. "I know convicted felons lie about their guilt. I've been lied to enough to have some sort of judgment about things like that. But after talking to Prejean, I think there's enough doubt that I hate to see him executed."

Annie Louvier studied the young woman carefully. "You have any kids?" she demanded suddenly.

"No, I'm not married."

Annie's lips twisted in a gesture hard to interpret. "I was a good mother when Cory was little. She never had a daddy, but I tried to make up for that. . . . "

Dani listened closely as the woman spoke of Cory's child-hood, and understood that no matter how hard the woman was now, Annie had had a real love for this, her only child. She spoke against the background of scraping fiddles and nasal voices, and the air was thick with the odor of beer and stale cigarette smoke.

"I loved her. But times was hard, and I couldn't make it no way—except this." Annie jerked her head around, indicating the darkened room. "She had to grow up in a joint—but I didn't have no other way to go—except something worse."

"I'm sure you did the best you could, Mrs. Louvier," Dani said quietly. "Life's been easy for me, but I can understand a little of what it must be like to have no help."

Dani's words seemed to break through the hardness of the

woman, and her lips grew softer. "She was such a pretty little thing, Cory was, and a sweeter child never drew breath!" A thought had its way with her, and she shook her head grimly, "If she'd been plain, it would have been better. Ain't no good for a woman in a place like this to be too good-looking!"

"I guess it's dangerous," Dani said. Then she asked cautiously, "Did you like Eddie Prejean? At first, I mean."

"Yeah, I did," Annie admitted. "He was different from most of the guys around here. Polite, you know? And educated. He was jealous, like all men, of course. They had some real fights when she went out with other men."

"But she liked Eddie, didn't she?"

"Oh, sure, she was crazy about him at first." Annie looked down at the table silently, then raised her head. "I talked her out of marrying him." Sadness washed across her face, and Dani read the grief. "I told her she could do better. That was when she was going with the governor."

"Annie—" Dani asked cautiously, "what does that mean—she was 'going with the governor'? He's a married man and a public figure."

"Layne Russell's a married man and a woman chaser," Annie snorted. "Always has been and always will be! Soon as I saw that big ruby ring he gave her, I knew what was up!"

"Did you think he'd divorce his wife and marry Cory?"

Annie shook her head. "I don't know, Miss Ross. I guess not. I thought she could handle him. And I still say she'd have done it," she said defiantly. "Cory never give herself away, I know that much! She was driving Russell crazy—which no woman ever done before!"

Dani felt that she was close to something, but knew that she must be very cautious. "Annie, before all this happened, would you have said that Eddie was a man who would commit murder?"

Annie shook her head at once. "No, I wouldn't. He fooled me bad. But you never know what a guy will do when he gets jealous. And they proved he done it—killed my little girl!" Anger swept over the woman, and she said, "I should have let Dax have him!"

"Dax—the man over there?" Dani stared at the bouncer who was standing behind the bar listening to the dark-haired waitress. A scowl was on his handsome face, and he looked across the room at her—or so Dani thought. His face seemed to be flushed, and he glared at her with such anger, she thought he was still mad that she'd turned him down.

"Yes, he was crazy about Cory—always was. He's my nephew, my sister Rae's boy."

"Did Cory have feelings for him?"

"No, not a bit. Oh, she liked him; they were close as peas in a pod when they were young. But when they grew up and Dax wanted to go with her, she just laughed at him. Said she'd never marry a cousin."

Dani stared at the man's broad shoulders. "He wanted to fight Eddie?"

"Wanted to *kill* him, honey!" Annie shook her head sadly. "Dax is good-looking and all—but he's not bright. Never got beyond the third grade. If I didn't keep him up, he'd be in jail or dead in a month. Got a strong back, but no mind at all. I caught him with a gun, and made him tell me what he was going to do with it—which was to shoot Eddie Prejean."

"That's very sad, Annie."

"Yeah, it is. Most things are." Annie Louvier leaned back against the scarred wood of the booth and closed her eyes. The jarring cacophony of the music beat against Dani's ears.

I could have been like this woman, she thought suddenly. *If I'd been born into her world, with no loving parents, no security—I could be in a beer joint waiting for the next cheap thrill with some man.*

The thought sobered her, and it saddened her as well. A great pity for Annie Louvier came to her, and she sat there longing to express the love that was in her, but she could find no way to put it into words.

"You really think Eddie didn't do it?"

Dani was startled by Annie's question but had her answer ready. "I'm not completely certain, Annie, but I've got a feeling that he's gotten himself caught in this thing because of some things he's doing that people high up don't like."

Annie opened her eyes instantly. "Like maybe Layne Russell?"

"Well—I think he's involved in it somehow."

"He's got it in him. He came from this part of the state. My daddy knew him. Worked for him some. He always said that there wasn't nothing too rotten for Layne Russell to pull."

"I have no proof," Dani said quickly. "And there isn't much time."

Annie sat wrapped in silence, the failures of a lifetime marked on her face. She looked across the table at Dani, then said, "I never said this to anybody—but I've never been sure Eddie killed my girl. He had a hot temper, but he's not a killer. And if he goes to the chair, that means the real killer will be somewhere laughing at how he got by with it." Taking a deep breath, she held it, then expelled it. She took a Virginia Slim from a pack in her pocket, lit it with a kitchen match, and let the smoke curl around her face. "What do you want to know?" she asked dully.

"I don't know, Annie," Dani admitted. "Somewhere in all this, there's a key. It might be in something Cory said to you that she never said to anyone else. Would it hurt too much to go over the last day or so of her life? To tell me what you two talked about?"

"No," Annie said slowly. "I don't mind doing that. I've been thinking about it a lot. Maybe it'll help to say it out loud."

Dani drank her Coke as Annie Louvier went over the last days of her daughter's life. She wished that she had a tape recorder, but it was too late for that. She strained to hear, not wanting to miss a word, and hoped that a word from the grave might fall, some word that would turn the key on Angola Prison and set Eddie Prejean free.

Finally, Annie crushed out her cigarette with a final gesture. "That's all, I guess." She got to her feet, saying, "I got to go to work." But she gave Dani a strange look and asked, "Any of this help you?"

"I'll have to go someplace where it's quiet and think about it, Annie. But it was good of you to tell me."

"If it helps Eddie, I wish you'd come and tell me about it." Her features softened, and she added, "I wish Cory had married him. Maybe things would have worked out."

And then she turned and left, crossing the crowded floor and disappearing through a narrow door to the right of the bar.

Dani had eaten none of the food, and discovered that the shrimp and boudin were cold, covered with a film of grease. She got up, aware of how tired she was and dreading the drive back to New Orleans. As she made her way to the door and several of the men made her a final offer, she was aware that the waitress was watching her.

Stepping outside into the cold March air was like entering an alien world. The sounds of the rasping fiddles and nasal singing were instantly muted as she closed the door. She savored the relative silence as she walked across the uneven concrete toward her car, wondering how anyone could stand having their ears assaulted by such a din for eight hours.

There was no moon, and the dim yellow lights over the

sign did nothing to illuminate the murky darkness of the outer edge of the parking lot. There was almost no traffic on the highway, though she heard the sound of the heavy tires of eighteen-wheelers humming dully in the distance.

She'd parked on the outer edge and saw the shadow of her Cougar only as a vague outline past two pickup trucks. She fumbled in her purse for the keys and was so preoccupied that she had no warning as a shadow came from between the pickups.

When a pair of strong hands closed around her, Dani knew she had made a bad mistake. Opening her mouth to scream, she managed only a brief cry before one hard hand clamped over her mouth.

"Keep your mouth shut and you won't get hurt!"

Dani began to kick backward, landing one blow on her attacker's shin. He grunted, then without warning, released his grip with one hand. Dani opened her mouth to scream, but she uttered only an abrupt grunt. A hard fist struck her in the temple, and she knew only a blinding pain—and then she slipped away, feeling her knees collapsing before she lost all sense of reality.

Later, she began to wake, struggling to come out of the blackness that wrapped her like a shroud. Her head was splitting with the worst headache she'd ever known, and a sudden jerking motion sent a blinding pain streaking through her head. The pain was so intense, she thought she'd throw up—and then she realized that her mouth was bound tight with some sort of cloth.

She lay there for a moment, fighting off the nausea, and the pieces began coming together. Her hands were tied behind her back, and she was lying across a circular form that she realized at once was the tunnel of a car. The bumping of the car struck her blow after blow, so she knew that she was being taken down a rough, unpaved road.

Desperately she tried to move and succeeded in rolling over until she was on her side, but that was no better, for the tunnel beat her side so brutally that she was forced again to lie on her stomach. Opening her eyes, she twisted her head and saw only a faint glow from the instrument panel. She was in the back of the car being taken someplace.

The cords cut into her wrists, and her hands had lost all feeling. Once before in her life she had been totally filled with mindless terror—when she had been confined in a silo by a madman. The memory of that fear had crawled over her mind like an alien beast and now flooded her once again.

The car rocked and the springs groaned as the vehicle bounced over the rough terrain. How long she lay there fighting against the waves of terror that threatened to engulf her, Dani never knew. It could have been hours, counting the time she was unconscious. She longed for the trip to be over, yet the thought of what might happen at the end of her journey was a specter that loomed darkly.

Finally she felt the engine slow down, and the bumping against her stomach lessened. Then the car stopped altogether. She heard the door open, then slam. The door by her head opened, and she felt herself hauled out of the car by rough hands.

"Come on, now—don't play possum on me!"

Dani recognized the voice, for she had heard it only a short time before.

Dax Fontenot!

She had no time to think, except to remember the look of anger he'd given her at Annie's Place. He released his hold, and she almost fell to the ground. Her ankles were tied, she discovered, and her feet had no more sensation than her hands.

"You won't run away, will you?" Fontenot jibed. A light went on, and the strong beam of a flashlight caught Dani in the eyes, blinding her. A push sent her to the ground, and Fontenot turned and walked away. Dani blinked in the darkness, finally able to see that he was doing something a few feet away. She heard the sound of his feet on wood, then the light disappeared. The smell of a bayou was strong in her nostrils, and she could see the faint reflection of stars on water.

The silence was broken by the rattle of an outboard being turned over by a rope. Twice it came, and on the third pull, the engine roared into life, breaking the stillness of the night.

Dani lay there, and without warning found herself picked up and thrown over the broad shoulders of her captor. She bounced along, and then was deposited in the bottom of a boat. Several inches of stale water smelling of dead fish soaked into her back, and she struggled to sit upright.

Fontenot ignored her, and when he'd backed the boat out into the water and wheeled it around, he sent it shooting ahead with such force that Dani fell over backward. Fontenot laughed, calling out over the roar of the engine, "Make yourself comfortable, baby. We'll have us a little romantic boat ride."

Dani struggled to a sitting position, and tried to make some sort of order out of the journey—but it was impossible. She was being taken into the depths of a bayou, and each tree that loomed overhead looked like every other tree. As for direction, that was impossible to tell as well, for Fontenot sent the flat-bottomed boat around groves of huge cypress trees, cutting back and forth so rapidly that Dani gave up.

The engine roared steadily, and for at least thirty minutes, Fontenot steered the small craft deeper into the swamp.

Finally, the roar of the engine lessened, and then shut off. The boat glided silently along, and by the dim light of the stars, Dani was able to see a slight bit of ground swelling out of the black water. She made out an indistinct shape on it, and as the boat ground to a stop, she saw that it was a very small cabin.

Fontenot leapt out, pulled the bow of the boat up onto the land, and then came and jerked Dani to her feet. "Come on, baby, I'll show you around your new home."

Once again he stooped, picked her up, and laid her over his shoulder. Dani knew that struggle was useless, so she lay still as he unlatched the door and stepped inside. He slung her at once to her feet, and she tottered briefly, then fell backward. The back of her head hit the wooden floor, sending fresh waves of pain through her skull. She lay still until most of the pain receded, her eyes shut tight.

A light came on, and she opened her eyes to see Fontenot moving around with the flashlight. He rummaged through a rough sort of cabinet until he seemed to find what he wanted. Dani heard the sound of metal on wood, and then after a moment, a match made a blue spurt in the darkness. She watched as the wick of a kerosene lamp suddenly glowed, breaking up the darkness.

Fontenot snapped off the flashlight and came to stand over her. The lamp made an amber glow on his face. Stooping down, he pulled the gag from Dani's mouth, saying, "Now, yell all you want to. Nobody to hear you but gators."

Dani's mouth was dry, and she gasped, "Why are you— doing this to me?"

Fontenot leaned over and caught her face with one hand. Pushing his face close to hers, he grated, "You ain't gonna stop Eddie Prejean from fryin' in the chair!"

He shoved her face back angrily, and started for the door.

"You can't leave me here!"

Fontenot turned, his handsome face smiling viciously. "You're a detective. Figure out how to get yourself out of this mess. Smart lady like you should be able to get loose pretty soon. But don't try wadin' through this bayou. It's stiff with big gators."

"Please—don't leave me—!"

"You ain't gonna' die," he said with finality. "There's food and firewood. Boil the water before you drink it. Soon as Prejean's dead meat, I'll come back and turn you loose."

And then he was gone.

Dani lay there as the engine roared into life, listening as it began to pull the boat away.

Finally it faded into nothingness.

She was alone now, as she had never been alone in her life.

14
No Exit

I've got to get out of here—!

As the sound of the outboard died away, fading into silence, Dani's mind fluttered like a bird in a sealed box. Coherence of thought gave way to a series of flashing impressions, and she kicked against the floor in an effort to roll over.

He may never come back—he may leave me here to die!

She succeeded in rolling over on her side, then tried to get to her feet. By doubling her legs she was able to get as far as putting her weight on her knees, but only by pressing her head against the rough planks that made up the floor could she maintain that precarious balance—and the pressure on her head brought the blinding streaks of pain to her temples.

With a short cry, she fell, rolling over on her back, her eyes closed against the pounding that seemed to drive the bones of her skull into her brain. The agony came like waves, beating against her like a hammer, then easing off, only to come again.

Lie still, don't try to move.

She had no choice but to rest the back of her head against the rough flooring, but the discomfort of that was nothing compared to the pain of the headache brought on by Dax Fontenot's blow.

Disciplining herself, she lay quietly, waiting for the pain to subside. When it faded into a dull throbbing, she opened her eyes and looked around the room carefully without moving her head suddenly. The room was small, no more than ten feet square. Along one wall was a pair of bunk beds with faded, flat mattresses. Across from the bunks, cabinets were nailed to the wall; Dani noticed some jars and boxes in the upper cabinet, and pots and pans in the lower section. At the far end of the room, just under a window covered with a wooden guard, two unmatched wooden chairs sat at either end of a small kitchen table. On the wall, various gear, mostly fishing rods and nets, hung from nails.

Dani became aware that she had a raging thirst. Her lips were cracked and dry, and her tongue was swollen.

Got to get a drink—! But how?

Dani ignored the thirst and lay quietly. She thought of the days she'd spent buried alive in the silo, along with Ben and Karl and the others. There had been times when she'd longed to run to the cement walls and beat her fists against them, to scream with frustration—but she never had.

But there had been light and others to share the prison with her. People to talk to, things to do.

She understood as she lay there that this was different. There was nobody—and there would be nobody.

But maybe somebody will come—Ben or Luke!

And even as the thought rose in her mind, a mocking reply seemed to rise from somewhere deep inside: *They don't even know you're a prisoner. Why would they even look for you?*

Dani closed her eyes and tried to reason out some hope. *When I don't come home, Mom will get worried. And the first thing she'll do is call Ben.*

But the question rose instantly, *Even if he knew you were missing, how would he find this place?*

It was a question that Dani didn't want to entertain—and yet it could not be ignored.

He'll go to the police, she thought slowly. *He knows I'd go there.*

And what will Catlow tell him? That you went to jewelry stores, right? And how long will it take Ben to find Blanchard's store? And if he does, what can Blanchard tell him that would help him find this place?

The logic that was part of Dani's mind and character became her enemy. The longer she tried to think of how someone could find her, the less likely it seemed.

Finally, she began to panic and only caught herself by saying aloud, "Look, Ross—you've got to stop crying like a big baby! First, get yourself out of these ropes!" There was a tough streak in Dani Ross, one that surfaced whenever she was faced with a difficulty. "Stop thinking about what *won't* work," she admonished herself sternly, "and think about what you *can* do!"

Don't try to stand on your broken head, dummy!

"Good idea," she muttered through dry lips. "Must be an easier way to stand up—"

Her feet were numb from the tight cord, but her legs worked fine. A thought came to her, and she said aloud, "You've got no arms, but you've got two good legs—so use them!"

Doubling up her legs, she shoved herself across the floor until she came to the wall with the bunk bed. Carefully she scooted along until her head touched the planks that made up the wall. Then, using her feet, she kicked at the floor until she was lying beside it. Taking a deep breath, she sat up, tightening her stomach muscles so that she rose slowly to a sitting position.

"See how easy? Now—for the hard part—"

She twisted around until her back was against the wall, then lifted her legs and gathered them up, so that her heels just touched her buttocks.

"Okay, thighs—" she whispered. "Do your stuff!"

Slowly she began to exert pressure, and by twisting her torso from side to side, discovered that she was moving upward. With a gasp, she made one final effort and came upright. Her head swam with the pain from the effort, so she stood there with her eyes closed, waiting until the dizziness passed.

Opening her eyes, she smiled—and was proud of herself. "Wonder Woman's got nothing on you, Ross! All you need is a costume, and you'd make America safe again!"

Then she took a deep breath, and looked around the room. The thought came to her that if Fontenot had left her in the dark, nothing would have been possible. She paused, then said quietly, "Lord, you've said to give thanks in everything. So thank you for life—that he didn't kill me out of hand. Thanks for the light, so I can see how to get loose. And thanks for the help you're going to give me to get that job done!"

She looked down at her feet, measuring the cord that bit into her ankles, then swept the room with a quick glance.

There's got to be a knife here somewhere!

The cabinet seemed to be a likely place, but it was ten feet away. Only two ways to get there, either hop across the room or wiggle around it, bracing herself against the walls and the furniture.

Better not do too much hopping—too hard to get up if I fall.

Carefully she began inching her way around, avoiding the

bunk beds by heading back toward the front door. It was a painful, laborious task, and by the time she'd gotten to the front door, her legs were trembling.

"Come on, come on, you can do better than that!"

She could see some tableware on top of the cabinet, and forced herself to complete the journey. But when she saw only two spoons, a bent fork, and a blunt table knife, she wanted to cry. Closing her eyes, she leaned back against the wall, then suddenly looked at the front of a cabinet, which had a small drawer.

"Got to have a paring knife or a butcher knife somewhere!" She moved to the front of the cabinet, stooped down, and groped for the handle. When she finally grasped it with numb fingers, it refused to budge.

"Come *on!*" she cried angrily, giving a forward jerk that finally freed the cabinet—but which also threw her off balance so that she fell face forward. She managed to twist her body so that she fell heavily on her side, but the fall jarred her head, bringing the pain back again.

She lay there, fighting off the nausea that came with the pain. The thought of going through the business of struggling to her feet as she had before was almost more than she could bear. For some time she lay there, her mind a blank. The room was cold, and her thirst grew worse.

"Lord, help me get loose!" she pleaded. "I can't do it—but nothing is too difficult for you!"

A little tune began chiming inside her head, and she began to sing a chorus she'd always loved, a simple little song that she'd always believed but had never needed so much as right now in this deserted bayou.

"Nothing is too difficult for thee," she sang over several times through parched lips. "Nothing, nothing—absolutely *nothing*! Nothing is too difficult for thee!"

Her voice sounded tinny and small in the stillness of the cabin. There was no organ, no piano, no choir with trained voices. But as she sang it over and over, somehow Dani began to experience something very unusual. The pain still beat against her head, her wrists and ankles were still tormented by the tight cords, and the thirst was not slaked—yet, despite all this, she began to feel an absolute certainty that all would be well! It was not that she psyched herself up, or tried to force herself to feel something. No, she was too far gone for that!

It was as if she were suddenly surrounded by some sort of bubble, a clear bubble of crystal. She was inside, but somehow all her pain and fear and confusion were *outside*!

With her mind she knew that nothing had changed. She was still tied hand and foot. No one was likely to come to her rescue. She was growing weaker each moment. And there was nothing to encourage her.

Yet somehow she felt—*protected.*

That was the essence of what she experienced as she lay helpless on the cold floor of the cabin.

I'm going to be all right! she thought as the sense of being protected continued to wash over her. *God is able—and he's promised never to leave me. I can't deal with the circumstances, but I can trust him to do whatever it takes to get me out of this!*

She lay there, and the fear and confusion and doubt faded.

And as she lay there, her eyes fell on the lamp.

The flare of the burning wick was reflected in her eyes—and she suddenly knew what to do.

Rolling and twisting until she was back against the wall, she struggled until once again she was upright. Then she moved along the wall until she stood beside the table that bore the lamp.

It was an ordinary lamp with a thick glass base and a chimney made of thin glass. It was resting almost on the edge of the table—exactly where Dani wanted it.

Carefully she began moving around the table until she was standing right in front of the lamp. She studied it carefully, knowing that if this failed she would be helpless. She could even die of dehydration before Fontenot returned.

The chimney sat on top of the reservoir. It was not fastened but was held by three bent metal wires that curved over a lip on the base of the chimney. Dani knew that it was a simple enough matter to remove the chimney—but only if one had hands—and that it was very hot to the touch.

How can I get the chimney off with my back to it and with my hands tied?

"That is the question," Dani whispered. Then she said, "Lord, help me—"

She leaned over and peered at the reservoir, noting that it was almost full. That was good—for it made the base heavier and less likely to tip over.

For a moment, she toyed with the idea of trying to knock the chimney off with her forehead—but discarded that notion. There was too much of a chance of knocking the base over, and the thought of being trapped alive in a burning building sent a chill through her.

She resolutely hopped around until her back was to the lamp. Carefully she reached back, touching the chimney. It was so hot that she withdrew her fingertips at once.

I'll have to do it in one smooth movement—spread my hands, close on the chimney, pull it up, then swing around and drop it.

She waited until she was breathing evenly—and then did it!

Her outstretched hands touched the sides of the chimney, and she closed them at once. The pain ran along her palms, but she lifted up, swung to one side, and released the chimney.

The sound of the thin glass shattering on the floor was a beautiful sound to Dani!

"Thank you, Lord!" she cried out, ignoring the pain of her scorched palms.

Once again she turned around and considered the lamp. The wick was burning in a yellow circle of fire, not more than half an inch high. The cord on her hands, she assumed, was the same as that on her feet—thick cotton cord which would burn easily. She was suddenly very glad that Fontenot had not used tough nylon rope!

"Going to hurt a little bit, Ross," she said. "But think about how good it'll feel to have these things off!"

She twisted around with her back to the flame, then reached out carefully to locate the exact position of the reservoir. It was about eight inches from the edge, and moving awkwardly, she pulled it forward until she felt the heat of it on the small of her back.

For one moment she hesitated, then she leaned forward, lifted her arms high, and moved backward. She lowered her hands and discovered that she could feel the heat of the flame well enough to adjust the position of her wrists.

When she felt the heat on her wrist at what seemed like the spot where the cords were tied, she lowered her hands—and at once uttered a small cry, for she had misjudged so that the flame touched the heel of her right hand.

Gritting her teeth, she moved her hands farther back, and this time, she felt the glow of the flame on her wrists.

She was very close, she knew, but there was no way to burn the cords without getting singed. Slowly she lowered her hands even more, and the flame seemed to bite into her wrists. Closing her eyes, she strained outward, putting all the pressure she could on the cords.

The pain grew worse, but she suddenly smelled something—and knew that it was smoke!

With a desperate wrench at her wrists, she moved her hands closer to the flame—and then she almost fainted, so terrible was the pain!

"Oh, God—!" she cried. And at that moment, the cords gave way!

Dani staggered and almost fell, as her arms suddenly swung forward. But she caught herself, and the pain of her singed wrists and hands seemed nothing to the relief of having the use of her arms! She stood there, swinging them back and forth, moving her shoulders as the muscles relaxed.

She was filled with an exaltation that had come to her only on rare occasions and expressed it by singing again, "*Nothing* is too difficult for thee—" as strongly as she could.

She sat down and untied the cord from her feet, then rose at once and looked for something to drink. She found two cans of Dr. Pepper, ripped the tab off one, and let the liquid trickle down her throat.

Nothing had ever tasted so good—and she knew that as long as she lived, Dr. Pepper would be her favorite soft drink!

She stood there, nursing the drink for quite some time. She finally went to the door and opened it. When she stepped outside, dawn was breaking over the bayou. The sun was a crimson arc peeping over the rim of the world, and its rays transmuted the waters of the bayou from black and brown to orange and gold.

Dani stared out at the huge trees standing as sentinels over the mysterious waters, and had no idea where she was. She had no boat and would not have known which direction to take if she had. She was all alone in the midst of danger with nothing to give her any hope.

Yet she *had* hope. As she looked out at the white egrets that dotted the burning water, she knew that she was *not* alone.

"Oh, Lord God, thank you for setting me free. Now I ask you to deliver me from this prison. You came to set the prisoners free, so your Word declares. Now—set this prisoner free!"

A bull gator grunted harshly somewhere to her left, but Dani only laughed. "Grunt all you please, but I know the One who made you, gator! And he's not going to let you have me!"

The echoes of her voice disturbed a solemn blue heron that had come to rest on a cypress knee beside the cabin. He spread his wings and oared himself away with a disdainful look on his long face—like a merchant prince who had come to a land looking for riches and had found nothing!

15

Savage Hits a Blank Wall

What do you mean, she's *missing?*"

Savage never spoke harshly to Ellen Ross—never! But she had caught him off guard, speaking in a voice that had a slight tremor in it he caught even over the phone. He was never at his best over the phone, and he had spent a hard day with Sunny, watching as she interviewed nerd-type bureaucrats in little cubbyholes called offices. He had deposited her in her apartment, driven home, and gone straight to bed—but sleep had refused to come until the early hours of the morning.

When his phone had rung, it had jerked at his nerves so badly that he was clawing under his pillow for his gun before he realized the source of the noise. He had groped in the darkness for the phone, knocked it off the nightstand, and when he had fished it off the floor, he placed it to his lips and growled, "What is it?"

"Dani's missing, Ben!"

The sound of the fear in her voice made him respond harshly, "What do you mean, she's *missing?*"

"She was supposed to be in last night," Ellen said, speaking jerkily. "But she never came home."

"Maybe she decided to stay over in Baton Rouge."

"She knows I worry, Ben. She'd have called if she was going to do that."

Savage's mind raced, but all he could come up with was, "Look, Ellen, maybe she had car trouble or something."

"Ben, you know Dani better than that! She's always good about letting people know when she can't make it to an appointment." Ellen Ross was not a nervous woman, but Savage sensed that she was on the verge of giving way to her fears. She paused, as if to get better control of herself, then asked, "What can we do, Ben?"

"Call Luke," Ben said instantly. "I'll be in Baton Rouge in an hour. Did she say where she was going—anything about her plans?"

"She said she was going by Angola to see Eddie Prejean," Ellen answered. "Then she said she was going to talk to the detective who was on the case. I don't think she mentioned his name."

"Anything else?"

"She—told me not to worry, that she might be late. But, Ben, Allison and I went to a movie last night. We were gone from seven until after ten."

"No message on the answering machine?"

"It quit working about a week ago."

"She probably left a message that didn't get on there,

Ellen," Ben said. "Did you call the office to see if she'd left any word with Angie?"

"It's too early. Angie doesn't get in until eight-thirty."

"Look, I'll go by the office first and check. I'll call you if she left word there."

"Call me anyway, Ben!"

"Yeah, sure." He tried to think of some way to make her feel better, but said only, "I hate people who say, 'Don't worry.' But it's probably okay. Call in thirty minutes."

He hung up the phone, threw his clothes on, and left without shaving. When he got to the office, he checked the answering machine, then dialed Ellen's number. "Nothing on this machine, Ellen. Call Luke and fill him in. Tell him I'll be talking to the officers at the Baton Rouge Police Department, but have him put an APB out on Dani's car. He'll know what to do."

"All right." She hesitated, then said, "Call me!"

"Sure. We'll find her, Ellen."

"I'm—glad you're here, Ben!"

Savage left the office, got into the Hawk, and left New Orleans at once, waiting until he got out of the city limits to break the speed laws. No creature on earth is more unreasonable or has a more erratic temperament than the traffic officers of the New Orleans Police Department. At times they jerk a hapless driver to the station for nothing more offensive than getting one wheel in the next lane of traffic, but at other times they ignore a clown who drives down the middle of the street at high noon.

He kept the needle of the speedometer hovering around eighty as the Hawk hurdled past the exits that led to the small towns lying off the ribbon of highway, and by the time he passed the sign proclaiming the city limits of Baton Rouge, a thin ray of sunlight illuminated the sky.

The parking lot behind the police station looked desolate

as he parked the car. *Too early for anyone to be on duty*, he thought, but he ran across the cement and into the building anyway. A heavyset sergeant looked up as he came in, his face phlegmatic as he droned, "Yes, sir?"

"I need to talk to one of the officers who handled the Louvier case."

The sergeant stared at him. "Hey, you're Savage, aren't you?"

"Yes."

Displeasure drew the lips of the officer down instantly—and then a thought came to him that he seemed to enjoy. "Why, sure, Mr. Savage. You want to talk to Detective Oakie. I think you two have met?"

Savage shook his head. "I'd rather talk to one of the other officers."

A deep laugh shook the belly of the sergeant. "I'll just *bet* you would! Okay, how about Lieutenant Catlow?"

Savage showed no trace of the disappointment that came to him. "Catlow will be fine," he said steadily. "Is he here?"

"No, he ain't. You'll have to wait until ten o'clock."

"Look, Sergeant, I know I'm not a very popular guy around here—but this isn't for me. A young lady is missing, and the lieutenant may be able to help." When the policeman hesitated, Savage added, "It might be crucial. I wish you'd let the lieutenant make up his mind if he'll talk to me."

"Well—I'll give him a call."

Savage stood in front of the desk, longing to break into action, but knew that he had to be patient. Inside, a fear that had been birthed when Ellen had first called was growing. He'd felt uneasy about the case from the beginning. Someone had killed Cory Louvier, and if it had not been Eddie Prejean, then that someone was still wandering around free. And if anyone got too close to him, he had nothing to lose by killing again.

"He says he'll be here. You wanna wait in his office?"

"Thanks, Sergeant."

Savage left the front desk, making his way to the office according to the sergeant's directions. Ignoring the chairs, he went to the window and stared out at the uninspiring view. He was still there thirty minutes later when the door opened and Catlow walked in, irritation in his gray eyes.

"Sorry to be a pest, Catlow," Savage said quickly. "But my boss didn't come home last night."

Catlow stopped abruptly, his brow knotting. "You checked around?"

Savage shrugged. "That's what I'm doing here—" He ran through the circumstances, stressing that Dani was punctilious about letting her people know where she was. He ended by saying, " . . . so she didn't call in to the office, which is odd— and she didn't call her mother, which she just *wouldn't* do."

"Got the stuff on her car?"

"Luke Sixkiller is handling that. She came to see you yesterday?"

Catlow nodded slowly. "Yeah. She was here."

"She say anything about where she was going?"

Catlow thought rapidly, then asked, "You know about the lighter?" When Savage gave his head a negative shake, Catlow gave him a quick summary of what he and Dani had talked about. When he was through, he stroked his chin slowly. "I think someone found that lighter at the scene of the crime, and she was shielding him. The way I got it, we missed it, and somebody else found it. And it wasn't one of us who lost it, either. I've checked everybody who was there, including the lab boys." He shook his head slowly, "I'm wondering now if she ran into whoever owned that lighter. I hope not."

"She left here to trace it? Where would she go?"

"She mentioned going to some jewelry stores."

"I better start running them down."

Catlow nodded at a phone. "Use Oakie's phone. I'll use mine. There's a thousand jewelry stores in this burg."

Savage's eyes narrowed. "Well—thanks."

"You don't know about this, do you?" Catlow said, noting the doubt on Savage's face. "Well, I sort of took to your boss, and—" He hesitated, then looked directly at the other man. "And the rest of it, Savage, is that this case has never felt right to me."

"You don't like Prejean for it?"

"The evidence said he did it—but I got a little built-in warning system. You been a cop, so you must know how it is," he shrugged. "It goes off sometimes when I least expect it. All the time I was working on the case, I kept looking around for something that said he didn't do it." He stared out the window for a moment, then turned his face back to Savage. "It's going off like crazy right now. Let's find out where she went with that lighter."

Most of the stores were not open, but Catlow left demanding messages on the answering systems. The few they did get were negative, but they kept at it doggedly. Lou Oakie walked through the door at 8:30, halting abruptly at the sight of Savage using his phone and making notes on his notepad. He glared angrily at Savage and turned to Catlow saying, "What's going on here?"

"Miss Ross is missing, Lou. Find a phone and start checking the hospitals."

"Oh." Oakie hesitated, then left the room. He came back in fifteen minutes to report, "Not in any of them." He fidgeted restlessly, then asked in a subdued voice, "Anything else I can do, Riley?"

"You might call the people who do engraving—fancy stuff in gold. She said something about looking into that."

Oakie left the room at once, and two minutes later Catlow stopped dialing a number when he heard Savage exclaim, "She was there!" Savage nodded at Catlow, then said, "I'll be right over, Mr. Blanchard." He hung up the phone, his eyes bright and excited. "She was there, Catlow. I'm going to talk to him."

"Okay. Call me if you get anything."

"Yeah, I'll do that." Savage hesitated, then nodded and said warmly, "I appreciate it."

"Well, you're a pest, Savage, but your boss has class."

"Whatever!"

Savage got directions to Blanchard's store, and fifteen minutes later he pulled up, parking the Hawk in a spot marked *Handicapped.* There were no customers, and the tall man who came to meet him said, "You're Savage? I'm Blanchard." He didn't offer his hand but demanded, "What's this all about? The young woman?"

"Yes. She didn't come home, Mr. Blanchard. I'm afraid something's happened to her. What time did she come here?"

Blanchard mentioned the time, then at Savage's request, related the details of Dani's visit. He spoke slowly and was meticulous in the way he went over his conversation with Dani. Finally he said, " . . . and so I told her I'd see if I could find out who made the lighter."

Savage stared at Blanchard's long face and asked without much hope, "Have any luck?"

"Young man, there is no such thing as *luck*." Blanchard's long thin lips curled upward in an expression of disdain. "If a man does what he can do, he will succeed. If he doesn't, he will fail." Then he nodded and a light of pride came into his eyes. "The answer is—no, I didn't have 'luck.' But through hard work and intelligence, I did find out who made the lighter."

Savage blinked, and then he shook his head with admiration. "I'll have to remember that, Mr. Blanchard. Who made the lighter?"

"Simon Westenthall—a very fine craftsman," Blanchard said. "I know him slightly. He was the third name on my list, and he knew the piece as soon as I spoke of it."

"Who'd he make it for?" Savage asked quickly.

"A young woman, he said." Blanchard took a piece of paper from his pocket, stared at it and read the name carefully, "Lila Dennois."

"Address?"

"She didn't give one. Just ran by and told Westenthall what she wanted. Then she came by later and picked it up. Paid in cash, he said."

Savage shook his head in a gesture of disappointment. "May be able to trace her by name. Can I use your phone?"

"Of course. Come back and use the one in my office."

Savage followed the jeweler, dialed Sixkiller's number, and got him at once. "Luke, any word there on her?"

"No. Nothing on her car either. You got any leads?"

"A real thin one that's about played out. Listen, I want you to find out what you can about a woman named Lila Dennois . . . "

Sixkiller listened while Savage rapidly told him the details of the lighter, then said, "I'll find her, Ben. I'll go by and make sure Westenthall can give a positive identification on her, too. What's your next move?"

"I have an idea Dani might have gone to the Leonard Hotel. She told me she wasn't happy with the story that Clyde Givens gave about seeing the murdered girl leave with Prejean. It's just a shot in the dark, but it's all I've got. Say, call Ellen and tell her all this—or as much as you think she needs to know. I told her I'd call, but I'm short of time. Tell her I'll call later—and if anything turns up there, call me at Catlow's office."

"Okay, Ben—and good hunting!"

Savage put the phone down and turned to face the jeweler who had taken the call in with obvious interest. "Did Miss Ross say where she was going when she left here, Mr. Blanchard?"

Blanchard thought hard, then shook his head. "No. I'm certain she didn't. But I don't think she would have gone to any more jewelers to find out about the lighter. She did say she'd come back and check to see if I'd found the craftsman who made the lighter." A troubled look came to his faded eyes, and he asked, "Do you think she's in real trouble, Mr. Savage?"

"I think she is," Savage nodded. "She'd have gotten in touch with her family if she was able. She's a very considerate young woman."

"So I would have judged."

"Mr. Blanchard, call me at the local police station if you think of anything that might be helpful, and ask for Lieutenant Catlow—he'll know how to find me. And thanks for all your help."

"It was nothing—nothing!" Blanchard sighed. "She mentioned God to me, and I spoke harshly to her." He looked down at his shoes silently, then lifted his gaze to Savage. "At times like this, I wish I *did* believe in God."

Savage studied the old man's face, and nodded. "I know what you mean, Mr. Blanchard. Well—I'll call you if she turns up."

Blanchard called out as Savage made his way to the door, "Yes, please call—" But Savage was gone. The old man turned and went back to his high stool at his workbench, then sat down slowly. He watched through the window as Savage pulled away, then a sound at his feet made him look down. A chubby calico cat was staring up at him with round eyes, and he slowly bent down and picked her up. He stroked her fur absently, and then whispered, "Yes, Dolly, I wish I could believe in God. Such a fine young woman—!"

Heading for the Leonard Hotel, Savage got only two blocks away when he had a thought. Ducking into an Exxon station, he used the pay phone to call Catlow. As soon as the officer answered, Savage told him what he'd found out from Blanchard.

"Lila Dennois? Don't know the woman," Catlow said slowly. "What now?"

"There's a chance Dani might have gone to the Leonard Hotel. The security guard, a big ox named Mullins, doesn't like me. Maybe you could give him a call—tell him what a fine chap I am and how nice it would be if he let me talk to the help."

"Have at it, Savage," Catlow said at once. "I'll rattle Mullins' cage. Let me know if you get anything."

"Sure. Oh, yeah, I gave your number to some people in case they get anything, so you may get a call. I'll check later."

Ten minutes later Savage was facing Mullins, who said with a red face, anger glinting in his small eyes, "Yeah, you can talk to the guys. No problem."

"Hey, that's real nice of you, Mullins," Savage said smoothly. "I appreciate it. Be as quick as I can so I don't slow them up."

"Always glad to help," Mullins said, forcing the words out through tight lips.

Savage nearly smiled, for he knew the big man wanted to chew him up and spit him out. But he only nodded, and left at once. He wanted to tackle them one at a time and found Bejay Guidry clipping the mock orange trees beside the hotel.

He recalled what Dani had told him about the man and said at once, "Guidry, I'm Ben Savage, one of Miss Ross's operatives." He flashed his ID and saw apprehension leap into the man's dark eyes. "You've gotten yourself in over your head, man," Savage said, deciding to handle the young man roughly.

"Hey, what's all that jazz?" Guidry held the shears in both hands, clipping a branch to show he was cool. "I told all I know about that dumb case. Go read the report."

"I've been reading reports, Bejay," Savage said, curling his lip in disgust. "You're going up the flue on this one."

Guidry gave up his pretense of clipping branches and dropped the shears on the ground. His eyes narrowed as he said, "What you trying to pull, you?" he said softly, as he balanced himself on the balls of his feet as though he were ready to throw a punch.

He knows something, Savage decided. *But he's a tough one.*

"I hope you do go down, Bejay," Savage said. "I told Miss Ross to let you go up the river, but she said to give you a chance."

"You're talking crazy!" A sudden thought came to Guidry, and he said, "You been talking to that crazy Dax Fontenot, ain't you?"

Savage had never heard the name, but said, "Sure, I have."

Guidry shook his head. "The guy's got the mind of a ten-year-old—and you're listening to *him*?"

"He made some sense, Bejay."

"Sense? Dax don't know enough to tie his shoes." Anger stirred the Cajun's face, and he added, "He's always hated me 'cause Cory liked me better than him."

"Not what he told me," Savage shook his head. None of what Guidry was saying made sense, but he hoped something would fall out of the man that would fit. "You're going to take a hit, Guidry. You been to Angola? You won't like it much."

Perspiration suddenly appeared on Guidry's forehead, and he looked around, then said in a lower tone, "You want some advice? Don't pay any attention to that nut. I talked to him, yeah, but he ain't got nothing that'll put me away." He lowered his voice, adding, "If you want to do some good, be sure your boss stays away from him. He don't like her. He told a friend of mine that Lady Detective .38 she carries won't help her if she don't stop poking her nose in his business!"

Savage's eyes sharpened. "What friend did he tell that to?" When Guidry hesitated, he snapped, "You're in a spot, Bejay! And for some reason my boss wants to help you. Now—what friend?"

"Annie Louvier," Bejay said reluctantly. "Now, I got to go to work."

"I'll be dropping by—or maybe it'll be Lieutenant Catlow."

Savage wheeled and left, not giving Guidry a chance to argue. He found Leon Williams stacking dishes in a cabinet in the dining room. The black man smiled at once. "Why, Mr. Savage, you back again?"

"Hello, Leon," Savage said hurriedly, then asked, "You haven't seen Miss Ross, have you?"

Williams stared at him. "You means recent? No, suh, I ain't." Seeing the disappointment on Savage's face, he asked, "Something wrong with Miss Ross?"

It went against Savage's policy, which was never to tell anyone anything he didn't have to, but he suddenly said, "She's missing, Leon. I'm afraid for her."

"No! Oh, Lord help that lady!"

"Listen, I'm going to be moving around, but if you hear anything, give me a call. I can be reached at Lieutenant Catlow's office. Here's the number."

"I'll pray on it, too," Williams nodded firmly.

"Miss Ross would like that, I think."

Savage left Williams and found Clyde Givens sitting at the desk in the parking lot. There was something about Givens that bothered him, but he couldn't put his finger on it. He quickly discovered that Givens hadn't talked to Dani—or claimed that he hadn't. But Ben didn't feel inclined to lean on him as he had on Guidry. He asked him to phone Catlow's office if Dani got in touch with him, and Givens agreed rather sulkily.

Savage left the hotel and drove around the city, trying to think. On almost every case there came a time when there was nothing to do but wait—but this time there *was* no time. He drove down to the river, parked by the levee, and then walked up to sit and stare out over the expanse of brown water moving steadily toward the Gulf. Tugs pushed long steel barges against the current, and when he glanced to his right, he saw the colorful platform just north of the *USS Kidd*—the spot where he'd asked Dani to marry him.

Usually Savage was able to handle things, even tough things.

But this was not something tough that affected only him. He sat there on the grass, gripped by the most depressing sense of helplessness he'd ever known.

The river surged past, roiling brown eddies against the bank, and the paddlewheeler, *The Samuel Clemens,* started churning the water as the pilot backed her out into the current.

The wind was brisk and chilly, but Savage didn't feel it. For thirty minutes he sat there, then got up and walked down the levee toward the bridge. As he walked along, he kept his head down, and images of Dani came to him. He thought of her as he'd first seen her in the silo, and remembered he'd had nothing much but contempt for her—thinking she was just another Jesus freak. He remembered the look on her face when the two of them had fought a desperate battle on the snow-covered top of that prison, a battle that seemed hopeless, so great were the odds against them. But at the most critical moment, he remembered her face, how it had not been defeated but how it had glowed with a faith that had shaken all his thoughts about religion.

He thought about the fights he'd had with her—and how her eyes seemed to sparkle when she was angry. He thought about how he'd kissed her, holding her tightly in a cabin on a bayou, with a giant gator bellowing below. The smell and the touch of her firm body pressed to his as he held her—he thought of that, as well.

But the more he thought of her, the more helpless he felt. He turned under the bridge, and made his way back to the car. Slamming the door, he sat there, uncertain about what to do and unable to put the rising fear that had been growing for hours at rest.

Finally he drove back to the Leonard Hotel and got a room. When he was alone, he called Catlow, saying, "I'm in room 314 at the Leonard Hotel. Got to do some thinking. If anybody calls, put him through here."

Catlow agreed, and then Ben called Sixkiller. The two talked for some time, wrestling with the matter. Savage could tell that Luke was getting shaky. The burly homicide officer was fond of Dani, and like Savage, he was a man of action. Finally he said, "It's in God's hands, Ben."

Savage stared at the phone, then said, "Sure, Luke." He hung up, then called Ellen. He spoke with her for a long time, not giving a great deal of hope, but just being company. He knew that she was terribly afraid, but he could only try to cover his own fears while he comforted her.

He soon discovered that he couldn't fool this woman. "Ben—" she said finally, "I know you don't believe much in what God is able to do. But you're wrong. I'm scared—can't help that! But I've got someone who keeps me from falling apart—the Lord Jesus!"

She said no more, and all Savage could do was say, "I'm glad for you, Ellen. I'll be at this number if you need me—or if I'm not here, get Catlow at the police station."

And then he hung up and lay down on the bed. The sun was shining through the window, and it fell on his face. He was too weary to do more than put his hand across his eyes to shield them. He lay still, his brain racing and every nerve tense. He discovered that his jaw was tired from being clamped and deliberately forced himself to relax.

He was more alone than he'd ever been, it seemed.

The silence of the room became somehow frightening, for in it he began to think of terrible things—things about Dani. He pressed the back of his hand against his eyes until they hurt.

And then he whispered, "Oh, God—! Don't let her die!"

It was the first prayer that Benjamin Davis Savage had prayed since he was ten years old.

16

A Message
for Ben Savage

Savage came out of the bed instantly, the knock on the door breaking into the silence of the room. Picking up the Colt he'd placed on the nightstand, he moved to the door and stood to one side of it before asking, "Yes—who is it?"

"Me, Mr. Savage—Leon Williams."

"Just a minute—" Savage stepped to the bed and put the gun under the pillow, then went and opened the door. Williams stood there, his face sober and somewhat strained. "Come in, Leon," Savage said. He stepped back, and when the black man had entered, he shut the door before asking, "Any word about Miss Ross?"

"Well, suh, not what *you* might call a word," Williams responded.

Savage, noting the small man's hesitation, frowned. "What does that mean—not what *I* might call a word?"

Williams came to a decision, nodding his head slightly. "I got a word from the Lord for you, Mr. Savage." Williams held up his hand, palm outward, as disappointment touched Savage's face. "Now, I know you ain't a man of faith, but God sometimes uses men who doan even know him to do his work. Why, when God was gettin' ready to send his people back to their homeland, Israel, he used a heathen king called Cyrus. And he said, 'I girded thee, though thou hast not known me.'" Williams's voice rolled a little as he quoted the Scripture, and Savage knew that if he had lifted his tone, he would have awakened the hotel!

"Sit down, Leon." Savage waited until the smaller man took a seat, then seated himself on the bed. "Tell me about it," he said quietly. He said nothing of how he'd been brought to prayer for the first time in years but waited to hear what his visitor had to say.

Williams cleared his throat, clasped his hands, and said slowly, "After you told me about the trouble Miss Ross was in, I couldn't get it off my mind—I purely couldn't!" He shook his head, looking at Savage with compassion in his eyes. "That happens to me sometimes, Mr. Savage. I get burdened for some poor soul, and I jes' can't shake it off! Sometimes it's somebody I see—like maybe a man who checks into the hotel. I come to his table and he orders breakfast." Williams spoke slowly, deep in his chest, his eyes half closed. "He don't look like he need help—maybe got on a diamond ring and a fine suit. But God whispers, *Leon—pray for that man!* And from that moment, Mr. Savage, I weep in my spirit for him." He looked up at the man who was watching him and said, "I reckon you think that's crazy, don't you?"

"No, I don't." Savage was moved by the simplicity of the man who sat before him. "I wish more people were like that."

Williams didn't speak for a moment, but he was pleased.

His eyes lit up and he said, "I think one day pretty soon, you'll be doing that kind of thing, Mr. Savage." He nodded as if he knew a fine secret, then he shrugged his thin shoulders. "Well, like I said, as soon as you told me about the trouble Miss Ross done got herself in, a burden for her came on my soul."

"I've got one myself, Leon," Savage nodded.

"Yes, suh, I knows dat. I seen it in your eyes."

Savage ducked his head, asking quickly, "What about a word from God for me?"

"It didn't come right off," Williams said, his eyes thoughtful. "I got a chance to git off by myself so I could focus on God. Went up to one of the vacant rooms, and I fell on my face before the Lord. And Mr. Savage—" he said solemnly, shaking his head, "I reckon every devil in Baton Rouge come to that room! It wasn't no fight against flesh and blood—no, suh! It was a battle against principalities and wickedness in high places! The devil told me I was crazy! He told me to stop making a fool of myself 'bout somethin' that wasn't none of my business!"

"I can't really understand all that, Leon."

"I knows you can't, Mr. Savage, not right now." Williams put his eyes on Savage, adding, "The natural man receiveth not the things of the Spirit of God. But one day you *will* understand!"

At one point in his life Savage would have smiled in disbelief at such statements—but he didn't find it amusing now. "I hope so," he said slowly.

Williams continued, "I pled the blood of Jesus over that woman, and told the devil to leave her alone. He was right persistent, old Slewfoot, but in the end he had to run. Ain't no devil can stand against the Lord Jesus!"

Savage was listening intently to Williams. Afternoon had passed into dusk, and the city lights glowed in the falling darkness, throwing their rays inside the window. He could hear the sound of traffic, muted and far-off, but he leaned forward, asking, "What happened then?"

"It got real still, Mr. Savage," Williams whispered. He leaned forward, his face tense and expectant. "I waited and waited. Sometimes we get in a hurry, but God ain't in no hurry. I done learned that when I done all I can, it's best just to wait on God! And then it come—as clear a word as this unworthy servant evah got from God, Mr. Savage!"

Williams shut his eyes, and his head swung slowly back and forth. "I never cease bein' amazed that the Almighty God will lower himself to speak with a piece of flesh like me! But he did! He did!"

Tears ran down the small man's cheeks, and Savage, who had seen fakes and charlatans by the score, knew that these were real!

"I don't know what it means, what God told me to tell you," Williams said. "And you might need to do a little waitin' yourself, Mr. Savage. Sometimes the Lord uses dark sayings. He done said, 'It is the glory of God to conceal a thing: but the honor of kings is to search out a matter.' So I can give you the word from God, but you will have to search it out for yourself."

Savage felt almost afraid. He had never believed in such things, and now he was being confronted with a situation that demanded either faith or outright disbelief. Reluctantly he nodded. "What was it, Leon?"

"The Lord said for me to tell you, 'You don't need to hunt anymore—the answer you seek, you already have been given.'"

Savage stared at Williams. He had expected more! "Is that all?"

Williams nodded reluctantly. "You're disappointed. But

you mind what I said about seekin' out the things of God. He don't cast none of his pearls before swine, no, suh! I think he tests us that way—like if you really want to help Miss Ross, you'll do *anything*. Now, you ain't a man who's afraid of much, Mr. Savage. I can see that. And if it was a matter of going up against guns and knives, why, you'd die before you quit—ain't that the truth?"

Savage nodded slowly. "Yes, Leon. I'd do that for her."

"Well, now, you done left that behind," Williams said, almost sternly. "This is a battle in high places—against the power of evil itself. And there's only one way a man ever wins *that* battle—and that's by *faith*!"

"Don't have much of that," Savage muttered.

Williams said nothing, but suddenly he stood to his feet. Before Savage knew what he was doing, the black man had put his hands on Savage's shoulders. The touch startled Ben, and he started to rise, but with a surprising strength, Williams held him in place—and then he began to pray.

It was unlike anything Ben Savage had ever experienced, that prayer. It was simple enough, lacking eloquence and rhetorical flourish. Williams began to praise God, naming the qualities of the Almighty. Then he began to pray that Savage would be a broken man!

" . . . he won't never be a whole man, Lord, until he's been broken, so break him! That life in him, that strength, it's got to die before he can be the man you want him to be! Even Jesus had to die, so that sinners like me could live! Every seed's got to fall into the ground and die before it brings forth life! He's hangin' on to his own strength, Lord, but I'm asking you to break him down so he ain't *got* no strength! He ain't got no show, Lord God, in the flesh! He can't help that poor woman, and he can't help himself! But I know that *you* can save him—and *you* can show him how to save that woman he loves so much! So give him faith, Lord, faith to believe in you . . . "

As the words rolled over him, something began to happen inside of Savage. He had always been a strong man, priding himself on his strength. He had taken his beatings, but he'd never quit, never given up. Every problem that came to him, he'd put his head down, gritted his teeth, and run right at it.

But as Williams prayed, from deep inside somewhere, a hard knot began to form, and as clearly as words carved in brass, he knew the truth: *You're not going to win. You're going to lose. You're not strong enough to handle this thing. So you will either have faith in God—or you will lose all that is precious to you!*

Savage began to tremble and was so shaken by the thing that had come to him that he didn't even know when Williams removed his hands, didn't even hear the final words of the preacher, or the soft sound of the door closing.

Ben wanted to run, but he could not get to his feet. He began to tremble, his hands shaking so badly that he clasped them together to try to control them.

And then he began to weep.

He had never cried much, even as a child. He'd learned to clamp down on his emotions, to fight off anything that threatened to destroy the wall he kept before the world.

But now, the wall was crumbling. He felt the hot tears, and without conscious thought, he slipped to his knees. Placing his hands on the bed, he buried his face in them and was swept by the release of grief that followed. He tried to hold back, but then something inside him snapped, and it was like a dam breaking!

He began to utter great sobbing, choking gasps, and his shoulders shook as though he were being twisted by a giant's hand. He didn't try to pray, for he didn't know how. He heard no voice, but he was aware that he was being dealt with by no less than God. Finally he slumped to the floor and lay there weeping for a long time.

Eventually, the wild storm of grief began to pass, and in its place came a quiet sensation. He lay there, not moving, not wanting to move. He had been so tense that the relief that swept over him was like coming out of a storm into a quiet harbor.

Then he began to pray.

He prayed for himself, for in that moment, he saw his need of God. He saw the waste of his past life, and for some time, he spoke to God, asking for forgiveness. And then he waited. As he lay there in the darkness, he began to remember the Scriptures Dani had spoken to him over and over. He had not realized how powerful the Scriptures were, nor how she had made them a part of his mind.

But they were there:

Except a man be born again, he cannot see the kingdom of God.

He that believeth on the Son hath everlasting life.

This is the work of God, that ye believe on him whom he hath sent.

The wages of sin is death; but the gift of God is eternal life through Jesus Christ our Lord.

Except ye repent, ye shall all likewise perish.

For whosoever shall call upon the name of the Lord shall be saved.

As Ben lay there, it seemed that he could almost hear Dani's voice speaking these and other Scriptures. They came slowly, and all spoke of Jesus Christ.

Finally that passed—and Savage knew he was standing at the crossroad of his life.

He knew he would either say *yes* to God and call on him for mercy—or he would say *no* and live the rest of his life not knowing God. He had no proof, but it was as if God were saying, *I've spoken to you. I'm asking you to trust me, to have faith in me. Now—what will you do with my son, Jesus?*

Savage began to feel a dark shadow of doubt rising—one he'd lived with for most of his life.

And with that shadow beginning to close in, he made his choice.

"Oh, God—" he whispered. "I'm afraid—afraid of lots of things! But most of all—I'm afraid I'll miss everything if I don't come to you right now! So I'm asking you to take me just like I am! I can't be good enough—but I'm asking you to clean me up and let me be a Christian!" He began to weep, but softly this time, and he shook his head. "Save me, God—for I'm asking it. And I ask it in the name of Jesus!"

As soon as he prayed that prayer, Savage began to grow very quiet. He'd heard of people shouting when they found God, but it was not like that with him. He came off his knees and stood to his feet. His knees felt weak, so he sat down on the bed. His thoughts had been wild and uncontrolled, but now they seemed to be very quiet and regular.

He sat there for a long time, and finally he began to pray, this time aloud. He told God how weak he was, but said, "I'll serve you as best I can. But I won't be able to do a thing—not unless you help me. I don't know anything much about the Bible—and I can't seem to learn it. You'll have to teach me how to study it."

He was not at all self-conscious as he sat there in the darkness praying. He would have felt foolish a short time ago, praying aloud, but now it seemed natural and somehow, very *right.*

Finally, he walked to the window and looked outside, thinking of what he had done. And without effort of any kind, a memory came to him. He remembered something that he had heard Bejay Guidry say about Dax Fontenot:

He told a friend of mine that Lady Detective .38 she carries won't help her if she don't stop poking her nose in his business!

Savage's back suddenly grew rigid. He stood there, thinking hard, and then whispered aloud, "Fontenot couldn't have known the gun Dani carried was a Lady Detective—not unless she showed it to him—and Dani never showed that gun to anyone!"

He stood there thinking hard, and came up with only one conclusion. "It has to be Fontenot! The only way he could have known what kind of gun she carried was if he took it away from her!"

And then he thought, *It's just like God told Leon—I already had the answer!*

He moved quickly, retrieving the Colt from under the pillow and shoving it into the shoulder holster. He put on his coat, then dialed the number of the station. When he asked for Lieutenant Catlow and was told that he was off duty, he said, "Tell him that Savage called—and that he was going to talk to Dax Fontenot."

He hung up and dialed Ellen. As soon as she answered, he said, "I think I've got a lead, Ellen. Tell Sixkiller if I don't call in a few hours to hunt up a guy named Dax Fontenot." He paused, then added, "I want to tell you, Ellen—I gave myself to God tonight."

"Oh, thank God!" Ellen began to weep but said through her tears, "Go find her, Ben!"

Then he hung up and moved to the door.

But when his hand touched the knob, he stopped short.

I may have to use a gun on Fontenot!

And then he knew more about the struggle Dani had had—the difficulty of serving God when it involved using force.

But he suddenly thought of how the message from God—delivered by Leon Williams—had been true.

"God, I can't think you'd help me figure out where Dani was unless you wanted me to help her—"

He stood there in the darkness, doubt creeping over him—and then he threw it off. "Lord, you know best. I think you want me to go to Dani, and I'm asking you to let me get her free without killing anybody!"

He waited for one moment, and when the doubts seemed to flee, he stepped outside and closed the door. As he got into his car and headed for Annie's Place, he seemed to hear Ellen's voice, echoing:

Go find her, Ben!

17
Escape!

Dani Ross was a woman of deep emotions, but they lay buried beneath an orderly surface. Years of training as an accountant had brought this to her, and she had fallen into the habit of treating life's problems as she had treated problems in her earlier profession.

"When you've got things that don't add up in the books," she had often said, "all you have to do is go over them. The answer is there—you just have to find it."

But this swamp was not a set of books. It operated on a far different set of laws than those that controlled accounting processes. Here life and death were close together. There was no "answer" when a thick-bodied cottonmouth moccasin sank his fangs into your calf and pumped his venom into your bloodstream. Gallons of white-out would not allow a second chance. Nor could you show a bull gator the error of his ways with a chart of figures if he seized you and started pulling you into some dreadfully deep den!

"There has to be a way to get out of here," Dani said forcefully. "This is a big bayou, but people come here to fish and hunt. Planes do fly over."

She began to wonder how she might attract the attention of someone who came close. Make a fire, a smoke signal? A grim smile touched her lips as she argued aloud, "Have to burn the cabin down—and then what if nobody noticed? Not a good idea, Ross!"

She eyed the span of open water and considered trying to make it to solid land. "Not too deep in spots—" she said slowly. "Maybe go from one tree to another."

But she had fished in Louisiana bayous for years and knew that they were as treacherous as any territory on earth. The surface might be only six inches deep, so shallow one had to drag a pirogue over it, but there were drop-offs so sudden that an unwary person could sink down to the ooze ten feet below and quicksand that could drag one to a gritty death, the silence of the swamp shattered by dying screams and a final gurgle.

"Can't walk out," Dani decided, accepting the inevitable. Then a thought came to her, and she stepped away from the wall and turned to look at the cabin itself. "But maybe a boat—?"

She dreaded the idea of spending long hours doing nothing, and the thought of spending endless nights in the cabin oppressed her. "Robinson Crusoe did it," she muttered—and then she remembered the way the famous castaway had fared. "But he never got off his island with it."

But she was taken with the possibility, and for the next two hours, she went over every board in the cabin, as well as every item inside the single room. The walls of the cabin were made of thick cypress boards, one of the best materials for building flat-bottomed boats. They were old and dark with age, but with cypress, that didn't matter.

"I can't even drive a nail without hitting my thumb," she muttered finally. She made a cup of coffee and drank it slowly, at first rejecting the idea of a boat and exploring other possibilities.

By ten o'clock the swamp was heating up, and she was weary of her efforts to figure a way out. Seeing circles appearing on the smooth surface of the water around the cabin, she searched for something to fish with. Finding some line and a few hooks, she rigged up a fishing line and baited the hook with a morsel of Vienna sausage—which she hoped the fish liked better than she did. On her first try, she caught a thumping half-pound perch, and in thirty minutes she had caught enough to feed herself for a week.

"I'm not going to starve to death, at least." She waited until noon, then cleaned the first fish and heated corn oil in the black skillet, which had obviously been used for such things before. After covering the perch with cornmeal, she fried it whole in the oil. When it was golden brown, she put it on a plate, got a bottle of orange juice, and went back out on the deck. After pulling the back fin out carefully, she ate the firm, delicious flesh along the backbone. She ate slowly, savoring the meal, then tossed the cleaned skeleton over for the blue crabs and small perch to finish.

The orange juice was not cold, but it tasted good to her. She sipped it slowly, watching a flight of snow white egrets fly over in strict formation. A snake made a wide vee of a ripple across the lagoon, and as always she felt a weakness at the sight. She would sooner face a grizzly bear than a small cottonmouth!

After eating, she moved restlessly, pacing back and forth on the narrow deck, straining her eyes for any sign of life, and listening for the slightest sound of some sort of human activity. Nervous and irritable, she went inside. The cotton mattresses were none too clean, but she lay down on the bottom bunk, trying to ignore the rank odors. Her wrists pained her, and her head was so tender where she had been struck by Fontenot's hard fist, that every time she shifted and it touched the pillow, sharp pains brought her wide awake.

Finally, after an hour of tossing restlessly on the mildewed pad, she gave it up and rose to go outside again. A cool breeze was beginning to whip the smooth, dark waters, forming fine patterns on the surface. She stood there, hesitating, then came to a sudden decision.

"Don't go down with your bat on your shoulder—go down swinging," she said aloud. "At least that's what Babe Ruth used to say. He didn't have to get out of a swamp like this, though—"

But she wheeled and began searching at once for tools to build a raft. There wasn't much—only a large screwdriver, a hammer, several small wrenches, one large crescent wrench, a pair of pliers, and a few other rusty odds and ends. She stared at the collection with dismay, but she set her teeth, saying, "It's more than Edmund Dantes had, and he burrowed his way through about a hundred yards of solid dirt!"

Using the screwdriver, she pried off some of the boards, choosing those that were not too solidly nailed. Most of them came off with a screech as the nails pulled loose. She pounded the nails on the sharp ends until they stuck out of the boards. She had no idea how to build a raft, but decided to nail short boards across the longer ones. But she had no way to cut the long boards she'd pulled off. Her eye fell on the window, and she went at once to remove the short boards that framed it. Some of them were firmly nailed, and she skinned the knuckles on both hands getting them off.

Finally she had enough to satisfy herself, and she began to assemble her raft. Laying three of the short boards down, she carefully put the longer pieces on top, forming a rectangle eight feet long and about three feet wide. It was a job to pull out the rusty nails, but with the pliers, she got enough to nail the long pieces down. She discovered the nails were so long that she'd nailed the whole thing to the deck.

"Oh—*blast!*" she exploded. Looking around, she saw that the sun was lower in the sky, and she knew that she had to hurry. Using the screwdriver, she managed to loosen one corner of the raft, and then by inserting the stubby broom under it, she was able to get it free. She pried one end and lifted it. Then walking it on the narrow end, she let it fall into the water below.

Staring down at her creation, she nodded with satisfaction. "It floats, anyway!" But when she went down the ladder and stepped on the raft, she was dismayed to discover that it sank alarmingly under her weight. She discovered that it would hold her up, but her weight pushed it so far down in the water that there was no way she could control it.

She climbed up the ladder and began searching for something to get the flat raft to ride higher in the water. Again and again she looked, until she'd exhausted the possibilities.

Her spirit sank as she slumped down on the blue milk carton. She dropped her head, bitterly disappointed. *Have to stay here until he comes back—and he won't do that until Eddie Prejean is dead.*

She picked up the large crescent wrench, staring at it. Then she thought suddenly, *The stovepipe!*

At once she ran inside and stared at the wood stove, then at the pipe. It was at least five inches in diameter, and when she moved to touch it, it remained firm, instead of crumbling as an old tin pipe would have done.

"Stainless steel!" Dani cried in astonishment. She'd helped her father install a woodburning stove, and she saw that this one was made out of the same material.

Quickly she studied the joints, her gaze going upward where the ceiling rose at a steep pitch. "Each joint is four feet, and there are four joints," she calculated. "That means two pontoons eight feet long—Hallelujah!"

She began taking down the pipe at once, sending black clouds of old soot in such a thick cloud that she had a coughing fit.

She hauled the pipe outside, then stared at the open ends. *Got to seal those ends and make the joints watertight!*

She did it at last, but she discovered that a number two can of tomatoes was just a fraction of an inch smaller in diameter than the ends of the stovepipe. She opened four cans, stuffed one in each end, and considered the result. "Still not tight enough," she muttered. "And the joints in the middle have to be sealed."

She solved it by discovering an old inner tube and a roll of rusty wire. Cutting off a portion of the inner tube, she held it over the end of one of the makeshift pontoons and wired it tightly. Just to be certain, she put two pieces of wire about six inches apart, then twisted them tight with the pliers. When she had made a similar seal for the joint where the two pieces were joined, she hauled the raft back onto the deck—which was almost beyond her strength.

Fortunately, there was plenty of wire, and after using some of the shorter pieces of wood on the raft to form a sort of cradle for the pontoons, she put the stovepipes in place and wired them firmly. Just to be certain, she put the rest of the wire around the whole raft, and tightened it well. Then she pushed her handiwork to the edge of the deck and shoved it off. It hit the water, sank as it nosed down, then popped back and floated neatly on the pontoons.

"Praise the Lord, I've got me an ark!" Dani shouted for joy.

Then she glanced at the sky, and saw that the sun was far down in the west. For a moment she stood there, thinking it might be best to wait until morning. But she didn't want to waste time, so she scurried around, throwing food and several bottles of water she'd boiled into a sack. She put them on the raft, then remembered she had no paddle—but she knew of something better.

Going to the back of the cabin, she used the pliers and the screwdriver to remove a long, slender pole someone had used for an antenna of some sort. It was at least twelve feet long—just right for poling a raft through the shallow waters of the swamp, much better than a paddle!

She tossed the pole down, then quickly tried to think what else she might find helpful. A thought came to her, and she went inside and grabbed up two of the yellowing sheets and the two old blankets. She looked around but felt the pressure of time.

Going to the ladder, she climbed down, tossing the coverings on the top of her craft beside the food and water bag. Carefully, she stepped onto the barge. It dipped alarmingly, but she was expecting that. Picking up the pole, she leaped to the center and was relieved to discover that the small barge held her easily.

Carefully she lifted the pole until most of its length was in the air, then lowered the end until it touched bottom. She'd poled flat-bottomed boats before, once even entering a pirogue race. It was a matter of balance, mostly. As she pushed on the pole, throwing her weight against it, the raft moved steadily forward. She quickly discovered that the blunt end of the raft dug into the water, slowing her progress, but when she moved slightly back, this lifted the end.

By the time she had reached the opening, she'd mastered the art. Giving one last look at the cabin, she steered the craft through and entered the world of thick trees. It frightened her somewhat, for at least in the cabin there was shelter and some sort of security. She'd heard of many who'd gotten lost in the bayous of the Atchafalaya Swamp—and were never found.

The temptation came to turn about, to do nothing but wait—but such waiting was not in her character. She shoved the pole and sent the small craft between two huge cypress trees that had been old when her grandfather had made his charge up the Little Round Top along with Pickett.

When she'd gone fifty yards, she paused and dropped her pole across the boat. Stooping, she picked up one of the sheets and tore it into ribbons. Then she tore some of the strips into short pieces about two feet long. One of these she tied to an overhanging branch, then she stuck the rest into her belt. Picking up the pole, she sent the barge deeper into the swamp, stopping when she could barely see the white strip and tying another.

"At least I can find my way back if I have to," she nodded as she drove her small craft deeper and deeper into the murky depths of the swamp.

For an hour she poled steadily forward, careful to tie strips to mark her way. Her arms grew tired, and she stopped from time to time to rest them, taking small sips of water from one of the bottles. She kept the sun in position, so that no matter how she had to steer around islands or impenetrable stands of cypress, she always came back to the same direction. She'd been unconscious for most of the trip into the swamp, but she knew that by heading north, she'd eventually have to strike either a road or a stream that flowed into the river itself—and that would mean safety.

What she didn't figure on was her own weakness. By the time darkness was no more than an hour away, she was trembling with weakness and had a splitting headache. Her eyes blurred, so bad was the pain that came to her temples, and finally she had to admit defeat.

"Got to tie up someplace—" she muttered and began to search for some sort of small island. But to her dismay, she discovered that she was in a part of the bayou where the waters were deep, and no land could be found.

Wearily, she pulled close to a giant cypress knee and tossed the loop of the rope around it, snugging the raft up as tightly as she could. She put the pole down carefully, then lay down and gasped for breath. By the time she had rested enough to sit up, darkness was almost palpable. She could see no more than shadows of the huge trees around her.

Saying a word of thanks that she'd thought to throw some of the candles into the food sack, she lit one of them, but almost at once, the hum of mosquitoes came to her ears. She used the light to dig a can of Vienna sausages out of the bag, along with a can of pickled peaches. She opened them and ate, letting the juice from the peaches dribble down her chin. She drank some water, thinking how wonderful a cup of coffee would be.

The mosquitoes were feasting on her, so she made a pad of the blankets and draped the sheet over herself to keep the pests off.

The little raft bobbed with each movement she made, and soon the sounds of the world she'd invaded began to come to her. Some were high-pitched and shrill, but some were hoarse and deep. From time to time, something would break the surface of the water. Once, something large surfaced nearby, making such a splash that it rocked Dani's small craft.

There were panthers in the swamp, she knew, and bears, too. Not grizzlies, of course, but the black bears could be dangerous at times.

And she was very much aware that her small raft lifted her only a few inches above the surface of the water.

A cottonmouth could slither right on top of me!

The very thought of such a thing made Dani's skin crawl. She tried to avoid the thought, and almost at once, she heard the hoarse grunting of a bull gator not far away. Ordinarily she was not afraid of alligators, for they were, for the most part, harmless to man.

But gators ate anything, and with one huge bull like the one that kept bellowing, who could tell what would happen if he found a tender morsel right on his level!

Time ran on, very slowly. There was no way she could sleep—not with that gator getting closer, or so it seemed to Dani, every moment!

Fear came, and Dani wished for a Bible and a light to read it by. Always that was her resource in times of trouble, but now she did what she could—which was to search her memory for favorite verses. And she knew a great deal of the Scripture by heart. She'd attended a Basic Youth Seminar when she'd first become a Christian, and the one thing that the speaker had impressed her with was the importance of memorizing Scripture. She had thrown herself into a program, and with her fine memory, she had stored entire chapters in her mind.

In her more recent past, she'd discovered that it was not the *amount* of Scripture, so much as the act of meditating on it, that was fruitful. She'd formed the habit of taking one small section, sometimes only a single verse, and thinking about it off and on as she went about her work or lay on her bed at night.

For half an hour she lay with her eyes half closed, whispering different verses—most of them simple praises from the Psalms, her favorite Old Testament book. They were filled with poetry in which desperate men poured out their needs before God—frantically, at times. Others were majestic and poetic statements made as men stood in awe of the God they served.

A calm came over Dani as she sat there whispering the ancient words. Finally, one psalm came into her mind with a vivid clarity, so sharply that she could visualize the words as they appeared on the well-worn page of her Bible. It was the third psalm, and she spoke aloud the heading: "A psalm of David, when he fled from Absalom his son."

Her mind went back to the tragic history of King David, the sweet singer of Israel, the man the Scripture eulogized as "a man after God's own heart."

She had often wondered why David should have been God's special favorite, for he had fallen into gross sins—adultery and murder. After thinking of it for a long time, she had decided that God loved David because David loved God! With all his faults, nothing in the literature of the Bible was more poignant than David's songs in which he poured out his love for Jehovah!

Dani thought of how the third psalm had come to be written. It was composed by David at a time when his favorite son, Absalom, had risen up to lead a civil war against him. Absalom, handsome and wise in the ways of politics, had won the hearts of the men of Israel, and David, with a small band of faithful followers, had fled the palace to save their lives.

Dani thought of that, then quoted the first verse of the

psalm: "Lord, how are they increased that trouble me! Many are they that rise up against me! Many there be which say of my soul, there is no help for him in God."

The words seemed to find a special lodging in Dani's spirit. As she sat there thinking of the hopelessness of her condition, she wanted to say, "That's exactly the way I feel, Lord!"

She thought of the trackless swamp and the unlikelihood of finding her way out. She thought it more likely that Fontenot might decide that it would be too dangerous to let her live. Fontenot, she knew, had such a simple mind, that if such a thing came to him, he would have no hesitation about carrying the thought through to a bloody finish. Easy enough for him to hide her body in this place!

She shivered slightly at the thought and quickly recited the next two verses: "But thou, O Lord, art a shield for me; my glory and the lifter up of mine head. I cried unto the Lord with my voice, and he heard me out of his holy hill."

Dani whispered those verses over, time and again, making a prayer out of them. They sounded feeble, the words in her whispered tones, and were lost among the sounds of the swamp.

Fear came to her, crawling along her nerves. It grew worse, and finally she began to weep. "Oh, God, help me!" she whispered.

And then she remembered verse five of the psalm she'd been thinking of:

I laid me down and slept; I awaked; for the Lord sustained me.

Dani lay there trembling and fighting back the tears, but she thought of David, too. Surrounded by his enemies, with death at his elbow—yet, he lay down and slept!

With an effort, Dani stopped weeping. She wiped the tears from her eyes, then closed them and said, "Lord, I'm not a good person like David, I know. But I know you love me—

and I'm going to do what he did! I'm going to sleep. If that ol' gator eats me, I'll be with you, so that's all right. Just take over, Lord—it's all in your hands!"

The prayer came to a close, and almost at once Dani's tired muscles began to relax. It seemed to her that the dreadful sounds of the swamp creatures were muted, as though they were far away. However it was, she slumped down and let her hands fall to the pad—and drifted off into a sound sleep.

Once it seemed she heard someone calling her name, but she could not move out of the warmth and comfort of sleep—and on her face was an expression of total trust.

18

"I'll Never Let You Go!"

Although Savage wanted to throw all caution to the wind, to go rushing headlong into action, he forced himself to turn off Interstate 10 at Baton Rouge and find a phone booth outside a gas station. He called Catlow's home number and got an answer on the third ring.

"Catlow."

"This is Savage—" Ben said, speaking rapidly. He gave a quick summary of what he had, ending by saying, "I'm going to wring that guy Fontenot, Catlow—but just in case he manages to nail me, I want you to go after him."

Catlow was silent for a moment, then said, "Okay, Savage. You want some backup?"

"Be safer if I go alone—but thanks. I'll get back to you as soon as I get something."

"Watch yourself. If Fontenot knocked off the Louvier woman, he'll be ready to do it again to cover up his tracks."

"Yeah, I'll do that."

Savage hung up, then ran to the car and sent it out of the driveway with a screeching roar. The dual glass packs on the Hawk made it sound like an express train, and now he regretted putting them on. "Not going to sneak up on anybody in this rig," he muttered. He kept the speed at an even eighty, hoping that none of the highway patrol noticed.

As he roared along, he thought for a time about what lay ahead—but there was no way to guess about that. He'd have to play it by ear. He thought of what had happened to him in the room at the Leonard Hotel, wondering at it greatly.

The thought came to him that he had merely had an emotional experience, but he rejected that at once. He was not given to fancies, and he knew that if he lived to be an old man, he'd never forget that time lying on his face in the darkness. The shrinks would tell him that he'd created the whole thing out of some inadequacy that had been caused by his early life.

As the highway unrolled beneath the tires of the Hawk, he thought about that. He'd had a terrible life as a child. No happy home life for him! His father had died before he'd been born, and his mother had been confined in a mental institution when he was twelve years old. He had run away from the orphanage and joined a circus—and it had been the kindness of Tony and Anna Rudolpho that had saved him. They'd taken him into their family and made a flyer out of him, the star of The Flying Rudolphos.

Savage thought of those days briefly—and of his later days. He'd had some tough times, but he knew deep down that what had come to him could never be explained by any psychologist. Even as he raced toward some sort of dangerous confrontation with a man who might be a killer, he had a peace that he'd never known.

When he pulled up in front of Annie's Place, he was not surprised to see that there were only two cars out front. Dives like Annie's were designed to operate in the darkness, not in the light of the sun. The people who frequented them were like the bugs and reptiles that made the dark underside of logs their habitat, and any light thrown on them made them flee for their lives.

He touched the Colt under his arm, then got out and locked the Hawk. The front door was locked, as he had expected. He knocked on it with his fist and stood there listening intently for any sound. He thought he heard something, and then the sound of a safety chain rattled, and the door swung open a few inches. A woman's voice said, "We're closed. Come back tonight."

The door started to close, but Savage said quickly, "I'm looking for Dax Fontenot."

The movement of the door halted, and the woman demanded, "What you want with him?"

"Well—it's private, you might say," Savage said. He smiled adding, "I'm not a bill collector."

"You look like a cop."

Savage made himself laugh. "Well, thanks for the compliment. But I'm not the law." He hesitated, then said, "I really need to see Dax. No trouble for him."

"Well—he lives in Lafayette. You can see him when he comes to work tonight."

"If you'd give me his phone number, I could call him."

"He don't have a phone. And he don't like to have his sleep interrupted. You'll have to come back tonight." Annie hesitated, then asked suspiciously, "What's your name?"

"Larry Jenson," Savage lied quickly. "He might not remember me, but we met in New Orleans a while back. I got a proposition he might like."

"Well, come back tonight around five. You can see him then."

The door slammed shut, and Savage knew he'd get nowhere by forcing himself into the place. Annie, he saw, was a pretty tough customer, and if she clammed up, he'd have no chance at all of finding Fontenot.

He went to his car, got in, and headed for Lafayette, thinking, *A guy like Fontenot's got to have some kind of record. Have to check with the cops.*

He drove at once to the police station, went inside, and soon found himself talking to the chief, a tall, white-haired man named Slaughter, with a set of light green eyes. He was polite enough, but he was not handing out any information to strangers. "Sure, I know Fontenot," he admitted readily. "Been in the tank a few times—but no real trouble. What you want with him?"

Savage hesitated, then made the decision to trust the system. "It's got something to do with the Eddie Prejean case, Chief. My boss and I've been working with Riley Catlow in Baton Rouge on it."

The name caused Slaughter's eyes to narrow. "I know Riley," he said slowly. "Mind if I give him a call?"

"No. He knows I'm here."

Slaughter dialed a number and sat upright until he got the other officer on the phone. "This is Slaughter, Riley. You know a man named Savage?"

He listened, his green eyes studying Savage carefully. Finally he said "Okay, just checking. See you, Riley." He hung up the phone, saying, "I don't know exactly where Fontenot lives, but maybe we can find out. We might spot his truck. It's a fire-engine red four-wheel drive Ford. Lots of chrome and a fine deer rifle across the back window."

"It's important, Chief," Savage said quickly. "I'm worried about my boss."

Slaughter nodded. "Come on, we'll go rat hunting."

For the next two hours, the two men drove around Lafayette, the Chief stopping from time to time to speak to people. Savage sat in the car, giving him the story little by little. He revealed more than he realized, and once Slaughter said, "You're stuck on your boss, aren't you, Savage?"

Savage nodded. "Yes. Have been for a long time."

"Well, I know you're anxious, but this is the only way I know to find out anything about this bird. Come on, I know an old friend of his. We'll put pressure on him."

But Slaughter didn't need to use force. He parked outside a bar, went inside, and came back almost at once, a smile on his face.

"Bingo!"

"You got him?"

"Yeah—at least I got an address. According to his buddy in there, Fontenot's got a room at a sleazy hotel."

"Chief—would you let me take it from here?"

Slaughter studied Savage for a long moment. "You're pretty uptight. Not planning to wipe him out, are you?"

"No. But if you pick him up, he won't have to talk. He'll start hollering about his rights and lawyers. But I can throw a scare into him. And if he won't talk, you got my word I won't do anything to him—nothing permanent."

Slaughter knew he was putting himself in a tricky position, but something about Savage made him say, "All right, Son. You go get him."

"Thanks, Chief!"

Slaughter took Savage back to the station and let him out, saying, "He's in the Fortune Hotel, Savage."

"Okay." Savage hesitated, then said, "Could I borrow a pair of cuffs?"

Slaughter pulled a pair out of the glove compartment and handed them to Savage. "Bring him in alive."

"Sure." Ben put his hand out. "I'll get back to you as soon as I get something. Even if this doesn't work out, I'll call you."

"Hope you find her," Slaughter nodded. "And watch yourself. Fontenot's not a shooter, but he's tough. Don't turn your back on him."

Savage nodded, then got into his car and pulled out. He followed the directions the officer had given him, and found the Fortune Hotel with no trouble. He pulled into the small parking lot, noting that the clientele of the Fortune didn't waste money on luxury cars. The few vehicles in the lot were either old sedans or pickup trucks—and the red Ford pickup stood out like a jewel among them.

Savage felt a grim satisfaction as he spotted the truck. *He's here—or at least his truck is.* He entered the hotel and stopped at the desk. A young black man turned and asked, "Yes, sir, you need a room?"

"No, I'm looking for Dax Fontenot," Savage said.

"Room 223."

"Thanks."

Savage nodded and moved to the elevator. It arrived with a creaking rattle, and when he got inside, it seemed to groan as he pushed the button driving it upward. Stepping off into the dark passageway, he found room 223 and knocked lightly on the door. There was no answer, so he knocked again. This time a voice came, muffled and thick.

"Yeah? Who is it?"

"Police. Open the door, Fontenot."

Silence, then the sounds of the lock being drawn and the door being opened. "What's this about? I didn't—"

Savage shoved his way into the room, pushing the big man backwards so hard that he stumbled and almost fell. Savage pulled his wallet out with one hand and flashed his PI license before Fontenot's startled eyes, then pulled out his gun and threw down on the startled man. "You're under arrest, Fontenot. Get dressed."

"Hey—wait a minute—!" Fontenot babbled. "I ain't done nothing!"

"Shut up, while I read you your rights."

Savage reeled off the formula he'd spoken so many times when he'd been a police officer in Colorado, then he waved the gun at Fontenot. "Now, get dressed."

Fontenot scrambled into his clothes, cursing all the time. When he was dressed, Savage took the cuffs from his pocket, saying, "Put your hands out." He ignored Fontenot's curses, clamping the cuffs on tightly. He then put his gun away and opened the door. "Come on, let's go downtown."

Fontenot argued all the way down to the ground floor, and the clerk eyed them nervously as Savage jerked the big man's arm, pulling him out the front door. But when they arrived at the Studebaker, Fontenot blinked and was silent. Savage pulled the passenger door open, and Fontenot said, "You ain't no cop!"

He tried to whirl away, but Savage was expecting it. He kicked the back of Fontenot's leg, sending him sprawling on the concrete, then grabbed a handful of the man's thick hair and yanked him to his feet. Shoving Fontenot inside, he slammed the door and moved around and took his seat behind the wheel. Fontenot began yelling, and Savage saw a young couple walking down the street stop and stare at them.

Yanking the Colt free, he rapped Fontenot across the wrists, bringing a cry of pain from the man. He shoved the muzzle of the weapon into Fontenot's side, saying, "You can either live for a while—or I'll blow a hole in your guts now, Fontenot. Which will it be?"

Fontenot swiveled his head around and something in the expression of the man beside him made him shut his mouth. "Don't shoot!" he said thickly.

Savage nodded and slipped the gun under his arm. Starting the car, he drove out of the parking lot, wondering if the couple would report what they'd seen. But he saw them walk on and decided that they wouldn't make the call.

Now that he had his man, Savage thought hard about how to extract what he wanted from him. He'd known a few officers who'd have beaten Fontenot, but he'd never had the heart for that.

But Fontenot doesn't know what kind of guy I am, he thought as he threaded the Hawk through traffic headed for the interstate. *I've got to make him think I'm going to rub him out.*

Fontenot began to talk almost at once. "Look, you got the wrong guy or something. I ain't never seen you before."

Savage said nothing, knowing from experience that silence was a potent threat—far more so at times than vocal ones. He kept his face still, turning occasionally to give Fontenot a hard glance. Turning west on the interstate, he tried to think of someplace to take the man where he could work on him. *Maybe one of those roads around False River,* he thought. He'd accompanied a friend from New Orleans on a weekend fishing trip on that lake and remembered that the country around it had plenty of lonely dirt roads. *Get him alone and make him think I'm going to shoot him—that's all I've got!*

Ben turned off the road that led to False River, which was not, in fact, a river, but an oxbow lake. It had once been a part of the Mississippi, but a change in the main channel had left the curving body of water isolated from the river itself. The shores were fairly well crowded with cabins, so the lake itself would be too public for what Savage wanted. But he remembered that he and his fishing buddy had wanted to test fire a new .45 and had found a dirt road that wound around in the bottoms, ending in an old gravel pit filled now with blue water. It was an isolated spot, and it would well serve Savage's purpose.

He remembered the dirt road, but it was almost overgrown with saplings and weeds. *That's good,* he thought with satisfaction. *Not likely to be very crowded.* He'd had the Hawk painted recently and hated to put it through the punishment of the raking limbs that clawed the sides and scraped the windows—but Dani was more important than any paint job! The Hawk pitched and bumped over the hard-packed ruts, and Savage ignored the pleas of Fontenot.

Finally he spotted the gleam of blue water and stopped beside the edge. He got out of the car, walked around, and pulled the gun. Opening the door, he said, "Get out!" as roughly as he could.

Fontenot stared into Savage's face and then glanced at the still waters of the gravel pit.

"What—what we doin' out here?" he bleated, fear making his face stiff.

Savage reached in, grabbed Fontenot's shoulder, and hauled him out. Fontenot had to scramble to get his balance, and when he turned, he saw that Savage had lifted the Colt and was aiming it right at his chest.

"Wait—!" he begged frantically. "Don't shoot me!"

"Back up," Savage said. "You're too big to haul around." He stepped forward, and when Fontenot stepped back, his face drained of all color, Savage thought of an extra touch. "Stand there," he commanded as he moved to the rear of the

251

Hawk. Keeping his eye fixed on Fontenot, he opened the trunk. Reaching inside, he lifted a heavy-duty scissors jack out and tossed it on the ground near Fontenot's feet. Reaching into the trunk, he picked up a roll of wire he always carried, and then he slammed the trunk. Carrying the wire, he moved to stand in front of the man.

"Hate to waste a good jack," he commented. "Just wire it to your ankle, Dax."

Savage had seen men come apart under pressure, but never so completely as Dax Fontenot did. He began trembling in every limb, and his face seemed to collapse. His lips moved, but the only sounds he made were racking sobs, not words at all.

"Come on, I'm not enjoying this," Savage said brusquely. "It won't hurt. I'll promise you that."

Fontenot dropped to his knees and began crying. He was a man in size and appearance, but he had never matured emotionally over the age of twelve. Now the tears ran down his cheeks, and he hiccupped as sobs jerked his body. "Why—why are you going to shoot me?" he finally managed to gasp.

Savage frowned, but hope was strong in him. "Because you killed my girl."

Fontenot stared at him wildly, shaking his head violently. "No! I ain't never killed nobody!"

"She's gone, and you killed her."

"Who you talking about—?" Dax suddenly blinked, and he said rapidly, "You mean the Ross woman?"

"That's right."

"No, she ain't dead!"

Savage felt a wave of relief wash over his body, but he allowed nothing to show in his face. "You're lying, man!"

"No, I swear!" The big man scrambled to his feet, babbling

in his anxiety to tell Savage the truth. "I took her, sure, but she's okay! I wouldn't kill no woman."

Savage shook his head. "You're just trying to get out of being killed, Fontenot—" He lifted the Colt, and it had exactly the effect he desired.

Fontenot cried out, "I got her in my cabin, my fishing cabin in the swamp. I'll take you to her!"

Savage lowered the Colt. "All right, I'll give you the benefit of the doubt," he said. "Get in the car."

Fontenot scrambled hastily, almost falling into the car. Savage picked up the wire and the jack, threw them into the back of the Studebaker, and then got behind the wheel. "Where's this cabin?" he demanded.

"Go back to the main road, then take the interstate to Whiskey Bay."

"There it is!"

Savage looked over his shoulder at the cabin inside the small lagoon, then turned back to face Fontenot, who was steering the boat. "All right—pull up slow," he ordered. "Cut the engine."

The engine shut off, and Savage turned to catch the ladder. He tied the rope tightly and said, "Up the ladder, Fontenot." The big man scrambled up the ladder and Savage followed.

"Where is she?" Savage demanded. "Why didn't she come out when she heard us coming?"

Fontenot was staring at the boards stripped from the sides of the cabin. He turned and went through the open door. When Savage came inside, Fontenot cried, "She ain't here! She must have got away!"

"Got away?" Savage was bitterly disappointed and considered the idea that Fontenot had been lying, hoping for a chance to escape. "Was there a boat?" he demanded.

"No," Fontenot said, looking around. He stared at the gaps in the cabin wall, and exclaimed, "Maybe she made some kind of boat!"

"You're lying," Savage said quietly. "Trying to save your hide. You brought her out here, but you killed her."

"No, she was alive when I left! Look, she's been eating the food—see? Most of it's gone." He stared at Savage and said, "She'd never make it in a boat—not through this swamp! "

Savage studied the man, then waved the Colt toward the door. "Outside," he commanded.

Fontenot stiffened. "You ain't going to shoot me?"

Savage shoved him outside, and looked across the lagoon, thinking hard. *She'd head north,* he thought. *She'd know that was the way out.*

"Get in the boat—and you better pray we find her, Fontenot!" He allowed the big man to go first, and when he was in the stern, Ben climbed down and took his seat. "You know these swamps," he said. "She'd head north."

"We'll find her!" Fontenot started the engine, turned the boat, and when they were clear of the lagoon, said, "She can't have gone far!"

Savage found himself praying, much to his surprise. *Help us find her, God!* was all he could say. He knew these swamps could be deadly, and the thought of Dani alone in the depths of this one pained him.

"Look—up ahead there!"

Savage jerked at the sound of Fontenot's shout, and when he looked ahead and saw the strip of white cloth, a thrill of hope shot through him. "She's marked the way!" Fontenot cried. "Keep lookin'!"

He need not have said that, for Savage was straining his eyes. It was growing darker now, the shadows falling over the waters as the sun dropped behind the tall trees. Then he saw another one. "There—to the left," he called out, but Fontenot had seen it at the same instant and had turned the boat toward it.

"Go faster," Savage shouted. "Dark's coming on and we won't be able to see her sign!"

Fontenot stepped up the speed as much as he dared, and they followed Dani's trail rapidly. Then, somehow, they made a wrong turn. When they found no cloth for some time, Savage grated out, "We've missed one. Go back to the last strip!"

By the time they got back to the point where they'd seen the last strip, it was almost dark. "Go to your right," Savage ordered. "She must be in there." He took the flashlight he'd brought from his car, and trained the feeble ray on the waters. *Batteries are almost gone,* he thought.

He sat in the prow, his eyes straining to see through the falling darkness. For a few moments despair came over him—and then out of the gloom he saw a faint strip of white.

"There it is!" he shouted. "Keep going!"

Five minutes later, the last feeble ray of light from the batteries picked up something white. Savage stood up in the boat, peering desperately at the object. Then he cried out, "Dani! Dani!"

Fontenot had seen Dani's small raft and had skillfully brought the flat-bottom next to it. Savage kept calling, and when the white sheet moved, he reached out and pulled it free.

And there she was!

Dani came free of the sheet, blinking against the dim light. When Ben called her name, she smiled and put out her arms.

Savage reached out, picked her up, and drew her into the boat, which rocked precariously, causing Fontenot to shout, "Hey—watch out. There's gators in here!"

But Savage was not thinking of gators. He was holding

Dani in his arms, crushing her to his chest. Dani threw her arms around him and buried her face against his chest. She began to cry, and for some time he held her fiercely.

Finally she looked up, but could see only the outline of his face. Reaching up, she touched his cheek—and was shocked to find tears there.

"Why, Ben—!" she whispered.

But she could say no more, for he held her too tightly.

"Dani—I'll never let you go again!"

She lay in his arms, listening to the hoarse tone of his voice, and suddenly she knew what it was she wanted.

"No, Ben," she whispered. "Don't ever let me go—not ever!"

19

A Slight Case of Burglary

Dani felt warm and secure as Ben sent the Hawk hurtling through the darkness toward Baton Rouge. The terror of the past hours still lurked just below the surface of her mind, and she realized that time would have to soften and finally erase it. She knew, also, that she would never forget the moment when Ben had lifted her from her small ark and had held her close.

He reached over now with his free hand and took hers, holding it tightly; she returned the pressure. Curiously she turned to consider his profile, thinking, *He's not as hard as I thought.* Nothing about him had ever shocked her so greatly as the tears on his cheeks when he'd held her. She had long known that he had a core of toughness—which she secretly admired. But now she was happy to have evidence that underneath that outer toughness was a tenderness that she had only seen briefly.

He turned to her suddenly, meeting her eyes, and smiled. "You gave me quite a scare," he said quietly. "I don't want to ever go through anything like that again."

Dani leaned against him, placing her other hand on his. It gave her a strange sense of completeness to hold his square hand, to feel the strength of his shoulder. "I knew you'd come," she said. "When things got bad, and I wanted to just scream or quit—something inside me kept saying, *Ben will find you.*"

Savage put his eyes back on the road, saying, "Got something to tell you—"

Dani listened with a growing sense of happiness as Ben told her how he'd found Christ. She held to him tightly as he spoke, and when he finished, she found that tears were running down her cheeks. "Ben—" she tried to say, but she could not speak. He glanced at her, leaned forward, and pulled a handkerchief from his pocket, handing it to her. She dabbed at her eyes, waiting until her voice was under control before saying, "I'm so happy, Ben!"

Savage said, "It makes a difference." His brevity told her that he meant much more than that. He finally spoke again, saying, "One thing bothers me about it, Dani."

"What's that, Ben?"

"I don't want you to think it's something I did just so you'd be pleased. It's more than that." He hesitated, seeming to try to arrange his thoughts, then said slowly, "I want to marry you more than I want anything in the world, Dani, but if that never happens, I *know* something's happened to me. All my life I've had some sort of strange feeling—even when I was a kid. Kind of hard to explain, but it's like I was made to do something and never found it. I guess I've been like the bear who went over the mountain to see what he could see. But until last night, the only thing I saw was the other side of the mountain."

"I felt like that, Ben," Dani nodded. "Maybe we all do. St. Augustine said once that there's a God-shaped cavity in man, and that no man will ever be complete until God comes in and fills it."

"That's it!" Savage exclaimed. "And I just thought of something Annie Dillard said. Something wonderful had just happened to her, and she said, 'I was still ringing. I had been my whole life a bell, and never knew it until that moment I was lifted and struck.' That's what it's like." He turned to her with a smile. "You've been waiting for this a long time, haven't you?"

"Since we first met, Ben. Now I wish—"

"Hey—what about me?"

Dani and Ben were both slightly startled by the sound of the voice that broke into their conversation. Fontenot had been quiet since Ben had stuck him in the back seat with his hands cuffed behind his back and a warning to keep his mouth shut. He said now in a worried voice, "What you gonna do with me, Savage?"

"My duty as a citizen," Savage answered. "Take you to jail."

"Aw, come on!" Fontenot argued. "I didn't hurt the broad, did I? She's okay. I was gonna go back and turn her loose soon as Prejean fried." He looked at Dani and said, "Look, it ain't gonna do nobody no good for me to be locked up, Miss Ross."

"And if we turn you loose," Dani said, "you'll promise not to ever kidnap anybody again as long as you live?"

Fontenot was so simple that he missed the thick irony in Dani's voice. Eagerly he nodded, saying, "Yeah, sure—that's it!"

Ben laughed shortly. He was still smoldering with anger at

the big Cajun. Dani had told him about how he'd left her tied, and it was all he could do to keep his hands off the man. "You clown!" he said roughly. "I hope they throw the book at you! In the good old days, kidnapping was a capital offense. Now about the best I can hope for is that you'll get twenty years with no good time and no parole. That's what I'm going to tell the prosecuting attorney to go for."

Fontenot blinked in the darkness, and fear began to work on him. He'd already forgotten his fear of death, for he knew that Savage would not hurt him. But he knew about being in jail, having served a year in Dixon Correctional Institute for robbery. The shadow of Angola lay over his mind now, and horror stories about what happened to men in there came to him. He began to beg.

"Please, listen to me—" he babbled. "It wasn't my fault— taking Miss Ross out of circulation. I didn't like her pokin' around, 'cause I liked Cory and I want to see the guy who offed her put away. But I never kidnapped nobody in my whole life."

A memory tugged at Dani, and she asked, "Did somebody call you when I was in Annie's place?"

"Yeah, sure, that's it!"

Dani said slowly, "I think he might be telling the truth, Ben. He came over and tried to talk to me. I guess he thought I'd be so impressed with his muscles I'd fall into his arms. He wasn't putting on an act, either," she added slowly, the memory growing clearer. "He's too simple for that." She turned around in the seat so that she could watch Fontenot's face. "But later I saw you glaring at me. You were standing beside a waitress, and you looked mad enough to kill."

"Well, I was sore, all right," Fontenot admitted. "But I get sore a lot. Got a bad temper, me! But it don't come to nothing usually." His brow furrowed, and he shook his head. "It set me off when I found out you was tryin' to get Prejean off. That guy deserves to burn! Cory was a nice girl."

"How'd you find out that's what I was doing?"

"Why, Skip told me."

At that name an alarm bell went off in Dani's head.

"Skip told you?" she said, thinking of the cigarette lighter with that name engraved on it. "How did he know I was there?" She turned her head to meet Ben's eyes and saw the fire in them. They both knew that this was the breakthrough they'd been needing. "How'd he know I was there? Was he in the bar?"

"No. Lila, she called him and told him you was there asking questions about Cory."

"Lila's the waitress you were talking to?" Savage demanded. "Her last name is Dennois?"

"Yeah, that's right."

"What's Skip's last name?" Dani asked, keeping her voice casual. It was a critical moment, for a man like Fontenot could be led, but if he got stubborn, hot iron would not wring anything from him.

But Fontenot was totally unsuspecting. "Skip Herndon."

At that moment it all came together for Dani, but she needed more. "Phil Herndon? The governor's right hand man?"

"Sure, that's the guy."

"Why would Lila call him?"

"Aw, ever since Cory got killed, he's been hanging around," Fontenot said. "He come to ask a lot of questions, and then he got tight with Lila. They been goin' together since then." He thought for a moment, then added, "She's a hot number, Lila is. We went together for a while."

Dani added it all up in her mind, then said, "Let me get

this straight, Fontenot. Herndon's been hanging around ever since Cory was killed. He asked Lila to call him if anybody came around asking questions about the murder?"

"That's it. I dunno what he's so uptight about, but he was pretty shook up when I talked to him."

"What'd he say to you?" Savage asked.

"Said that the Ross woman could make a lot of trouble," Fontenot answered. "Told me she was trying to get Prejean off the hook and said that could cause lots of trouble for lots of important people."

"He mention any names?"

"No. Just said for me to take you someplace and keep you quiet until Prejean fried." Anxiety threaded Fontenot's voice, and he begged, "Look, Miss Ross, that's all it was. I was a little rough, I guess. I'm sorry about that lick in the head, but twenty years in Angola is a bad scene. Just let me go, huh?"

Dani was only half listening. "Did Herndon ever give Lila expensive presents?"

"Presents? Sure, all the time—jewels and stuff."

"What about her? Did she ever give Herndon anything?"

Fontenot paused, and Dani and Ben held their breath.

"Oh, sure," Fontenot nodded. "Not expensive stuff, I guess—except for the lighter."

"The lighter?"

"Yeah. Skip's a big hunter—deer and bear. He bagged a record buck, and Lila had a lighter made for him. It was pretty nifty—gold and made out of a rifle shell."

Dani touched Ben with her elbow slightly. "Fontenot, we are going to take you to the police, but maybe the charges won't be so bad. That is—if you cooperate with us."

Fontenot said at once, "I don't want no twenty years in Angola. What kind of deal you talking?"

"You tell the police what you just told us, and I'll drop the kidnapping charge. Just assault and battery."

"Why, that'll only be a month or so in the county jail," Dax said with surprise. His face grew crafty, and he asked, "What's the catch?"

"We don't think Eddie Prejean killed Cory," Dani said. "And we want the real murderer to pay for killing her."

Dax Fontenot was not much as a man, but he had a primitive streak of blood justice in him. Cory was his kin, and among Cajuns, that exceeds most other facts. He sat there thinking in his slow fashion, and neither Dani nor Ben spoke, knowing their man well.

Finally he said, "I want the guy who killed Cory to burn. If Prejean didn't do it, I'll do anything you say to get the guy who did into the chair."

The Hawk probed the highway relentlessly, the twin beams dividing the darkness, and the three occupants grew silent. Dani wondered about Eddie Prejean, what he must be thinking as the fated hour drew closer. Ben's mind was going over the hours he'd spent seeking God at the Leonard Hotel. Dax Fontenot slumped in the back seat, thinking of the time he and Cory Louvier had gone to Mardi Gras in New Orleans. The thought of her as she'd been when the police had taken her from the raw earth came to him, and a smouldering anger began to build in his primitive spirit.

"Time to get you home, Dani," Ben said as they left the Baton Rouge police station. The session with Catlow and Oakie had been long, for the two officers had been cautious. Both Dani and Ben were glad that Catlow was in charge, for if the case against Eddie Prejean was set aside, they would come in for some censure.

Catlow had pressured Dax Fontenot relentlessly, until finally he was content. He'd said, "Book him for assault, Lou."

Oakie had been angered by the minor charge. "He'll be on the street in an hour, Riley!"

"Can't help that." When Oakie had left, taking Fontenot with him, Catlow had turned to the pair and studied them with half-shut eyes. "Well, what does that get us?" he asked. "Nothing here to get a new trial—and we all know the governor's not going to give a stay."

"But the lighter was found at the scene of the crime!" Dani protested.

"No, it wasn't. It was found at the grave. The girl wasn't killed there. And it wasn't found by the police, but by a twelve-year-old kid. Who knows what he'd say on the stand? Might deny the whole thing."

"But what about Herndon? He ordered me to be kidnapped."

"You hear him say that? No, all we have is the word of a slow-witted roughneck with a bad police record. And he might change his story at any minute. You both know that."

A wave of fatigue washed over Dani, and she was aware of the aches and pains that probed at her body. Worse than the fatigue was the sudden sense of hopelessness that accompanied it. She slumped in the chair, saying no more.

"Look, Miss Ross," Catlow said, a ray of sympathy in his eyes. "I know you were hoping for more, but Savage has been in my spot. He'll tell you there's not much I can do at this point."

"That's right, Dani," Ben nodded. "It's just not enough."

Dani nodded and got to her feet. She tried to smile at Catlow saying, "I know, Lieutenant. Thanks for trying."

Catlow rose, and as the two turned, he said, "We'll keep working on it, Miss Ross."

But when Dani and Ben got back to the car, and Ben said, "Time to get you home, Dani," a streak of anger ran through her. She settled down in the car, and when Savage slid behind the wheel, he noted the look on her face. "What's that mean? That look on your face?"

Dani turned to face him, her lips drawn tightly together. "Ben, we don't have *time*. Eddie's going to die if we don't do something!"

"Do what?"

"Oh, I don't know!" Dani wanted to go home, to fall into bed and sleep—but she shook her head rebelliously. "The killer is laughing at all this! And Eddie's going to die!"

Savage sat quietly beside her, his mind racing. Finally he said, "Look, we've tried the cops, and that's no good. Catlow's a good man, but he's got to have something to work with."

Dani looked up at him quickly. "You've got some kind of idea?"

Savage shook his head, and there was a determined twist on his lips. "Nothing brilliant. Like I said before, you poke a stick down a hole and see what comes out."

"Which hole are you thinking about?"

"The only hole we've got—Phil Herndon's place. I think we ought to burgle it."

Dani's mind rebelled against the idea. It was the sort of thing that Savage would do, but all her training went against it. She stared at him, forming arguments, and then saw that he was waiting for her to do just that. She hesitated, then after a long pause as she wrestled with her conscience, nodded, saying firmly, "All right, let's go, Ben!"

Her agreement caused shock to leap into the eyes of Savage. He knew her very well and had fully expected her to throw the suggestion out at once. A smile touched his lips, and he suddenly reached out and put his arm around her. Drawing her close, he kissed her cheek, then released her and started the Hawk.

"Okay, we start your new career," he said. "Dani Ross—girl burglar!"

"You're a bad influence on me," Dani said. "Now, how do we find where he lives?"

"You ask me that? A trained detective? Wait here."

Dani sat in the car while Savage went into the police station. He was back inside of five minutes, saying, "Got it!"

"How'd you get it so quick? Ask Herndon?"

"Nope. Looked in the phone book." Ben grinned at her as he started the engine, saying, "That's your trouble, Boss. You think everything's complicated."

He drove out Highland Road, which was a strange anomaly of sharecropper shacks wedged between mansions worth millions. Herndon's house was one of the more modest ones, a small stone-and-cedar affair set way back off the road on what must have been at least a ten-acre plot. The drive wound around through large live oaks, and when Ben nonchalantly turned off Highland and headed for the house, Dani stared at him, exclaiming, "What are you doing?"

"Finding out if anybody's home." Savage seemed to be enjoying himself. "Good chance everybody's gone this time of day. That's what America's come to—no little mothers home tending the kiddies. Gone to the office and parked the kids at daycare."

The carport was a huge affair built on one side of the house, and there were no cars in it. "Stay here while I see what we've got," Savage said. He got out of the car, walked to the door under the carport, and rang the bell. Dani watched as he stood there waiting, and finally after several tries, he turned and motioned to her. "Nobody home," he called out.

Dani got out of the Hawk, and when she got to the door, she found that he had already opened it. He was putting a credit card back into his billfold, and nodded cheerfully. "Good thing Crimestoppers doesn't let folks know how easy it is to open these simple locks." He pushed the door open and stepped inside. When Dani hesitated, he turned with one eyebrow lifted. "Well—you comin' in or not?"

Dani moved inside, feeling extremely nervous. "What if he comes back while we're here?"

"Then he'll catch us," Savage said practically. "But we can hear the car coming, so I figure we can get back outside in time to convince him we're selling aluminum siding or something. Come on."

Savage moved through the kitchen and passed down a short hall that led to a study. "You go through that desk over there," he nodded. "I'll check his bedroom."

"All right—but let's hurry."

"Haste makes waste," Ben said severely, then turned and disappeared down the hall.

Dani moved to the desk, an old rolltop that had been meticulously restored. It was not locked, and soon she was going through the papers and documents. Herndon evidently kept most of his records here, for she found his income tax records in one file drawer. A quick glance at the past year's taxes made her wonder, for it seemed a small income to own such an expensive house. He was, she discovered, a careful bookkeeper, retaining receipts, even from Wal-Mart, going back five years.

But despite the plethora of papers, there was nothing in the desk that would prove that Herndon had anything to do with Cory Louvier—or even with Lila Dennois for that matter.

"Hey—come see!"

Dani looked up and saw Savage standing in the doorway,

a wide grin on his face. She scrambled to her feet and followed him down the hall into what seemed to be the master bedroom. "What is it?" she whispered.

"What are you whispering for?" Ben asked loudly. "Nobody here but us burglars." Then he pointed to a wall safe with a door that stood open. A print of one of Hopper's paintings was leaned against the wall, which obviously had been used to conceal the safe.

Dani gave Ben a startled glance. "How'd you get that safe open?"

"Cheap safe," he shrugged. "Opens with a key—and anything that opens with a key can't be hard to handle. Look inside."

Dani moved to the safe, reached inside, and took out a small green box made of some sort of metal. She opened the lid and saw that there were three rings and a Rolex watch inside. One of the rings was the largest ruby ring she'd ever seen—with a band made out of a golden serpent. She looked across at Savage who nodded. "Bingo!" he said. "That's got to be the ring Cory Louvier was flashing around."

Dani turned her eyes back to look at the ring. "Will this be enough for Catlow?" she asked.

"I'd guess it might. It'll be interesting to hear Herndon explain how it got off her finger and into his room."

"Do we take it in?"

"No. We go tell Catlow about it. He gets a search warrant and finds it himself."

Dani put the ring inside the box, closed it, and replaced it in the safe. Savage came to close the door, and when it clicked, he replaced the picture. "Let's get out of here," he said, and the two of them left the house at once.

As they drove away and headed for the police station, Savage said, "This will be circumstantial, Dani. It'll take more to get Prejean off the hook."

"I know." Dani looked across at Savage, then asked, "I have a feeling you have another idea. And why do I have this feeling it's something illegal?"

"You hurt me with suggestions like that!"

"It'd take a crowbar to hurt you! What is it?"

Savage began to explain, and Dani listened carefully. By the time they pulled up in front of the police station, she was convinced.

"I'm going to hate being married to you," she said suddenly. "You have such a—a *devious* mind!"

"Yeah, but I can do one-hand pushups!"

"Well, that makes it all right," Dani smiled. She put her hand over on his, and said quietly. "We're going to have a fine time, aren't we, Ben?"

"The very best, Dani!"

20

The Trap

Phil Herndon was tired, but happy.

"I'm going home and sleeping for twenty-four hours, Grace," he said to his secretary. "If anybody important calls, tell them I'm in conference with the governor, and that I'll get back to them."

"Yes, sir." Grace Thomas had learned long ago to conceal her contempt for her employer. She did it now out of pure reflex, smiling as she said, "Will I be your secretary when you're elected attorney general, Mr. Herndon?"

Herndon came over and ran his hand down her arm. "Why, you and I will be going up together, honey," he said. "Course, you'll have to be a little less formal—"

The woman kept her smile, saying, "You'll be in the big time after that election, and it could be just a stepping stone to something even bigger."

Forgetting his impulse to pursue his secretary, Herndon let his thoughts jump ahead. He was a man of overpowering ambition and had spent the day courting prospective supporters. It was something he did well, but it was tiring. They were all careful men and demanded more than any official would be able to give, but he knew how to play them very skillfully.

"Good night, Grace," he said, thinking of how he could put his prospective opponent in the race out of the running. Leaving the building, he went to the parking lot and got into his Corvette. The luxury of the car pleased him, and he enjoyed out-gunning those who pulled up beside him at traffic lights—leaving them behind as he sent the car hurtling ahead with a scream of the tires.

He pulled into his driveway and thought for one moment of his wife and son. He'd built the house for them but had lost them in a nasty divorce case. He hadn't loved either of them, but any man with political ambitions needed a showcase, a family to stand with when the television cameras were rolling.

Getting out of the car, he groped across the carport toward the door—but halted abruptly when a voice spoke out of the darkness—

"Been waitin' for you a long time, Skip!"

Herndon thought of the .38 in the glove compartment of the Corvette, but he knew it was too late. "Who's that?" he demanded.

"Me—Dax."

Herndon cursed him roundly, then demanded, "What do you want? I told you never to come unless I called you."

"I been in jail," Dax grunted. "And from what I hear, you'll be going that way yourself."

"What!"

"Listen, Skip, we're in big trouble! We gotta talk."

"Come inside."

When they were in the house, Dax said, "Gimme a drink, Skip. I need it!"

"Come on to the study."

Herndon led the way to the study and poured a large drink for Fontenot, then when the big man drained it down, he demanded, "What's all this about jail?"

Fontenot shook his head, glaring at the other man angrily. "You know that guy Savage, the one who had the trouble with the local cops?"

"Yes, I heard about it."

"Well, he's a rough cookie, Skip!" After taking another swallow of his drink, Dax began to speak rapidly. "He caught me off guard, Skip. Made me tell him where the woman was."

"You told him that? You're a fool!" Herndon said angrily. "They can nail you for kidnapping."

"I'd rather be alive and facing that, than dead in the swamp—which is where I'd be if I hadn't told him!"

Herndon was alarmed, but he forced himself to conceal it. "Just tell me everything that happened, Dax." He stood there as Fontenot spoke, not missing a thing. He was a lawyer and a shrewd one. When Fontenot was finished he said, "So you told them I was the one who called you and told you to take the woman?"

"Yeah, but I didn't have no choice!"

"It doesn't matter. They can't prove it, and you'd be a fool to try to drag me down with you." Herndon sipped his own drink, going over Fontenot's story. Finally he shook his head. "It's too weak, Dax. They can't touch me. As for this kidnapping charge, I'll get that reduced—wait a minute, what are you doing out? You couldn't make a bond that big."

"They didn't charge me with kidnapping," Fontenot said. "Just assault."

"Why'd they do that?"

"The Ross woman said she knew I didn't mean no harm. I told them how Cory and me was kin, and she said she could understand how I could have gone off the deep end." Fontenot thought hard, then said, "And she said for me not to worry—that Cory's killer was about to get his."

"She meant Eddie Prejean!"

"No, Skip," Fontenot shook his head. "Her and Savage and that woman on TV, Sunny Sloan, they've all found out who done the murder. Well, the Sloan woman don't know yet. Ross and Savage said they've got the proof just about nailed down. Said in a day or two, they'd have it all, and then the Sloan woman would break the story on TV."

Herndon's lips grew thin. "Did they go back to New Orleans?"

"I don't think so, Skip. I heard them say something about gettin' rooms at a hotel until they got it sewed up."

"Which hotel?"

"I think it was the Majestic, the old one out on Airline."

"Okay. Now, Dax, you get out of town for a few days. I don't want any reporters or cops grilling you."

"I ain't got no cash, Skip."

"Here—" Herndon fished out his billfold, removed several bills, and thrust them at Fontenot. "Call me in a few days, but don't use your right name. I'll tell you what to do."

"Okay, Skip." He hesitated, then asked, "You think I better take Lila with me? They'll be talking to her, too, I guess."

"Yeah, take her."

"Take a little more dough!"

Herndon gave him more money, then he waited until he heard an engine start. Picking up the phone, he dialed a number, and after several moments, he said, "Layne—I've got to see you. No, right *now*! It's a hot one this time. Yes, I'll be right there."

273

Hanging up the phone, Herndon hesitated for a moment before going into his bedroom. He took off his coat, pulled a shoulder harness with a .45 in it from the nightstand beside his bed, and put it on. As he pulled on his coat and left the room, he muttered, "They'll have to go! No other way."

Layne Russell listened quietly as Herndon spoke, his face impassive. He was a poker player of renown, and he let nothing show on his handsome features. But all the time he was listening, he was making plans. He had survived in a jungle worse than any that Africa had to offer by being shrewder and more ruthless than any of the other carnivores on the Louisiana political scene—and he had no intention of going down now.

"So the Ross woman and Savage have got us—is that it?" he asked when Herndon finally grew silent.

"That's what Fontenot says, but you know what a simpleton he is, Layne."

"I don't think we can ignore it, Phil."

"No, I don't either. What we've got to do is buy them off."

A light touched the cold eyes of Russell, and he seemed interested. "What if they won't be bought?"

Herndon shifted nervously in his chair. The two men were sitting in a small room located on the first floor of the governor's mansion. It was one of the few rooms not bugged, so the governor used it when he wanted to be certain that he wasn't going public. Herndon said quickly, "I think it's just a matter of price, but if that doesn't work, we can put pressure on them. Have their licenses revoked."

Instantly Russell knew that was futile. And the fact that Herndon offered it only increased the governor's contempt for the man. "Well, you may have something there, Phil," he said slowly.

"But we've got to do it quick, Layne," Herndon said. "If that Sloan woman goes on TV with something, it'll be too late."

"You're right, Phil." Russell looked at Herndon steadily, an idea taking shape in his mind. He came to a sudden decision, saying firmly, "You've got to handle it, Phil. I'll get the money, but I can't go to them. You understand that? If anything happened to me, neither of us would be in office for long."

Herndon nodded, but he grew wary and there was a trace of a threat in his voice as he said, "Look, Layne, I'll handle it, but I'm not going to do time. If I get caught, you'll be in it."

"Why, you're not going to get caught, Phil!" Reproach was on the governor's smooth face, and he shook his head with a mild rebuke. "You're a smart man—otherwise I wouldn't have you at my right hand!" He smiled then, and nodded. "Go as high as you have to. Fifty grand—a hundred. They've got a price, so find it. Set up the drop, then come back and I'll get the cash. We pay them off, they don't sing to the reporter, and Prejean goes down. Then you and I can get ourselves into this election—and we'll win, Phil."

"Sure, Layne!" A burst of confidence rose in Herndon, and he got to his feet. "I'll call them right now!"

"Use this phone, Phil," Russell nodded toward the one on his desk. He sat back as Herndon found the number and dialed.

"Hello, is this Dani Ross? Okay, this is—a friend of Dax Fontenot. I need to talk to you and Savage." A look of surprise came over his face and he nodded slowly, "Yes, it's me. Where can we meet? No, not at the hotel—too public." He thought hard, then said, "You know the old River Road? Well, six miles out of Baton Rouge there's an abandoned store set back off the road. Meet me there in an hour—and no cops!"

"Good thinking, Phil," Russell smiled. "Now, get back here as soon as you can. I want to be on top of this."

"Sure, Layne!"

Russell waited until Herndon was outside, then picked up the phone and dialed hastily. "Johnny? Layne here. Got a job to be done, and I mean like in an hour." He settled back in his chair, his eyes turning hard as agates. "You know where that abandoned feed store is about six miles out on the old River Road? Well, in an hour there'll be a meeting there. Now here's what I want you to do—" He spoke rapidly, then paused to listen for a few moments.

A frown creased his smooth brow, and he said, "Johnny, the woods are on fire. This one is for the whole thing, so don't miss. What?" He listened, then said carefully, "Yes, Phil, too. Sorry about that, but it's him or us. Now, call me when it's over."

Hanging up the phone, Governor Russell slowly leaned back in his chair. He looked up at the clock on the wall, marked the time, then locked his hands and waited.

The odor of the river came to Dani and Savage as they sat in the Hawk with the windows rolled down. Fifty yards behind them, the levee rose to conceal the brown waters of the Mississippi, and as dusk began to close in, Dani turned to look at the green banks that stretched in both directions.

They sat there keeping an alert glance on every car that appeared, and finally Ben said, "I still think you should have let me handle this."

Dani shook her head. "He'd see I wasn't here, Ben. We're the bait, and it's got to look good."

"May not work, anyway," Savage remarked. "It seemed like a good idea, but right now it looks pretty flimsy." He shifted around, peered down the road, and shook his head. "I hope Catlow and Oakie are better at hiding out than most cops are. All Herndon needs is one hint of cops around, and the whole thing's blown."

"I've got a feeling Catlow's pretty good at his job," Dani nodded. "It's Fontenot I'm not sure about. He's not too swift, and it's asking a lot for him to fool a smart operator like Herndon."

"I think he'll do fine," Ben said. "All he had to do was stick to his story."

The idea had been to get Dax Fontenot to go to Herndon with a scare story—to tell him that unless something happened, Herndon would be in trouble. Ben had argued that if Herndon could be stampeded, he might make a mistake. And the bait in the trap was themselves.

They had gone to Catlow with the plan, and he'd hated it. But in the end, he'd agreed to cover them. Now the trap was set—but neither of them was convinced that it would work.

"It's the only thing to try, Ben," Dani said, trying to console him. "We'll just have to go with it."

But Savage was only half listening. He sat up, straightened, and peered into the distance. "Car's slowing down," he murmured. The two of them watched, and finally he said, "It's him. Watch yourself."

They waited, watching the red Corvette as it swung into the graveled area overgrown with weeds and stopped. The door opened and a man got out, leaving the engine running. He called out, "All right, get out, and let's talk. Leave your engine running."

"The noise of the engines would ruin any recordings if we were wired. There might be somebody in the car, but I don't think so," Ben muttered. "Come on." The two of them got out and walked over to where Herndon was standing. Savage could see the bulk of the weapon beneath Herndon's jacket and kept his eyes on the man. "All right, Herndon," he nodded. "We're here. Start talking."

Fixing them with a hard stare, Herndon shrugged. "It's quite simple, actually. I want to buy you off."

His blunt remark made Dani blink. "Well, that's pretty plain," she said. "How much are you offering—and for what?"

"I think you know what we're talking about, Miss Ross," Herndon said. He looked nervous, but he was determined. "You lay off the Prejean affair. That's all I want."

"And how much are you willing to pay?" Dani demanded.

"Fifty thousand in unmarked bills."

"Not enough," Dani said at once. "And who are you fronting for, Herndon? You don't have that kind of money."

"Never mind that," Herndon snapped. "I can get the cash, but you've got to be reasonable." He scowled and tried a threat. "I didn't have to offer you this deal," he said. "There are rougher ways than this to get you off my neck."

"You had some practice getting rough with Cory Louvier, didn't you, Herndon?" Savage said. "But we'll be harder than she was to take care of."

"Look, I didn't kill that girl," Herndon hastened to say.

"You buried her," Dani shot back. "Who are you covering for?"

Herndon started to answer, but Savage said, "Look out!"

He'd been watching a car that had appeared out of the falling darkness, and when it slowed down and swerved toward the old parking lot, he knew it was trouble.

Herndon threw one quick glance over his shoulder, whirled, and made a run for his car. He had yanked the door open when the boom of shotguns shattered the air. Something struck him in the arm, and he fell to the ground, grabbing wildly at the .45 under his coat. The shattered glass from his window fell on his face, and he was blinded for a moment. He heard the booming of the shotguns and the sharper cracks of handguns. The Corvette was rocked as blast after blast riddled it. Finally, Herndon was able to open his eyes. The windows of the black car were open, and shotgun muzzles were extended, jumping as they fired.

Herndon knew at once what had happened, and he leveled the .45. He began firing, noticing at the same time that Ross and Savage had taken shelter behind their car and were blazing away at the big sedan.

"Keep down, Dani!" Savage shouted. "Those shotguns will go right through the glass!"

Dani had known that, for the windows of the Hawk were shattered, and she had heard the pellets striking the old building behind her. Her greatest fear was that she would be shot in the feet or legs, so she moved down and got behind the wheel of the Studebaker. When the firing of the shotguns lessened, she lifted her gun and threw a shot at the car. Savage, she saw, was raking the sedan steadily with his Python Colt.

"Hold on!" Savage yelled. "Here come the cops!"

The driver of the car heard him, for he yelled and sent the big car spinning away, throwing gravel as it dug into the rough earth. As it took off, two police cars came roaring down the road from the east, and as they shot past, Dani saw Oakie driving one and Catlow leaning out the window, blazing away at the rear of the black sedan.

"Are you all right?" Ben was at her side, and Dani nodded. Her face was pale, but she said, "Yes, I'm all right."

"Come on, let's go see about Herndon."

They ran to the Corvette and found Herndon getting to his feet. He held the .45 but offered no resistance when Savage took it from him. His eyes were wide open and his mouth pulled tightly together as if he'd bitten into something spoiled.

"They were out to get you, Herndon," Dani said. "Who knew you'd be here?"

Herndon began to shake. His arm had taken some pellets, and the blood was running down from his cuff. He lifted the bloody hand, stared at it, then said woodenly, "He tried to take me out—after all I've done for him!"

Dani and Ben exchanged quick glances. "The governor?" Dani asked quietly.

"Yes, it was him!" Herndon dropped his hand to his side and began to curse. He called Layne Russell every vile name he could think of, then stared at the two. "He killed that girl—Cory Louvier."

"Russell killed her?" Dani whispered.

"Yes. It was at that party. He took her off, and when he tried to force her, she held him off. He's got a mean temper, and he hit her, knocking her against the sharp edge of the mantle. Freak accident—but he was the one, not me."

"So he came and got you to take her out and bury her?" Savage asked.

"Sure—and I did it! I bribed that guy at the Leonard to say he saw the Louvier woman leave with Prejean. I took care of all of it."

The sounds of gunfire came to them, sounding like faintly popping firecrackers. Then they stopped, and Savage said, "That's the end of that, I'd say."

Dani said, "We've got proof that you buried the girl, Herndon. You'll have to stand trial."

"But not for murder," Herndon said angrily. "No, it's Russell who'll have to answer for that!"

"You'll testify against him?" Dani asked quickly.

Herndon, staring at his bloody hand and at the wreckage of the Corvette, nodded. "For that—and for many other things. I know enough on him to send him to jail. He'll probably get off from most of it, but he won't be governor anymore. I'll have that to laugh about!"

"Better let me look at that arm," Savage said. "You're losing a lot of blood."

"If it wasn't for getting even with Russell, I'd bleed to death," Herndon mumbled grimly, but he made no protest as Savage stripped off the coat and examined the arm. By the time he'd made a bandage to stop the bleeding, a police car roared back, and Catlow almost fell out of it in his eagerness.

"Just like the good old days in Nam," he said. He nodded, saying, "Well, Phil, you've gotten into a bad one this time. I'll have to arrest you."

"Layne Russell killed Cory Louvier," Herndon said at once. "Take good care of me, Lieutenant. I'm your star witness."

Catlow's face showed shock, but when Dani and Savage nodded, he murmured, "I'll do that. Come along and we'll get that arm seen to."

As Oakie put Herndon in the car, Catlow stared at the couple. "Well, it all winds down like a real bad movie, with all the ends neatly tied together. Eddie Prejean will be glad." He suddenly grinned and put his hand out, "For a pair of PI's, you two aren't so bad! Now, you'll have to go to the station. Won't take long."

"Have to bum a ride, Riley," Savage said. He stared at the Studebaker, then shook his head sadly. "Sure hate to lose that Hawk."

"I'll buy you another one, Ben," Dani said, bringing a huge grin to Ben's face. "A man's got to have a few toys."

They rode in the back of the police car with Herndon all the way back to town. Dani held one of Ben's hands, and he held her tightly with the other. She was so tired that, when she lay back on his arm, she went to sleep.

Oakie looked back and grinned, but said nothing. Turning back to Catlow, he remarked, "I knew all along that Savage was a good one!"

21
From This Day Forward

Sunny Sloan smiled into the camera, radiating confidence. " . . . and so we have the fall of a titan! When Governor Layne Russell was arrested by police this morning, it marked the end of a giant. Not a gentle giant, but a colossus who took what he pleased, plundering an entire state. The charge was not first degree murder—as some critics insisted would have been fair. But when a governor who has manipulated the law for years is charged with manslaughter, that's news!"

At her home, Dani and Ben were sitting together on the couch in the den, sipping coffee and watching the special report. The other viewers included her family and Luke Sixkiller. The burly police officer squinted at the screen, observing, "That outfit is pretty revealing for a reporter, isn't it?"

Savage looked more closely, then shook his head. "No, looks about right to me."

Dani yanked her hand away from Savage and glared at him. "I noticed you noticing it."

"I'm a trained detective," Savage grinned. "And besides, I noticed you noticing me noticing Sunny. I did it to make you jealous."

"You sound like you work in the Department of Redundancy Department!" Rob said. He looked back at the screen and asked, "When does she tell about how it was you two who did all the work that's making this broadcast possible?"

"Coming right up," Savage promised.

Sunny was winding up the program. " . . . and in the future, we will be bringing you up-to-date reports on the sordid saga of Louisiana's reverse Robin Hood governor, who robbed the rich to give to himself!"

"Did you give her that line, Ben?" Dani demanded.

"No, I guess her writers came up with it. All I ever heard Sunny say on her own was, 'Do you like this dress, honey?'"

"Will you two hush?" Ellen spoke up. "I want to hear this."

Sunny had reached the end of the program, and now she said, "I want to thank everyone who helped me on this special report—" She began to name people, including the producer and the cameramen, and finally paused and said, "My thanks to all of these. But there are two people who deserve special thanks. Without the help of these two, you would not be watching this story tonight—"

"Here it comes!" Sixkiller said loudly.

"Be quiet, Luke!" Ellen said with exasperation. She was leaning forward, her eyes glued to the screen.

Sunny Sloan paused dramatically, then said soulfully, "And these two wonderful people are—my mom and dad!"

As Sunny smiled and was faded away by the TV people, a groan went up from Dani's family.

"Why—that ungrateful *wench!*" Rob yelled. He took off his

moccasin and threw it at the TV, missing it by a broad margin. "She'd have been zilch without you, Sis, and here she thanks her *parents!*"

Ellen tried to conceal her disappointment. "Well, it's nice that she remembers her parents."

Ben laughed suddenly. "Sunny hasn't spoken to her parents in years," he said. "Her father abandoned Sunny and her mother when Sunny was a baby. And she's fought with her mother ever since she grew up. They don't even send Christmas cards to each other!" He shook his head with admiration. "That was pretty good drama, though. Almost as good as Nixon's Checkers speech. I predict great things for Sunny Sloan."

"Move over, Dan Rather," Allison said with a sour grin. "But I'm glad she didn't take you away from Dani."

"Take him away from me?" Dani exclaimed. "Why, that piece of fluff couldn't take her own temperature."

"A sexist remark if I ever heard one," Sixkiller spoke up. Then he got to his feet, saying, "Well, enough of life's little pleasures. Got to go catch some criminals."

"Oh, Luke, can't you stay longer?" Ellen asked at once. "We're going to make some fudge and then play Trivial Pursuit."

Sixkiller shook his head regretfully. "Next time, Ellen. Thanks for the meal." He waved his hand at the rest of the group, saying, "See you later, guys."

When he left the room, Dani got up suddenly and went out after him, a disturbed look on her face. When the door closed behind her, Allison said, "Luke's taking losing Dani pretty hard, isn't he?"

Savage nodded soberly. "Yeah, he is." He got up and wandered off to the kitchen, adding, "I know what I'd feel like if it were the other way around."

Allison turned to her mother, saying, "I hate it when things like this happen!"

Ellen shook her head sadly. "Luke's such a fine man! But he'll find somebody. God will bring him just the right wife."

Outside, Dani had caught up with Luke just as he got to the car. He turned and faced her, his expression unreadable, but Dani knew the big man better than most. She put her hand on his arm, her eyes filled with grief.

"Oh, Luke—" she said, her voice breaking. "I feel terrible!"

Sixkiller grinned and shook his head. "That's not right," he shrugged. "You're getting the best guy there is."

"I know," Dani whispered. "But I know that you—"

When she couldn't finish, Sixkiller nodded. "It hurts, Dani. But the Scripture says that God sets the solitary in families. God's chosen Ben for you, and somewhere out there he's got somebody for me. I'll just have to wait. But don't be sad. It wouldn't be fair to Ben."

Dani blinked the tears back and summoned up a trembling smile. "I know the theory, Luke, but putting it into practice is what's hard."

Sixkiller suddenly reached out and enfolded her in his strong arms. He held her tightly for a long moment before releasing her. "You brought me to know Jesus," he said. "I can't ever forget that. But the rest of it, God will take from me. Now, you go in and tell Savage he'd better treat you right— or I'll arrest him and throw him in the slammer!"

Dani watched as Sixkiller got into his car and drove away. She had a strange, empty sensation in the pit of her stomach as though she had lost something that could never be replaced. Slowly she turned and walked back into the house.

The den was empty, and Dani wandered into the kitchen where she found Ben and her mother sitting on high stools talking quietly. They both looked up when she walked in, but neither mentioned Sixkiller.

"What are you two talking about?" Dani asked. She moved to the stove and after getting a cup of coffee, turned to face them. "What are you plotting? I can't trust either of you."

"'Oh, we're just deciding about the future," Savage shrugged. "After we get married, we'll have to have a place to stay. Don't think you'd enjoy my apartment all that much."

"It's not a maiden's dream," Dani admitted. "But I like your cat."

"I'll share her with you. But I have a plan—a master plan," Savage said. "It's a stroke of genius!"

"It's his idea, Dani," Ellen said quickly. "I didn't have anything to do with it."

Dani stared at her mother, wondering why she seemed so defensive. Then she shifted her gaze back to Ben. "What's this wonderful master plan of yours?"

Savage grinned at her, saying, "I've always been sort of a freeloader. So I've been asking myself, 'Savage, where could you get free room and board? Where could you get the best cook in the world? Where could you live where someone could take care of you when you get sick?'"

Dani stared at him. "And the answer is—?"

Savage waved his coffee cup toward Ellen. "Why, I'm planning to move right in with my mother-in-law," he said airily. "Just what she needs—a son-in-law under her feet, bumming free room and board!"

Dani glanced at her mother quickly, and in that instant, they both understood what Ben was up to.

He knows Mother is having a hard time, Dani thought. *He's willing to give up his privacy to help her through this time—and to help with Rob and Allison. They've all been unhappy since we lost Dad, and Ben sees that.*

"Well, that's a fine way to start a marriage, mooching off my family!" Dani exclaimed, hiding the sudden surge of affection that had come to her. "Don't I have anything to say about this?"

"Nope, not a thing." Savage reached out, picked up a brownie, and took a bite. "I've got no character at all, Sweetie. You'll just have to take me as I am. What you sees is what you gets."

Ellen rose and went to Ben. She bent down and kissed him, whispering huskily, "Thank you, Ben!" and then she left the room hurriedly.

"Now, you see what an operator I am?" Ben nodded at Dani. "Here I am moving in like a parasite, and *she's* thanking *me*!"

Dani moved over and sat down on Ben's lap. Putting her arms around his neck, she kissed him long and hard. Then she moved closer and put her head on his shoulder. "Oh, Ben, I just *love* masterful men!" she whispered.

He held her close, and for a long time they sat there clinging to each other.

Finally he pulled her back and stared at her. "That's good to hear— that you love masterful men."

"Oh, I *do*!"

Savage stared at her suspiciously. "I have what is called the Savage method of handling wives and children. Want to hear it?"

"Yes!"

Savage said with great firmness, "My plan is to give wives and children anything they want, and then they'll hush and let a man alone." He kissed her firmly, demanding, "How do you like it?"

Dani Ross, who had made a career of being independent, put out her hand and stroked Ben's cheek. "I call that the Ross plan for keeping a husband happy," she murmured. Then she smiled brilliantly, saying, "Oh, Ben, it's going to be wonderful being married to you! We're going to have a great time!"

Savage held her tightly and whispered, "From this day forward!"

They got up and walked outside, holding hands and looking up at the stars which glittered across the sky. A star burned its way across the velvet blackness, scoring the night with a silver line that slowly faded.

"Make a wish, Dani," Ben said, squeezing her hand.

Dani turned to him and whispered, "No, Ben. God's given me so much—there's nothing left to wish for!"